By day a mild-mannered real estate attorney based in Oak Park, Illinois, after hours the author moves willingly into the dark worlds of the whodunnit, immersing himself in the intrigue of murder and mayhem. When dragged out of the shadows, he fills his time by cursing at his garden, trying to stay relevant to his daughters, and making artisanal ice cream every chance he gets. He has one prior published work, *Serendipity: Seemingly Random Events, Insignificant Decisions, and Accidental Discoveries That Altered History.*

As always, to my daughters, Tierney, Lourdra, and Gilleece. Maybe they'll read this one.

Thomas J. Thorson

HEIRS APPARENT

A Malcom Winters Mystery

AUSTIN MACAULEY PUBLISHERS™

LONDON • CAMBRIDGE • NEW YORK • SHARJAH

Ordering Information:
Quantity sales: special discounts are available on quantity purchases by corporations, associations, and others. For details, contact the publisher at the address below.

Publisher's Cataloging-in-Publication data
Thorson, Thomas J.
Heirs Apparent

ISBN 9781647503185 (Paperback)
ISBN 9781647503192 (Hardback)
ISBN 9781647503208 (ePub e-book)

Library of Congress Control Number: 2020904907

www.austinmacauley.com/us

First Published (2020)
Austin Macauley Publishers LLC
40 Wall Street, 28th Floor
New York, NY 10005
USA

mail-usa@austinmacauley.com
+1 (646) 5125767

Times change. Chicago's hulking 2.7 million-square-foot Old Post Office, vacant and decaying since the government left it for more modern quarters in 1977—and the site of a pivotal scene in this novel—is finally being renovated and recently welcomed its first tenant. Real estate development may be fluid, but what remains forever constant is my gratitude toward all the people whose support help make my writing life easier. For this book, that includes my three daughters and my sometimes roommate Christina Michael, all of whom suffer through alternating periods of being totally ignored and nonstop rambling about murder weapons and character development; super estate planning attorney William Ellsworth, whose war stories over lunch provided the plot point that pulled the whole story together; my editor Kristen Wise, who pushed through my stubbornness with gentle persistence and whose ideas that I vociferously railed against actually made the book so much better; HVAC technician extraordinaire Tom Hack, who somehow dug out photos of the inside of an ancient boiler; graphic designer Stephanie Rocha for her imaginative ideas and invaluable contributions; and my beta readers: insurance agent Richele Brainen, IT guru Curtis Rangel, and Steve Kirshenbaum of the wonderful The Looking Glass Books. I gratefully thank them all.

Prologue

The rising sun's rays glistened on the surface of an eerily calm Lake Michigan, portending the first stage of the transition from the overcast bluster of late winter to the deceptive sunshine of early spring in Chicago. Slowly, stealthily, it rose until it glanced off the barren trees lining Michigan Avenue, dapples of light breaking through the branches to cast upon a silent, still figure seemingly asleep on one of the many stone benches lining the sidewalk. The speckles of light beckoned the man to awake and to bask in its pledge to banish the cold, to celebrate the rebirth of a season long-awaited by the city's many frozen souls.

But the occupant of the bench was not asleep, nor deceived by the sun's false promise of warmth. Movement was the last thing on his mind. On the contrary, he focused on keeping so still that his body would appear to be one with the bench, unnoticeable to the occasional passersby or the pigeons that normally assumed anyone in his position was only there to toss breadcrumbs at their feet. This was no easy task, as he was cursed by an abnormal height that made blending in a near impossibility. The multiple layers under his winter coat also added undesirable bulk.

The tall man understood this, so he had come to the same bench at the same time of day and sat, motionless, for hour after hour until his knees ached and his back seemed to fuse with the slats upon which it rested. By this, the fifth day, he no longer garnered glances from the early-morning joggers and dog walkers, and the park's panhandlers left him alone. He had become one with the bench, a fixture, an unimportant blotch no more worth considering than the bench itself. He had made himself invisible.

He thought back to the debate he had with himself the night before. Part of him felt that it was time, that he had waited long enough, but something from

9

the deep recesses of his consciousness objected. What's the harm in waiting a few more days, it said, just to make sure that he had achieved complete inconspicuousness? There was no timetable here. An overabundance of caution never hurt. Ultimately, he was able to block these thoughts, in part due to the feelings of paralyzing trepidation that arose at the prospect of further delay. There may be no timetable, but at any time someone, somewhere could speak out and ruin everything. There was still more to do to assure that wouldn't happen. He needed to get this one behind him and move on to the next.

As he contemplated moving off of the bench, though, doubts arose once more. Was his decision soundly thought out, or was it influenced by the stiffness deep inside his joints and the chill that never seemed to dissipate after a day of sitting? A sudden rage at his own indecisiveness gave him the impetus he needed. He was certain that he could take action without being seen. In the unlikely event that the park's denizens would be questioned later, they would not recall seeing anyone who didn't seem to belong there nor would they be able to describe the man whom they had come to ignore, if they remembered him at all. As methodical as his quest for anonymity had required him to be, he was not a patient man. It was time to accomplish his goal and to give up these long, uncomfortable, bone-chilling sessions. He was a man of action and it was time to act. Just a few more minutes would be enough. And so he sat, motionless, as the sun continued to rise and the brisk air refused to warm.

When the clock in his head told Tall Man that it was time, he rose slowly and made his way up the path to the street, keeping his head lowered and his pace steady. From his time sitting on the bench, he knew the pattern of the stoplights. He could reach the intersection at the very instant the walk signal made it safe to cross, preventing the need to stop and wait among the others. Taking deep breaths to keep calm, he entered the lobby and glided past the disinterested man at the front desk, invisible once more. Just as he exhaled in relief and turned toward the elevators, disaster struck.

A figure emerged from the elevators, striding purposefully toward the revolving doors to the street. Tall Man cast his eyes downward and tilted his head away from the individual in an effort to hide his face, but a flash of red brought his eyes involuntarily upward, like a bull transfixed by a matador's cape. Just as he did so, the person caught his gaze, smiled, and greeted him with a cheery, quiet "Good morning." The interchange was over in an instant, but this seemingly innocuous greeting threw Tall Man into a panic. He relied on routine, on predictability, before committing himself to his task. Should he abandon his plans completely? Would it be better to start over, to commit himself to sitting on the bench for five more days?

No, he told himself, he had to do it today. He actually never saw the person's face other than the smile. A woman, he thought, mostly from the tone of her voice, although even of that he wasn't sure. A glimpse of what may have been red hair, or perhaps a scarf. Tall Man had trained himself to be observant. If he was this clueless about the greeter's features, she probably didn't get a good view of him either. He told himself that he was overreacting. He had other places to be and other people to visit. The longer he stood frozen in indecision, the more visible he would become. He hurried toward the elevators.

He knew that his target was home. The young man had arrived back from his night shift about four hours earlier, the same time as every other day. Pressing '18,' Tall Man huddled in the corner of the elevator in the hope that other passengers would ignore him, but luck was with him and he ascended alone. Shuffling down the hallway of the eighteenth floor, he found his destination and quietly knocked, not expecting the sleeping man to respond. Using a universal key card he had obtained at great expense, Tall Man pushed the door open inch by inch so as not to make a sound, closing it with equal care.

Inside at last, he moved swiftly now, anxious to get the actual killing behind him. This was not the part he enjoyed. He was no murderer. This was business. Slipping a cord from his pocket, he pushed his elbow against the bedroom door and burst into the room, his adrenaline urging him forward.

Before he could reach the prone figure on the bed, Tall Man stopped short, a jolt of surprise stopping his momentum. The young man lay on his back, his lower body sprawled halfway onto the floor. Blood barely bubbled out from the single bullet hole in the middle of his forehead, puddling onto the sheet below. The stench of voided bowels and a trace of burned fabric filled the room. Tall Man silently gave thanks that there was no need to check a pulse, with the chance of leaving a trace of himself behind.

A sudden realization of how recently the man died jolted him and Tall Man scanned the room quickly to make sure the killer was no longer in the room before slowly backing out to survey the rest of the apartment. A bitter bile rose into his mouth in response to his fright. Only when Tall Man completed his tour without encountering another soul did he dare to swallow, grimacing at the taste. He didn't like the unexpected and it unnerved him. There was no time to think about it now, though. He returned to the bedroom.

Tall man surveyed the scene from the doorway. A pillow with a hole and scorch marks directly in the center lay near the man's head. Two empty wine glasses and an unopened bottle of red sat on the nightstand. Each side of the bed showed signs of having been occupied, and both pillows still had the indentations of a head. The curtains were drawn tight, leaving only thin vertical stripes of dulled light to shine past. Curiosity tempted him to stay to reconstruct what had happened in the short time the victim had been home, but for all he knew, the police were already on their way, or perhaps the killer lurked nearby. No good would come from lingering here.

Tall Man silently departed, his head throbbing as he wondered who had done his work for him, and why. Did he (or possibly she, based on his observations in the bedroom) have the same goal or was this some random act? It would take some thought, but not here. As unobtrusively as he had arrived, Tall Man returned to the main floor, walked out the front door, and disappeared, as if he had never been there at all.

Chapter 1

Six Months Earlier

If the Greyhound bus you're riding is going to break down, Rapid City, South Dakota is as good a place as any. There's not much temptation that's going to lead you astray or cause you to spend money you were saving for a snow globe of Mount Rushmore, available at discount prices at Wall Drug. Getting lost and missing the bus when it's ready to move on would take a good deal of effort, and getting mugged would probably make you somewhat of a local celebrity. Maybe they'd even throw you a parade. For me, the peacefulness of being caught in the middle of nowhere might be a blessing in disguise for a traveler with a lot on his mind. No distractions.

Not that my fellow passengers would all agree. Self-proclaimed 'Big Bob,' the rotund hardware store supervisor in the third row, made it clear that heads would roll if he missed the opening of the wrench and plyers convention at the casino hotel in Hammond, Indiana. In row seven, the young mother of the twins who had taken turns screaming since we left Sheridan, Wyoming, simply looked like she was going to cry. Ditto for the elderly woman occupying the seat to my left, who was returning home to her cat, the subject of dozens of pictures to which I'd been subjected for the past several hours. Me? It doesn't matter much. I'm not sure where I'm going anyway, so getting there faster seems a bit existential.

I'm less interested in a destination than in leaving behind where I've been. Even that's more of a mindset than a place. For longer than I care to admit to myself, I earned a living of sorts lurking in the shadows completing tasks for people whose main focus was deniability. I had no title and you wouldn't find my name on any list of Uncle Sam's employees. Violence and near-death experiences were the norm. As long as I shut out all thought, never questioning the tasks at hand, everything was fine. And I was good at it. Damn good. But one assignment brought all of that crashing down. I began to question the job, to question my role. Thinking made me less effective and more vulnerable. I made mistakes, almost got killed. More than once. My time was up. I either needed to get out or I would die. I knew it, they knew it. I think they would have preferred the latter scenario, but they reluctantly released me. The question facing me now, is now what?

There are only so many pictures of a cat you can feign interest in, even if she is dressed as a reindeer or a leprechaun. Faking sleep soon became my escape, but closing my eyes opened up the door for my thoughts to wander and that can be a dangerous thing. I've become preoccupied with a single thought, the threshold step to beginning over again no matter where I end up, and there isn't much I can do about it sitting on that bus.

I need a name. Escaping my past and running to a new life is something I don't have any experience with and copies of *Escaping Your Past for Dummies* are scarce, so my plan up to this point has been to wing it and hope for the best. I'm pretty sure, though, that at some point I'll have to identify myself and it would help to be prepared. I obsessed over it during my faux naps, but my imagination couldn't come up with a name I felt comfortable with or that seemed in the least bit plausible. I even considered using the name of my seatmate's feline, but 'Fuzzy Whiskerface' would probably draw too much attention. The best I came up with on my own was 'Dolph Greenburg.' I need help.

With the better part of an afternoon to kill before an overnight stay in a bus station lobby chair, I'm off to wander the streets of Rapid City looking for inspiration. If Main Street is true to its name, that's where most of the businesses will be. Maybe something will jump out at me. Or maybe the modern world hasn't quite caught up to rural South Dakota and I'll find a phone book.

My assumption about the businesses was dead on, but the first ten blocks or so are a wash with no phone books in sight. It's been almost an hour and I'm losing faith. As I near what appears to be the end of the business district, I begin to pass a homely cinder-block building sitting on the side of a dusty section of road. It's seen better days and gives all the appearance of a typically anonymous administration building. Maybe a social security office. But as I draw near, with every intent of walking by, I realize how myopic I've been. Idiotic might be a better word, but I'm being kind to myself. There's another obvious place to browse thousands of names and I'm standing in front of one right now. A bookstore, right here in Rapid City. What better place to find free access to a nearly unlimited selection of names? I can enter as one man and emerge as another.

Coming in off the glare of the street, it takes a few seconds for my eyes to adjust, but when they do, I get a welcome surprise. Crammed into this squat building with the colorless exterior are endless shelves of bright paperbacks, with waist-high stacks sitting on the floor in indiscriminate piles. I must have gawked.

"Welcome, stranger. You must be from out of town. You just found the best bookstore in all of the Dakotas. We have over 35,000 titles. If you can't find it here, you won't find it. And because they're used, you can get several books for the cost of one new one. Can I help you find anything?"

I decide not to share the fact that I'm looking for a name, not a book, so I quietly demur and head into the fray. The man behind the counter watches me for a few seconds then goes back to reading, looking up now and then to gauge my progress.

Funny how the names of authors seem to reflect the subject of their books. The economics book writers' names are too stodgy, the romance novelists are too, well, feminine, and the guys who write fantasy conjure up images of geeks with acne, thick glasses, and polyester plaid shirts. Probably unfair, but that's how I see it. I need something unique but not so audacious as to draw attention.

My frustration begins to increase, and I sense the clerk eyeing me is growing suspicious of this customer who gives equal time to travel guides and women's studies texts. Close to giving up, I spy a tattered and torn hardcover hiding behind a stack of pop psychology tomes. It's some sort of a guide to creative writing for the masses subtitled 'Find Fame and Fortune Writing Best Sellers!' It appears old, probably out of print ages ago. The back cover lists rave reviews from journals and individuals I've never heard of, but they're certainly enthusiastic. The photo of the author on the inside back flap is the clincher. If I squint my eyes a bit and use creative license (see, I'm learning from the book already), he kind of looks like me. 'Kind of' with a liberal interpretation.

I browse around a bit more to give myself time to make up my mind, but by the time I get to the locked case with the sexual self-help books (*How to Be a Slut While Retaining Your Womanhood*), I know it's right. I feel guilty not buying it, but I want the name, not the book.

"Thank you very much, you have a nice store here," I offer to the clerk at the cash register as penance for not spending any money.

"I'm sorry you didn't find anything," he replies. "Maybe next time, Mr...."

"Winters. Malcom Winters."

I've kept few of my contacts from my previous life, figuring that if I could find them, they could find me, but Freddy Four-Fingers is far too useful to cut off. I don't know his real name, but how he got tagged with his nickname was all too obvious. Missing the pinkie fingers on both hands (maybe he should have been 'Freddy Eight-Fingers'), he's still the most skilled forger I've ever encountered. Rumors abound as to how he lost those fingers, from mob enforcers to cannibalism, but the unwritten rule is if you ask, you can never use his services again. I've never asked.

I head back in the direction of the bus depot, but not before finding an isolated doorway in an abandoned building just off Main Street. I pull a burner phone out of my backpack, hesitating only a moment when I realize my supply of phones is at a crisis level, but this call is essential in establishing my new identity as Malcom Winters.

Information connects me to the classified department of the Tennessean, the daily paper in Nashville, Tennessee. While on hold, I scribble down the message I want to place. One letter out of place could mean paying a fortune for an ID for an Asian toddler, so it's critical that I get this right the first time. "Denny G: First, Mal can come and last win was terse when ignoring the last half of me. Wants it all as usual. Cindy K."

Okay, so the code is a bit juvenile, but it's effective, and not so wild as to raise any suspicions. As if anyone is out there is scouring the Nashville papers looking for secret messages. I've also heard that Freddy uses a different code for each one of his customers so as to avoid any spying on the classifieds. Never hurts to be cautious, though.

'Denny G' is, of course, Freddy, but it also indicates what set of documentation I'm requesting, and the 'wants it all' is the full treatment, the deluxe version of his services. Not only a birth certificate and passport, which I'll use to get a driver's license myself, but a whole history in the various government databases, school records, employment histories, tax returns, and a social media presence through Facebook and Twitter. For whatever reason, Instagram costs extra. He'll even make sure I get a mention in a few news articles throughout the years. I don't know how he does it, but anyone who Googles me will see a full, if uneventful, life through the miracle of the digital age. 'Cindy K.' is me. Freddy already has my photograph and an embarrassing amount of personal information on me in his files.

I have the woman in the classified ads department read back the wording twice. She must get a lot of odd requests, as her voice never left the range of 'bored beyond belief.' I head back to the bus depot but not to the same bus. The cat lady has probably imported more pictures of Fuzzy and will be disappointed to lose her captive audience, but now I have a destination. I have to find a way to get to Nashville within the next thirty-six hours.

Chapter 2

It's hard to imagine a counterfeiter with the nickname 'Freddy Four-Fingers' setting up shop anywhere but New York, but there he is 900 miles away in the middle of the country music capital of the world. To dispel even more of the typecasting, he isn't some skinny, mole-like guy with a bad case of the twitches. He looks like a middle-aged accountant, speaks softly and politely with just the slightest hint of a drawl, and actually wears a tie when he works. Which he does alone. Who wears a tie when no one is around to see it? I only hope that he doesn't own the complete collection of the albums of Conway Twitty or I'll be completely disillusioned.

The travel gods are good to me, I get lucky on connections, and the sassy Greyhound ticket agent with big hair gets me on the first of three buses that will eventually get me to Nashville by tomorrow night. I settle in a window seat halfway back, leaving room for other passengers to keep on moving after they get a glimpse of my 'crazy face,' which I've actually practiced in front of a mirror. My facial muscles ache after the first ten minutes or so, but by the time the bus pulls away, I have the entire row to myself. No cat pictures for now.

After pulling into Nashville only seventeen minutes late, I scout out the closest newsstand looking for the present day's edition of the Tennessean. Discarding the front section, which is too depressing anyway, and paging nervously to the back section of the paper, I'm pleased to see that the disinterested woman in classifieds got everything right. Now, it's a waiting game. I have my usual dives to crash for a night in many cities, but Nashville isn't one of them, so I wander a bit before choosing my target. After sleeping in buses, on floors, and occasionally on a park bench for weeks, I feel a little luxury is in order. And I could use a shower. It might not have been my crazy face that kept potential seatmates away after all.

After making a slow 360-degree turn scouting the area within easy walking distance, I set off in the direction of the tallest building, often a good sign of lodging outside of the downtown area. Sure enough, before long, a Fairfield Inn appears before me. A modern, eight-story architectural disappointment more suitable for an airport, my guess is that its dismal façade doesn't translate to a discounted room rate. I'm low on cash and don't carry credit cards or an ATM card, so I need to devise a plan. It's nearing dinnertime, which is the perfect time to pull out Diversion Number Three. It works about half the time, but I'm a bit desperate and have no better idea. Besides, it's kind of fun when it unfolds as it should.

Strolling into the spacious lobby, trying to look like I belong there, I'm pleased to find the stand of local tourist flyers that seem endemic to all hotel entryways immediately inside the doors within easy listening distance of the front desk. As expected, the two clerks look harried as they cope with tired and ornery travelers and a shrieking baby. They're probably hungry and half their mind is focused on their upcoming dinner break while the line to check in grows longer and unruly. I stand quietly, all the time attempting to give the impression that I care about The County Music Hall of Fame or ziplining over the city. While my eyes stare unfocused at the splashy colors of the flyers, my ears' attention stays zeroed in on the front desk, ten feet to my left. About fifteen minutes pass without a suitable mark, and I begin to worry that my fixation on whether to go see the Patsy Cline Museum before or after the Johnny Cash Museum might draw some unwanted attention. Grabbing a handful of flyers at random, I move to a vinyl couch in the lobby and spread them out, keeping one eye on the never-ending flow of guests. Too young, kids in tow, not bedraggled enough. Dammit.

Just about when I'm ready to actually start reading the brochure for the Dukes of Hazzard Museum and to reconsider my life's choices, a middle-aged couple with identical Elvis t-shirts and matching luggage approaches the front desk. Best of all, from the wilted look on their faces and the sweat drops on the husband's brow, they'd spent a long, overly warm day visiting the sights. They probably know whether Patsy or Johnny was worth a look.

Within a minute, I commit their names and room number to memory and wander to the far end of the lobby near a plastic potted plant, looking impatiently at my wrist where a watch would be if I had one, as if I've been kept waiting too long. Out of the corner of my eye, I watch the couple enter the elevator, luggage in tow. I count slowly to one hundred, saunter casually over to the lobby men's room, and enter a stall. Taking a whole roll of toilet paper and wadding it up, I proceed to flush it down the toilet. Or at least try to, several times. I add more paper as I continue to flush. Eventually, the bowl begins to back up and overflow, my signal to move on upstairs. The weary couple should have had time to enter the room and flop on the bed by now. Combing my hair the best I can, I ride up to the eighth floor. Standing outside Room 813, I clear my throat and knock gently.

The same haggard and sweaty man I'd followed up from the lobby opens the door a crack, appearing a bit annoyed that his intended nap has been delayed. I'm momentarily distracted by the neon Elvis staring back at me from his chest.

"Mr. Evans? Mr. Buddy Evans?" I try to sound as official as possible. No reaction from Buddy, just a blank stare. "Mr. Evans? From Akron, Ohio? I'm the assistant manager of housekeeping. I'm afraid there's been a bit of a mistake in giving you this room. May I come in?" Without waiting for an answer, I push the door open and step past my portly friend, who still hasn't said a word, glancing into the bathroom as I pass. As I presumed, there's been no time for anyone to try out the shower yet.

"Who is it, dear?" comes a shrill voice from the other side of the room. "Did he say housekeeping? Did he bring up more towels?"

I turn my attention to the prostrate figure on the far bed. "I'm sorry, Ma'am, but as I was telling your husband, there's been an unfortunate error. This room should never have been assigned. I'm afraid the shower isn't working. No water, you see. I have to ask you to go back to the front desk to get another room."

"Well, of all the nerve!" Mrs. Evans is clearly the alpha here. "We just got in here!"

"I understand, Ma'am, and on behalf of the hotel, I apologize. Perhaps they'll give you a coupon for a free drink in the bar."

The prospect of anything free usually does the trick, and this time is no exception. With exaggerated sighs for my benefit, in case I don't know how inconvenienced they are, Mr. and Mrs. Evans pull their luggage out into the hallway and head for the elevator. Elvis has left the room.

From experience, I know I now have about ten minutes, but I only need three. Unscrewing the showerhead, I place a quarter neatly in the path of the flow then screw it back on tight. Before slipping out of the room, I take a quick inventory of the room. Sure enough, sitting in plain sight on the nightstand is the room key. No sense taking it with them since they weren't coming back. I place it in my pocket.

I linger in the hallway for about six minutes before the night maintenance man makes his appearance. The first-string crew will be on their way home by now and the second shift is typically limited to one guy. Invariably, this guy feels so put upon if asked to do any actual work that whatever he can save for the day shift, he will. Only full-blown emergencies require immediate attention. Fortunately, I had created just such an emergency back in the lobby. He just doesn't know it yet.

Leaning against the wall just outside Room 813, studying a brochure listing all of the food options within walking distance, I hear the squeak as the bathtub faucets are turned and the shower lever is pulled, followed closely by a loud curse. Before there was time to find the cause of the issue, though, the man's radio squawks.

"Lenny, we have a problem down here in the men's room. Major overflow. We need you right away."

More cussing and the sound of tools being thrown back into a box is my signal to move down the hallway a ways. True to form, Lenny hangs a 'Do Not Disturb' sign on the door and ambles angrily toward the elevator. Chances are slim that he'll be back. If he surprises me, he'll find an irritated hotel guest who insists that the shower works just fine, thank you, and if he doesn't leave me alone, the front desk will hear about it.

Using the key kindly donated by Mr. and Mrs. Evans, I enter the room and lock the safety latch behind me. Time for that long and much-needed shower. I can only hope that it works.

Chapter 3

If there's any upside to being forced to read countless tourist brochures, it's that I now have my evening itinerary firmly set in my mind. I clearly want to avoid the rowdy, hard-drinking 'I came to Nashville to have a great time, and damn it, I'm going to have a great time if it kills me' tourist crowd around Second and Broadway. The fact that there's a Hard Rock Café on that very corner tells me all I need to know. Luckily, the Fairfield is in the Gulch, a trendy neighborhood that provides all I require within easy walking distance.

First stop, some dinner. Without any real plan, and an even worse sense of direction, I wander slowly away from the hotel, enjoying the night air. I haven't ventured very far before I spy what appears to be a miniature red Cracker Barrel in the next block. Always one to impose guilt by association, I've already written it off before I notice the line out the door. A good sign, maybe, so I join the queue without even asking what type of food it serves. My bare wrist tells me that about twenty minutes pass before I'm seated at a table with a couple from Georgia who are kind enough to lend a chair and perceptive enough to avoid extended conversation. A scrawny server with acne descends upon me with pen in hand before I have a chance to review my options, but I'm hungry so I just randomly point at a spot on the menu and hope for the best.

The catfish po'boy that arrives later is a little spicy for my taste but the collard greens and the banana cream pie I request make up for my disappointment with the fish. The burning in my mouth after the first bite of my sandwich made my brain go numb, which is the only explanation I can think of for why I order tea south of the Mason Dixon line. Any beverage that begins with tea in bags which then tries to cover up the taste of the tea with a truckload of sugar isn't meant to pass through these lips. A fine tea is like nirvana in a cup. Is it too much to ask for a barbecue joint to offer a Japanese Sencha? Okay, point taken.

The meal, while flawed, is still far better than the truck stop slop I've been picking at for the last chunk of time. As I make my way toward the exit, I decide to walk around the city for a while to work it off. I have no intention of stopping in a club to hear the music for which Nashville is famous since most of it has a bit too much twang for my taste, but that was before I stumble upon a dive called the Station Inn. A squat, forlorn-looking stone building with a red door, I would have driven right by if I'd been in a car. Good thing I'm on foot.

From the lineups listed on the posters masquerading as glass in the windows, this place isn't immune to the plague of country music, but it appears to focus on bluegrass, which is a whole different thing. Tonight they have some string players whose names I can't place but which tickle a memory cell somewhere in the recesses of my brain. I figure it's worth a chance and the small cover charge. I'm early, but as I enter, a crowd is already beginning to monopolize the folding chairs up front by the miniature stage, which is fine by me. I settle in the rear where my back can be against a post and my glass has the honor of resting on the wobbliest table in the joint.

I'm nursing my third drink and about the forty-seventh minute of studying the faded and tattered posters on the walls, some of them going back decades, when I feel a presence nearby. The presence speaks before I can take a second to turn in that direction.

"Do you mind if I join you?"

Oftentimes, the voice doesn't match the image conjured up in the nanosecond before seeing its source, so I'm prepared for disappointment because this voice is sultry, intelligent, ultra-feminine in a tom-boyish way, and drop-dead gorgeous. Okay, so maybe I'm projecting a little. Once I look up, though, if anything, I've sold her short. The first thing I notice is her hair, a brilliant mane of infinite shades of red, clearly not from a bottle because of its diversity and the fact that it suits her so perfectly. The waves at its ends fall past her shoulders, framing a mature but beautiful face with the deepest brown eyes, nose rounded just the right way, and a spattering of freckles. God, the freckles. I'm a sucker for them in a grown woman and hers will fuel my fantasies for years to come. She wears a deep auburn leather jacket, worn at the elbows, over a vintage Rolling Stones t-shirt, faded from too many

23

washings, with the smallest rip in a location that would tempt more than a glance if I weren't a gentleman. I won't mention the tight jeans because I'm not staring at them. I swear I don't even notice. She's every man's fantasy of the farmgirl next door, although I have the feeling that she's never seen the underside of a cow.

"Um, well, yes, please. I mean, no one is sitting there." Smooth.

I feign interest in the posters as she removes her jacket and eases into the chair, but the corners of my eyes work overtime to catch her every move. I do notice that there are still a few empty spots closer to the stage, making me wonder why she would choose to sit next to me. Maybe she likes shaky tables, but is it possible that she's flirting? I've never been quick on the uptake when a woman shows interest in me, and the last few years of generally avoiding people and eyeing every new encounter with suspicion have done nothing to hone that skill. I figure I have to say something anyway, just to be sociable.

"Have you been here before?" See what I mean? Hopeless.

"No."

Does a one-word answer mean that the conversation is over? I'd love to keep it going, but the awkward silence has me once more looking at my wrist to see if it's time for the entertainment to begin. Maybe one of these days I should buy a watch.

"I'm Felicity. My friends call me Fyre." I swear, she pronounces her name with a 'y.' I don't know how, but she does.

"Malcom. Nice to meet you, Fyre." See how subtle I am in putting myself in the 'friend' category? Gee, maybe she'll let me carry her books home from school. "Are you here on vacation?"

"No, business. Yourself?"

"The same. Where are you from?"

"Chicago."

"Never been there. Do you like it?"

"Very much. You should visit sometime."

Does she mean visit the city or visit her? I really need to find a class on deciphering what a woman says because too often, it means nothing close to how I interpret it. Or maybe a Google translator. There must be someone, somewhere with a degree in 'Woman-speak as a Second Language.'

Anyway, the conversation moves on to topics such as favorite types of music to what we do for a living. Given my line of business, if you can call it that, I'm fairly skilled at deflecting questions about my life or when pressed, getting creative in making something up. Today, I only fumble a little when describing my life as a writer. Fyre doesn't seem to notice. I'm also pretty damn good at knowing when someone is doing the same thing to me. Fyre is a decent liar, but not decent enough deceive the likes of me. I don't mind, not really, but a slight catch in her voice and a look in her eyes reveal an actual fear that I would discover something about her that she doesn't want me to know. That arouses suspicions and warning bells ring loud and clear in my mind. Something here is not right.

Beauty does have its advantages, though, and combined with the fact that we're both just passing through each other's path convinces me to set aside my doubts and to just enjoy her company for the night. I allow the conversation to move on to favorite parts of the country we've visited. Not exactly scintillating, but at least it's a topic I can handle without making a complete fool of myself. Either that or she's kind enough to pretend not to notice.

Just as we're ready to move on to more important issues such as whether we own any pets, the band starts shuffling out on stage. Seizing the opportunity, I leap into deeper waters.

"Have you heard these guys before?"

"No, but I've heard of them. The vocalist supposedly sounds a bit like Jimmy Martin in his prime, but I prefer more the jazz influence, like Vassar Clements."

I eye my new best friend Fyre with a combination of admiration, curiosity, and more than a little suspicion that she's testing me. I've never heard of those musicians and wasn't about to try to pursue that topic as if I did. I like some bluegrass music and can drop a name like Bill Monroe, but that's as far as it goes. So, instead, I do what comes naturally. I sit with my mouth slightly open, gawking, and say nothing. Meet Malcom Winters, master of the awkward silence.

Fyre smiles at me then turns toward the front of the room. Following her lead, I do likewise. The band turns out to be more than good, with a searing fiddle player who could make his instrument cry or fly and a singer who may or may not be reminiscent of Jimmy Martin. The overall effect on everyone in the room, including two strangers sharing a table at the back, is to magically bring us together in a sort of euphoric unity.

Fyre and I continue to make small talk between sets, my curiosity about what she's hiding unabated, although I can't shake the feeling that we were connecting. Part of my brain—the alpha male part—wonders if she would object to sharing a hotel room if she knew that any activity that might occur there would be subject to possible interruption by a maintenance man with a passkey and a wrench.

Any thoughts in that direction are dashed when she stands up after a rousing edition of 'St. Anne's Reel' and puts on her jacket, extending her hand across the table.

"Malcom, it's been a pleasure."

I stand, take the proffered hand, and hold it perhaps a bit longer than necessary. It's warm, soft, and oddly sensual. "The pleasure was all mine." Probably true. "You can't stay until the end?"

"I have an appointment. Have a good evening, Mal."

Mal. I like that and vow that if she can be 'Fyre' to her friends, I can be 'Mal' to mine. If I ever get any. I watch as Fyre slips through the crowd standing at the rear of the room, her hair seemingly changing hue as she moves.

I wait around awhile, but my interest in the music has waned. When I notice a young couple eyeing the empty chair at my table, I rise and motion for them to sit. Too bad Fyre is no longer around to make note of my chivalry and to give me credit for a few brownie points. With that, I head back to the Fairfield, confident that the room with the broken shower will still be mine.

Chapter 4

I'm up the next morning before 5:30, making the bed, cleaning the bathroom, and removing any sign that someone had spent the night there. Unnecessarily early, perhaps, but I'm also anxious to grab the morning paper to check the classified section. Mild-mannered Freddy can also be demanding, fickle, and temperamental, so if I miss an appointment to pick up my documents, he's likely to reschedule it for a week or even a month later, or to go completely silent on me. Throwing my damp towel into a maid's cart down the hall, I make my way to the lobby.

Hair tousled and damp, looking every bit a registered guest, I grab a complimentary paper off a stack near the front desk and settle into a well-worn but remarkably uncomfortable chair. I needn't have worried. Freddy's cryptic message is there, nestled between 'Looking for the woman wearing a Predator's jacket riding the #34 bus Wednesday afternoon' and a legal notice disclaiming some ex-loved one's debts. My package won't be ready until tomorrow morning. Damn. I have over twenty-four hours to kill.

Housekeeping is still setting up the free breakfast buffet. My impatient stomach may not agree, but eating will have to wait. It's not necessarily a bad thing, as I need to clear my head and start working on ideas for how to score a room for that night, so I exit the revolving door and start walking. It's going to be a wet day if the dark, threatening clouds are any indication, so I keep a brisk pace, traveling in a wide circle so as not to be too far away from the Fairview lobby. There's little traffic and not a single business shows any signs of life. Nashville residents like their sleep.

Less than an hour later, I'm back in the hotel lobby, still dry but no closer to any thoughts as to how to occupy myself for the next twenty-four hours nor what kind of scheme I can conjure up for free bed and board. Maybe I'm not doing my best, thinking on an empty stomach, and the smell of waffles and eggs is enticing. I pivot left and follow my nose to breakfast.

Hotel breakfasts are all pretty much the same, down to the overworked toasters, chunky scrambled eggs, and stale-looking pastries. Sadly, this is no exception. Being free, though, makes it more appetizing, which I guess puts me in the company of the Evans couple. Trying to balance the demands of my growling gut with the knowledge that consuming too much of the vittles here will give me something to regret later, I settle for a bagel, bowl of mock-Cheerios, and watery orange juice. Scanning the small room for a table, I immediately spot a very familiar back of the head, although today the colors seem momentarily stable.

"Do you mind if I join you?" I try to appear nonchalant as I approach the table's empty chair.

Fyre jumps, clearly startled, and I feel a bit guilty for having pulled her out of whatever reverie she had been lost in. She recovers nicely, brushes her hair back out of her eyes, takes a quick sideways glance at her reflection in the window, and points to the chair with her open hand.

"Um, well, yes, please. I mean, no one is sitting there."

Great, a smartass with a good memory. I ignore her jibe, set my plate down (grateful I hadn't piled it high), and take a seat across from her.

"I guess we're both staying here." Mr. Obvious. "How did your appointment go?"

"Very well. In fact, I thought I might have to stay another night but I got lucky. I'm headed home this morning. Are you staying in Nashville?"

"Unfortunately, yes. I had the opposite luck. I was hoping to be done today but it looks like my business won't be concluded until tomorrow. After breakfast, I need to see if I can extend my stay another night."

"Why don't you take my room? I have it reserved through tomorrow, so it's already paid for."

"I couldn't—" I stop suddenly when she held up her hand up to cut me off.

"Don't worry about the cost. I paid for it with points, so they won't give me a refund. Consider it my gift to my bluegrass compadre."

I sit back, slowly chewing my bagel, trying to see the downside to this unexpected stroke of good fortune. There isn't any. Before I can respond, Fyre continues talking.

"Before you make a decision, I'd like to make a suggestion. If you're like me, you can be pretty particular about where you sleep. I can show you the room to make sure it meets your standards. I think it would be an especially good idea if you give the bed a try."

"That won't be necessary. In this hotel, I'm sure all of the…" I cut myself off upon seeing the disappointment spread across Fyre's face, suddenly realizing how slow I am on the uptake. I take a quick study of her eyes. Beneath the clear anticipation and a healthy dash of desire, there remains the sadness I first noticed last night along with a deeper, disturbing sense of something I can't isolate in the fraction of a second we lock eyes. It's unsettling and I wonder if she truly wants me or if she's using me as a momentary, physical escape from whatever is haunting her. My hesitation is quickly buried by my own baser instincts. I take one last bite of my cereal, rise from my seat, and take Fyre's hand.

As we make our way out of the breakfast lounge, a familiar-looking couple is on the way in. Mr. Evans seems focused on breaking his fast, his eyes glued on the waffle maker, but Mrs. Evans stares at me with suspicion as the signs of recognition and the beginnings of a tantrum begin to spread across her face. I hustle after Fyre before she can say anything or rat me out to the front desk as the man who falsely claimed they would get a free drink due to the room snafu.

Not a word is exchanged as Fyre and I ride the elevator up to the fourth floor, each of us suddenly shy in the presence of the other. The silence continues as we walk to the door of her room. Her hand trembles a bit as she inserts the key card into the lock. I stay close as we enter, irrational fears that she'll close the door between us flooding my addled brain.

She's already packed, a small hard-shell suitcase standing at the foot of the bed. The only sign that she had been there at all is the rumpled sheet exposed by the flowered bedcover folded neatly at a diagonal. She turns to me and for a few uncomfortable seconds we both stand, frozen still, the heat in the room rising rapidly as each of our minds race to find the appropriate thing to say.

Simultaneously, we both realize that no words are necessary. We melt together as if drawn by invisible forces, our arms encircling each other in an embrace that fuses our two bodies into one. An annoying but persistent voice inside my head tries desperately to reign in the raw force of instinctual passion, reminding me to be tender. Against my will I listen, lifting my hand to the back of Fyre's head, pulling it gently toward me as my lips part. I can smell the scent of her shampoo along with the warm sweat of her desire, I also sense the slightest undercurrent of fear and uncertainty, although in all honesty that's probably coming from me.

Whatever inner voice is speaking to Fyre is on a totally different page from my own. As my lips softly, tentatively brush against hers, in a single motion she grabs my hair while she leaps into my body, wrapping her legs around my waist. Her hot breath singes me as she moves in, her tongue forcing itself deep within my mouth. To hell with tenderness. I respond in kind, placing my hands beneath her rear as we stumble toward the bed.

After several sultry minutes, neither willing to break the embrace as our hands begin to explore, I push her away slightly while still keeping her close. My fingers tremble as I begin to unbutton my shirt. Wordlessly she pulls my hands away, guiding them to the front of her blouse before bringing her own hands back to my chest. As my frantic fingers stumblingly work at freeing her top button, Fyre rips my shirt apart, buttons flying, pulling it down over my arms and binding me momentarily. She giggles as she takes her own top off, lingering after every button, finally revealing a lacy beige bra which barely has enough material to support the breasts beneath.

"I'll save you the trouble," she whispers seductively, unhooking the bra while I'm finally able to shed my own shirt. As we gaze at each other, lust permeating the air, I see that the hint of freckles I had first seen in her face the night before extends down to her chest. Oh my.

Fyre rises to her knees, forcefully pulling my face to her chest. I plant a warm and sloppy kiss where my mouth lands then playfully bite the inside of each breast before tracing my tongue slowly down her stomach to just below her navel. Impatient, continuing with an almost frightening abandon and aggressiveness, Fyre pushes me down onto the bed and straddles my chest. This time, no games as we each deal with our own belts. In moments, both pairs of pants hit the floor. Fyre moves my arms to my sides, pinning them between her thighs. Edging forward on her knees, she brings her glistening black panties just outside the reach of my mouth, rocking so that they would come tantalizingly close but never within range. A sly smile appears behind the hair hiding her face as she senses my frustration.

It's my turn to be impatient. Freeing my arms from their sweaty prison, I grab Fyre by the waist and lift, pushing her onto the bed at my side. Quickly, I roll on top of her, putting my finger to her lips. Fyre instantly recognizes that it's her turn to accept what I have to offer.

I begin running my fingers through her hair, barely exhaling a warm breath into her ear before nibbling the lobes on each side. Kissing her forehead, my lips travel down to her eyes, each closed in concentration, to the tip of her nose, then to her cheeks, brushing her lips on my way to her chin. Flicking my tongue on the nape of her neck, I kiss her deeply before diving into her bountiful breasts, nipples firm and welcoming. Licking, flitting, then sucking each one, trailing my tongue down her stomach. Reaching her panties, I grab the waistband in my teeth and gently pull them down her legs, only using my hand to free them from her feet.

As I move back northward, Fyre grabs hold of my hair, lifting my head away from her body. Sitting up suddenly, she flips me over so that now she's back on top. She proceeds with uncanny precision to mimic my every kiss, every flick of my tongue, moving down my body at the exact same pace before pulling my own underpants off with her teeth.

Now fully naked, we instinctively merge together, the heat of our bodies melting us into a single mass, so that I can't tell where I end and Fyre begins. We move together, first with me on top and then below and then not knowing where I am. The final, simultaneous shudders bring us both crashing down upon the mattress, drenched in our own perspiration, still holding each other tight as the adrenaline seeps away. In the afterglow, we continue to stay close and silent, limbs intertwined. Neither of us speaks and neither of us moves for one glorious minute after another.

Eventually, we pull away long enough to look into the eyes of the other. I don't know what she sees in mine, probably a sense of deep satisfaction and maybe even some affection, but I'm disturbed not just by what I see in hers but by what I don't see. There is no contentment or fondness, only an overwhelming melancholy and a distance that seems to put her miles away from the bed we are sharing. My mind races to find appropriate words to bring her back to me and to help her share in my post-coital bliss, or at the very least a bit of peacefulness. I'm saved the trouble by a loud knock on the door.

"Housekeeping!"

The corners of Fyre's mouth rise slightly as she turns her attention to the anonymous voice. Spell broken.

"Give me five," she yells at the door. Time to move on.

We walk quietly hand-in-hand to Fyre's car, where she presses her room key into my palm followed by a quick brush on my lips. No words are spoken. A minute later, I'm alone in the parking lot watching as she drives away. Rather than return to what is now my room—a problem solved—I choose to wander the city. I find a small shop where I buy a supply of burner phones for a decent price, then use one of them to make a call to arrange a money transfer into Freddy's account.

Eventually, boredom and a sense of restlessness overtake me, and I return to my room, where the lingering scent of passion infuses me with a sense of both exhilaration and loneliness.

Chapter 5

Freddy, being ever cautious, won't answer the door if you show up at the time he specifies in his classified ad. It has to be eleven minutes later. Not ten, not twelve, but eleven. I get an early start, as it's about an hour's walk to the apartment that doubles as his office. Located under Highway 40 over a bagel shop near the Tennessee State University campus, it isn't the most conspicuous spot. It's been a while since I've been there and my memory has disappointed me more than once lately, so I have concerns about whether I'll recognize the building. I'll never get my new identity if I'm late. The plan is to find it then camp out in a coffee shop nearby, grab a pastry, and wait out any excess time.

The route to Freddy's lacks the distraction of any visual appeal, allowing me to ignore my surroundings and to mentally revisit my tryst with Fyre. She's attractive, intelligent, and vibrant, which should be enough for any man, including myself. On the negative side, she's secretive and clearly is haunted by something, causing loud warning signals to sound inside my head whenever we're together. It's possible, even probable, that I'm so accustomed to being put in situations where not being able to read what's going on inside an individual's head means almost certain death, that I'm overreacting. I have the ability to track Fyre down if I want to, but is that what I want? Something to think about on the next Greyhound.

Having settled that issue through procrastination, I look up and find myself thirty yards from the bagel shop. Score one for my subconscious memory. From there, though, my plan rapidly falls apart. Walking a one hundred-yard perimeter around Freddy's base of operations, I barely catch any sign of life at all, much less a Starbucks. In a way, that isn't a bad thing, as their uninspired selection of hot teas shows why they're known for their coffee. I stand on a corner, frustrated and cold, contemplating whether to hang out in the 24-hour laundromat when a revelatory thought enters my head. Freddy lives above a bagel shop. Moron (me, not Freddy). I had to skip the Fairfield breakfast when it became clear that Mr. and Mrs. Evans were going to make a morning of it over coffee and Froot Loops, and a toasted wheat bagel with vegetable cream cheese sounds palatable. If they don't have tea, juice will do.

The bagel is better than good and the juice is cold. I'm just finishing when chimes sound from the phone in my pocket. Exiting the revolving door and circling to the rear of the building, I climb up a rotting wooden staircase to the second floor, staring at my phone and counting down the last few seconds before knocking on a faded green door. Two knocks, pause, one knock, pause, then two more. I wouldn't be surprised if Freddy has a different code for every customer.

The door slowly opens to a six-inch crack, the business end of a high-caliber handgun emerging right at eye level.

"Password?"

The request startles me. He's never required one before, although it's been at least five years since I last used his services. I'm not scared but I'm not happy either. Mostly, I'm just pissed off.

"How about if-you-don't-open-the-door-to-let-me-in-I'll-bust-it-open?"

"That'll work," he mutters. He opens the door just wide enough for me to slip in sideways before quickly shutting it and engaging a Rube Goldberg-esque set of locks.

"Since when do you require a password?"

Freddy grins, then shrugs his shoulders. "I don't. A few months back, I used an acquaintance to whisper to certain sources that the password 'Key Largo' would gain entrance. If you had used that phrase a minute ago, I would've blasted you without a second's pause. Keeps the riff-raff away." He shrugs again, a nervous habit. "You can never be too careful."

With that, the old man turns and straggles back to an old banker's desk set in the corner of the room, its top obscured by at least a dozen lamps of various intensities. For now, the room is darkened. Freddy has aged since I last saw him, having added deep stress lines across his forehead. His gray hair has turned a cream-colored white, a stark contrast to his coal-black face. Five years before, I would have guessed his age as around 50. Now, maybe closer to 80. And yes, he's wearing a tie. Purple with red stripes, if you must know.

"This business is getting harder every day," he grumbles as he lowers himself into his chair. "I'm too old to keep up with the technology. Thinkin' about retiring."

As he speaks, Freddy leans down and opens a drawer, which lets out a loud squeak in protest. He pulls out a thick envelope. "Good name, I like it. Solid. You'd be surprised what some people want. Won't even do some of them, draws too much attention."

Freddy's fingers quiver as he opens the clasp on the envelope, pulling out a stack of documents and pushing them across the desk. "If you ever need to do this again and I'm still kickin', I'll need a more recent picture."

I pick up the passport, turning it over in the dim light. Exquisite. Freddy sighs, then speaks again. He's talkative today.

"Kept your same birthdate. You know the drill. Take these to the chair over there and start learnin' about yourself. Before you leave, they go in the fire."

My memory may not be what it used to be, but I've been trained to zero in on the most cogent facts and lock them away forever. I can always Google myself later to fill in any gaps. I was apparently born in a small town outside of Toledo, won an award in a 7th-grade science fair, and was a two-sport star in my high school. And knowing Freddy, if you look up the class yearbook online, there I'll be along with every other student. Freddy has pictures of me at a variety of ages, from early childhood on, stored in his database. I'm not worried about security, though. The first time I met him, Freddy told me that if anyone's fingers but his own touched his keyboard, all of his stored data instantly dissolved.

I've been married, moved to Cleveland, then got divorced. Worked in sales for a while before accepting a manager's position with a flooring company. My interests include golfing—which I hope I'll never have to prove—and collecting beer cans. I'm pretty sure I hear Freddy chuckling as I snort in disgust.

There's more of the same, but I don't stay the whole hour. I throw my new life's history into the fire, shake Freddy's hand, and make a quick exit. Leaving his shop, I have a decision to make. Where to? My default plan is to go to the bus station, take the first bus that has a final destination at least two hundred miles away, and hope that the fates will be kind. I descend the stairs and plot my course to the Greyhound station. Heading back, a chilly wind flies in my face and I bury my hands deep into the pockets of my jacket.

As I walk, I feel a slip of paper at the fingertips of my left hand that hadn't been there the day before. Curious, I pull it out, read it, and give a mental tip of the hat to the fates. No words, only ten digits. 773-555-3589. I recognize the area code. Looks like I'm headed to Chicago.

Chapter 6

It doesn't take long to all but cross Chicago off my list of locales in which to leave the past behind and start anew. New York, no one makes eye contact and you can be safe in the knowledge that as far as your neighbors are concerned, you don't exist. Los Angeles, unless you're Somebody with a capital 'S,' people pretend you aren't in their line of sight. Within my first few minutes in Chicago, strangers looked at me as I passed and actually smiled. If I appeared a little lost for more than three seconds, passersby would ask if they could help. Big city, hell. I might as well be in Cheeseville, Wisconsin where everyone knows your life history before you finish unpacking. Not the easiest place to keep a low profile.

If it hadn't been for Fyre, I would have turned around and boarded the next bus to anywhere. I'm still undecided whether I'm ready to let her—or anyone—into my life, especially given my suspicion that there's a hidden side to her that I may not want to uncover. The easy route is to just move on, but I don't want to be halfway across Ohio when I realize I want to give the relationship, if that's what it is, a chance. To kill time while giving myself time to think this through, I begin to wander the neighborhoods of the city to see if I was too hasty in my initial impression of the place. I long ago composed a list in my head of certain specific requirements for where I would park my ass for a while. Quiet, hidden away, easy to fortify. An area where I won't attract attention. Oh, and no vermin. I'm done with the vermin.

I cover maybe half of the neighborhoods on the North Side without finding what I'm looking for. Too open, too dense, too anything-to-not-have-to-make-a-decision. It's beginning to get dark. My frustration brings on nostalgic feelings for the Greyhound seats and I even think back with fondness of my feline friend, Fuzzy. I make up my mind that if I can't resolve my intentions by morning, it's time to move on. To celebrate my historic non-decision, I make my way into the nearest tavern that doesn't serve fifteen-dollar cocktails.

I don't remember the name of that bar or where any of the next ones in which I imbibed were. I don't remember what I drank, or for that matter drinking at all. Hell, I don't remember much of anything before this awkward moment, waking up under the evergreen shrubs of a stately old dame, a cup of steaming coffee and a guava-filled turnover sitting by my side. I swallow my principles, apologize to the tea gods, and drink a couple sips of the java to warm up, then eat about half of the most godawful pastry I've ever tasted before abandoning it. Sitting up, trying to figure out where I am and why, and whether I have any broken bones from a forgotten fight, I look around trying to get my eyes to focus. That's when I become aware of an imposing presence standing only a few feet away. From my perspective on the ground, he appears eight feet tall and almost as broad.

"Yew ahl rite, mah frond?" Yes, that's exactly how he sounded and no, I'm not going to try to duplicate it any further. Just pretend that his accent sounds kind of what you might hear in Cuba but doesn't really, that it varies from one sentence to the next, and that no ethnic group in the history of this planet has communicated in this dialect. I'll supply the words; you bring the imagination.

"Where am I?"

"America. Chicago. Ukie Village. Under a bush. Leo." He taps his massive chest in case this prostrate idiot didn't catch the reference. Leo looks stern and sounds angry. A bloody apron hangs from his neck. I expect to see a sharp meat cleaver in his massive hands, but instead notice the slightest upturn at the sides of his mouth. His version of a grin.

"You need to move, my friend. Owner coming by soon. Bringing a buyer, maybe. Mean man. Nasty man. You can't be here, he'll bring cops. Maybe this time he'll sell. Always good to hope."

"Sell? What does he want for it?" I'm not sure why I ask, except to give me time to stand without wobbling and to get my defenses up before the hidden cleaver makes an appearance. I'm a little dizzy and wonder if all of the alcohol has left my system. Or maybe I hit my head on the ground on my way to the bush. In any case, I'm not so hungover as to miss the slight glint in Leo's eyes when I pose the question.

38

"Go now. Come back later."

Going now is at the top of my agenda already and I don't need any further encouragement. After moving through the old, dilapidated red iron gate, which squeaks painfully, though, I can't help but look back at the building in whose shadow I had slept. Its old, weathered red bricks have faded but remain defiantly solid and provide a base for the weedy green vines that creep up the front and sides. Cracked concrete steps framed by short, tiered brick balustrades lead up to a cavernous landing, behind which sits a thick wood and glass door with a leaded glass panel of abstract flowers situated above.

At first, the building appears four stories tall, but on second glance, I see that it's only three, with deceptively high, vaulted ceilings and bay windows on each floor. The entrance to the bottom unit, to which Leo returns, is four steps below ground level, its doorway hidden behind the front steps. Pots of spindly herbs line and partially block the steps down to his unit.

Respectful of Leo's request that I vanish before the building's owner appears, I shuffle uncomfortably down the block, appearing to the world as someone who had just spent the night under a bush. Gradually, the stiffness in my joints loosens and I begin to notice my surroundings. Each structure I pass was clearly built with the pride of its craftsmen. Mostly brick but several of stone, they're solid and imposing, but with an aura of stateliness. A good working-class neighborhood. Having nothing better to do, the trip to the bus station temporarily shelved, I think I'll look around a bit.

A few blocks away, bolted to a streetlight, a faded metal sign that had seen too many sunny days informs me that I'm in the Ukrainian Village neighborhood of the city. Sixteen square blocks of workers' cottages that housed German, Polish, and eventually Ukrainian immigrants who came here in the 1800s looking to start over. The homes that they built were meant to last because, after their long journey to the middle of a strange new country, they intended to stay.

And stay they did. It didn't take a whole lot more wandering to discover why it was called 'Ukrainian Village.' Witness the Ukrainian Cultural Center, the Ukrainian National Museum, and massive Ukrainian churches. Store signs in a language that I haven't seen in a long time. Then there's the Tryzub Restaurant, whose enticing aromas lure me inside. Service is prompt, and my first bite of their pierogis leads me to indulge in the palyushku. Soon, the warm meal and hot tea flavored with wild thyme and bilberry have me feeling almost human again. More importantly, both staff and patrons are welcoming but keep their distance from a stranger, content to give me my space.

Leaving the restaurant, a nagging memory flits halfway to my consciousness. Did Leo tell me in my addled state to come back later? Whether he had or not, I want to get another look at that building. Retracing my steps, I can't find the right block. For thirty minutes, I walk down blocks of brick and stone homes until they all seem to blend together. As time wears on, my frustration morphs into elation. A block unintentionally hidden from the world. As if by magic, at that very moment, I find myself in front of my destination. It's time to see Leo.

It shouldn't surprise me that I'm expected. As I reach for the handle of the outside gate, Leo emerges from the stairway leading up from his apartment. His dark eyes belie his welcoming smile, and I know that I'm being evaluated. For what purpose, I'm not yet sure.

We stare at each other for a few moments before I break the silence, deciding that the friendly approach is the way to go. "Hello again, my friend. Thank you once more for the kindness you showed me earlier. How did the showing go?"

The old man frowns and spits onto the ground; whether a commentary on myself or the potential buyer, I have no clue. "*Cara de monda. Un hombre mal.*" He spits again for emphasis. "He will not be coming back again, I'm afraid." With a wicked grin, Leo brings his hand out from the folds of his blood-soaked apron to reveal the cleaver I had expected that morning. I assume that the blood dripping off the razor-sharp blade is from an animal he was prepping for dinner and that the buyer thought better of purchasing a place with a seemingly insane man with access to sharp instruments as a tenant. Then again, I wouldn't swear that the cleaver hadn't been put to a different use.

"Come inside, *mi amigo*. We talk."

The most dangerous people I've ever encountered, and there have been many, were those who mouthed words when they read or couldn't add simple sums, but who, as soon as you underestimated them, struck with a cunning that you didn't see coming. Leo is unquestionably in that category. He knows what I want to do practically before I do.

"It is a good building. *Bueno*," he says as we sit at his kitchen table, each in a wobbly but surprisingly comfortable chair that must predate the Crusades. "You would like it here. Safe. *Solitario*. Good place to build new life."

As he says those words, Leo's eyes take on a distant look, for an instant focusing not on the stranger across the table, but on painful memories he cannot forget. At the same time, I know he sees the identical look in my own eyes and recognizes that we are kindred spirits. He knows nothing about me yet senses all that he needs to know, and it's crucial to both of us that we share the silence of the haunted.

"Top floor empty. I have key," he continues. "You stay, call owner. I have number."

He stands as I do, each of us simultaneously reaching a hand out and gripping a survivor's handshake. He holds me tight in his calloused and scarred hand, testing me with a progressively stronger squeeze. I'm proud to say I hold my own.

I follow Leo up the steps to the landing, through the door beneath the flowered glass, which is propped open by a brick, and up a long flight of worn, uneven wooden stairs. Seconds later, I stand inside the door of the upper unit, my breath echoing in the empty space. I don't move for a long time as I visualize the changes I could make and where each piece of furniture I don't own will go. And, of course, where I would sit for my morning tea. Just as my eyes reach the kitchen, the sun breaks out and casts its rays through the skylight and directly onto the island where my imagination has conjured an image of me sitting with a steaming mug. I turn and leave the unit without even looking into the other rooms.

Chapter 7

The combination of a seller who has seen too many deals derailed by the presence of a crazed tenant, and a wanderer anxious to settle down and start a new life, made the deal quick and painless. Within weeks, I became the owner of a three-flat in Chicago. I've wasted no time in my attempt to blend in and to erase my past. Of course it's impossible to completely drop off the face of the Earth, but when one yearns for a semi-normal life under a new name, the best way is to hide in plain sight. To do that, I've had to quickly become a Chicagoan, just one more face in the crowd who has suffered too many harsh winters, too many disappointments with the Bears, and too many political scandals. It's critical that I don't look, speak or act like someone from somewhere else. I've studied the locals, absorbing the small details that distinguish true natives from the transplants. I've learned that no one who grew up here calls the city 'Chi-town' or puts ketchup on their hot dogs and that the only acceptable time to visit Navy Pier is if you're being kidnapped with a gun to your head. I know who Casimir Pulaski was, but, like every other resident in the city, don't understand why there's a city holiday in his honor. Even though I haven't yet experienced either, I complain about the heat in the summer and the cold in the winter and discovered that the lakefront has weather systems all its own. I know the trains are called the 'el' (and never the 'subway') even when they run underground. That tall building on Wacker Drive will always be the Sears Tower, no matter whose name is above the door. I've become a native with a capital 'N.'

And I can do all of this in obscurity in my little corner of Ukrainian Village. Leo and I have become fast friends, bound by the present as well as by our unspoken secrets of the past. Life overall is good, although I need to consider finding employment. Finding a job would not only be a great way to enhance my cover, it may actually be a necessity at this point. Unfortunately, my current skill set doesn't exactly lend itself to most occupations. I'll need to give it some thought.

In the meantime, I could use a bit of recreation. Between unpacking, painting, and a bit of custom remodeling and spending what seems like forever immersing myself in the city and trying to acclimate, I haven't taken any time to enjoy myself. I decide to further my Chicago education while absorbing a little culture and head downtown to the Art Institute. Climbing the steps between its two guardian lions, I find myself silently scoffing at the clusters of tourists checking their maps for the route back to their hotels. More tourists pack the lobby, and there's little relief even after working my way past the ticket-takers. My intent is to wander in the direction of the Monet haystacks, but I find myself fighting my way through a crowd of well-heeled people surging into a room. After about the third sharp elbow finds my ribcage, I figure why fight them when I can join them? Maybe they know something that I don't. I follow the flow into the room.

When I see what's in store, though, I instantly wish I had pushed through the crowd a little more aggressively or headed toward the modern wing instead. Apparently, I'm about to be treated to a lecture by a 'noted art historian' who isn't noted enough to plebeians like myself, because I don't recognize her name and probably won't remember it five minutes after she's done speaking. According to the program thrust into my hands as I enter, her talk is entitled 'Notable Frames of the Impressionist Galleries 171–247.' The frames, really? I grab a folding chair close to the door. I assume I don't need to explain why.

I'm not alone in choosing to be near an exit. Plopping into the seat immediately to my right comes a short, painfully thin, wisp of a man who is just on the far side of forty but sliding quickly into old age. Thick glasses hang from a cord slung around his neck. In contrast to my blue jeans and sweater, he wears tan slacks and a button-down shirt covered by a tweed jacket. All it would take is patches on the elbows and he would be the perfect poster child for an English Literature professor. I'm not far off.

As the introduction of the speaker drones on by a portly woman who clearly craves her share of the limelight, my neighbor leans over to whisper in my ear.

"You were smart to get a seat back here. I heard her speak on the use of red pigment by female Medieval painters at the Cincinnati Art Museum two years ago. You would think with a subject like that, the audience would be rapt, but she just never connected. It was all I could do to stay awake. Have you heard her speak before?"

"No, and if this woman doesn't give up the mike, I may not hear her today either."

He snorts a girlish giggle, or maybe it was a titter, nodding. "That's Sylvia Pathman. She wouldn't know a Picasso from a Pizarro, but she's responsible for half the artwork in Gallery 151." He extends a hand. "I'm Stuart Vanguard."

I oblige. "Malcom Winters."

He releases my hand but holds his gaze. As the main speaker finally takes center stage, my catty companion looks up to the front of the room but within minutes, is openly staring at my face. Only when I show my annoyance does he resume speaking, so softly he's hard to hear above the conversation about the frames containing—wouldn't you know it—Monet's haystacks. I keep my eyes on the slide being projected to the front of the room.

"I apologize for being rude, but you do look familiar. Are you the Malcom Winters who wrote, um, what was it exactly? 'Make a Fortune Writing…'" He pauses, flustered.

"'Find Fame and Fortune Writing Best Sellers,'" I corrected to put him out of his misery.

"Yes, yes, that's it exactly!" he says, a little too enthusiastically, drawing a few scolding 'hushes' from those around us, who certainly seemed rapt, at least for now. Stuart brings it down a notch. "This is so exciting. Fortuitous. I have a proposition for you. Let's sneak out of here and go to the member's lounge." A guilty look comes over his face. "Unless, of course, you want to wait until the end of the lecture."

Tempting, but I shake my head and stand. I consider letting him know that I'm not *that* Malcom Winters once we leave the hall, but then again, coming into the orbit of one of maybe thirty people who bought the real Malcom's book is obviously the work of fates with a wicked sense of humor, and I want to see how they plan to finish this off. I'm also more than a little curious about this proposition. At least for a fleeting moment, I don't mind posing as a quasi-celebrity. I picture myself as fodder for Stuart's cocktail party conversations for months, so in a way, I'm doing him a favor.

We walk at a brisk pace past ancient ceramics and far too many headless statues to the rear of the museum, then down a set of stairs to the lounge where I'm able to enter as his guest. They have hot water and a decent selection of teas—nothing close to mine, but who does—and my selection seems to excite Stuart further and endear me to him like the best friend he's never had.

"Mr. Winters…"

"Malcom." I correct.

"Yes, of course, thank you. Mr. Malcom, as I told you my name is Stuart Vanguard. I'm the head of the English department at UIC. Meeting you here today was clearly destiny because I'm facing a crisis that you could solve with a simple 'yes.' I do so hope you're available."

He pauses and looks at me expectantly, apparently forgetting that he hasn't actually explained his proposition. My blank stare gets him talking again.

"Every year we, that is the English department—did I tell you I'm its head—invite a distinguished author or poet to be our visiting writer in residence to teach a few classes, give some lectures, and to just interact with the students in general. This year we have Claire Longstreet. You've heard of her, of course."

I nod. Who hasn't heard of Claire Longstreet? Besides me, I mean.

"She hasn't been quite as popular with the students as I had hoped. Sometimes, writers' brilliance doesn't translate to the classroom. But a contract is a contract, and I had intended to honor hers through the Spring Semester. Then, just last week, she told me that she was offered a chair at the University of Tokyo beginning in January and that she intended to take it! That was quite a blow to the school, naturally."

I nod again. I have an inkling where this is headed but want to hear it from him.

"Anyway, in short, I need to replace her for next semester. Your book was so inspiring, and you would be perfect! You would still have plenty of time to write, and the position comes with all sorts of perks. What do you say, Mr. Winters? Are you interested?"

In truth, I am interested. While the thought of trying to impart knowledge that I don't possess to a room full of disinterested young people is a bit scary

—all right, terrifying—I was just ruminating about the usefulness of a job as cover, and how I could use a little income to fill in the gaping hole my purchase of the three-flat made in my bank balance. Also, in my younger years, I sometimes dreamed of becoming a college professor, picturing myself with a tweed jacket and pipe, surrounded by stacks of colorful books in my office. I would work in an ivy-covered brick building, built before anyone still among the living was born, and filled with history and charm.

We agree to meet at his office tomorrow, which leaves me time to check into the real Malcom Winters. The identity forged by Freddy only goes so deep and makes no mention of my literary skills since I only intended to steal Winters' name, not his identity. And what if the real Malcom Winters is dead? The whole scheme could be brought down by a curious student finding my obituary online.

As soon as I get home, I jump online. Fortunately, Malcom Winters is not only alive, he's never set the literary world on fire. He must never have followed his own advice because the book advising other people how to write best-sellers was the only thing he ever published. He sold more copies than the thirty I gave him credit for earlier, but not by much. It only sold about 300 and has been out of print for years. While that means that I can't read it without going back to Rapid City, no one else can either. Maybe I could ask to borrow Stuart's copy. As a cover, it's a little public to be considered ideal, but then, no one who might be looking for me will be searching on a college campus.

Tomorrow comes, I put on my best and only suit, and Google how to get to campus. While sitting on the el, I realize that I should know something about the school to avoid looking like a complete ignoramus, as I've actually never heard of it before meeting Stuart. The University of Illinois at Chicago has been around in some limited form for a long time, but only became a degree-granting university in the 1960s. It bounced around a bit, even spending a few years out on Navy Pier, before landing a prime location southwest of the Loop. Most, if not all, of its buildings have been erected since that time, so no brick and no ivy. I look up the building in which the English department is housed and it doesn't even have a cool name like 'Lincoln Hall' or even 'Casimir Pulaski Hall.' It's 'University Hall,' which must have taken some administrator about ninety seconds to come up with. A tall steel and glass tower that houses several departments in all, it takes quite a bit of the romance out of the whole professor thing.

Visiting professor, actually, although in either case, it's a misnomer when applied to me. The interview turns out to be little more than a formality and I've barely warmed up my seat before Stuart is gleefully welcoming me as the newest member of the UIC faculty, officially the 'Morrow Visiting Professor of Creative Writing and the Art of Language,' which sounds much more impressive (but no less pompous) than it is. I try my best to mimic his excitement as he walks me down the hall to my new office, which, to put the best face on it, shows how useful closet organizers can be.

I have until January, the start of the winter semester, to learn all I can about the creative writing process. What could possibly go wrong?

Chapter 8

I've been in Chicago just over a month, and even I'm surprised at how far I've come in setting down roots. People who knew me in my old life would hardly recognize the formerly scruffy, dirty, smelly, furtive, lethal loner who avoided eye contact and only felt at home sleeping in fleabag motels or in greasy alleyways while on a mission no one else would want. Now, I'm practically respectable. I own my own home, have tenants, will soon be starting a job, albeit temporary, and haven't killed anyone lately. I'm almost content.

But the 'almost' is a huge one, coming in the form of a red-haired puzzle of a woman who walks these same streets and enters my thoughts and dreams nearly every day and night. Hers was the first number I programmed into my new cell phone, although realizing I didn't have a last name to type in only emphasized how little I know about her. I gave myself an ultimatum at that time, to either call her by the end of the month or delete her number and relegate her to my personal history as a one-night stand.

That thought, and that awful label, is what tips the balance in my ever-indecisive mind. The only women I've loved and left were doing the same thing to me, where each of us had a primal need that required a partner but nothing lasting longer than the lust that drew us together. Fyre deserves better and it was she that slipped her number into my pocket. Not only that, I feel an inexplicable compulsion to draw out and slay the demon inside of her, if that's what's behind the faraway, tortured look in her eyes. If she's reconsidered and decided that Nashville was as far as we should go, I'll be good with that. Maybe then she'll stop making unwanted visits into my brain.

So, what's stopping me? I stare at my phone as if it's to blame for my angst, drawing out memories of a scrawny, pimply faced teenager petrified of rejection by Carolyn Frost, a sophomore bassoon player three points too high up on the high school social scale. But even then, I eventually manned up and made the call. Come to think of it, the caustic rejection I received was every bit as horrible as I had feared while staring at that phone so many years ago. Maybe that's not the lesson I need to draw upon right now.

I take in a deep breath, close my eyes, and punch the button. Sweat emerges from different pores with every ring on the other end along with a welcome sense of relief that she isn't picking up. After the fourth ring, I mentally try to put together a few words that won't make me sound as stupid as the first thing that came out of my mouth when we met, but then the rings suddenly stop before voice mail has a chance to ask me to leave a message. Four rings, that's it? Did she see who it is and deliberately hang up on me?

It's a sign of how addled I am that it takes me a moment to realize that she wouldn't recognize that I'm calling because she doesn't have my number and I have my identity blocked on my phone. She may not pick up numbers she doesn't know. Now that I took the first step, I'm irritated at the delay and need to see this through. It takes me twenty minutes of continual typing and deleting before I compose a text that satisfies me: "Fyre, this is Malcom Winters. We met in Nashville. Please give me a call if you want to."

Malcom Winters, college professor and literary giant, a man, who in only eighteen words, can make himself sound like a complete imbecile.

I won't say my heart has leaped every time my phone has rung over the past three days. I won't say it because it would make me sound like I've had Fyre on my mind without pause for seventy-two hours. What I will say is that I eventually programmed the ringtone for her number to a distinctive tune so that I will know when it isn't her, which it always isn't. Some people might think using Sting's 'So Lonely' is pathetic. I mean it as irony. Really.

I've just crammed a scalding hot, oversized potato dumpling into my mouth when I hear strains of The Police coming from somewhere in my bedroom. I dash in the direction of the ring and in my haste trip over a shoe, causing the dumpling to jam in my throat, grab my comforter in an effort to break my fall, pull it completely off the bed, and in the process fling my cell phone which was apparently sitting on the bed against the wall. I dive for the now-silent phone and bring it quickly to my ear.

"Hfmmph?" You try talking with a hot dumpling halfway down your throat.

"I'm sorry, I must have the wrong number."

"No! Fyre, it's me. Malcom."

"Are you sure? I thought I might have called the primate house at the zoo."

How does one respond to that? By ignoring it, I'm guessing. "I apologize. I was eating when you called."

"And you answered before you finished swallowing. Your mother would be so proud." This is not starting out as well as I had hoped. I wait for her to continue, but the silence stretches to what seems like a full minute. "Malcom? You called me, remember?"

"Yes, of course. I found your number in my pocket and, um, I'm in Chicago now and I'm hoping that maybe you would like to have dinner."

"I always like to have dinner. Do you mean together, with you?"

I had forgotten this side of her. The smartass side. "Yes, please."

"Do you know where Glenn's Diner is?"

"No."

"Then it's perfect. I'll see you Thursday night at 7:00." And with that, she was gone.

Well, that went well.

Glenn's Diner is in a northside neighborhood I haven't been to yet and I've learned not to trust the Brown Line, so I leave plenty of time to get there. It's not difficult to find, with its optimistic outdoor tables beckoning the cold-blooded and a busy brown awning doing the same for those who prefer a warmer environment in which to eat. I step inside ten minutes early and only now discover how small the restaurant's single room is, with no more than ten or twelve tables and a waiting list to sit at one. I join the queue and hope that Fyre won't be disappointed that I didn't think to make a reservation.

I kill time memorizing the long list of seafood options written on chalkboards covering two walls, mentally debating what options would make me appear to have a more sophisticated palate than I actually possess, finally deciding on the Arctic char just because I have no idea what it is so it must be special. Time passes, the diners lucky enough to have snagged a table don't seem in any hurry to give them up, and the aromas drifting from passing plates begin to give my stomach fits, wondering when its turn will come. I resist pulling my phone out to check the time but find myself stealing a glance at the wrist of the man invading my personal space. 7:10. I look again fifteen minutes later. 7:12.

I'm now convinced either that I've been stood up or that Fyre got kidnapped by a band of gypsies on her way here, so I pull out my phone to check for texts or gypsy alerts. Just as I open the screen, I feel a presence at my elbow.

"I'm a few minutes late and you text your back-up date, do you?" Fyre's face hovers only inches away, making it difficult to see if she's teasing. "I'm here now and I'm worth waiting for."

I'm about to stammer an apology for something I wasn't doing and for my position in the long line, which, come to think of it, isn't my fault either, when she catches the eye of one of the more senior waitstaff.

"Ms. Stockton! How good to see you. It's been too long. Just give me a minute." We watch as the waiter hustles over to a table by the wall where a young couple appears to be lingering over coffee and dessert. As both man and woman watch in bewilderment, he produces a check, slaps it on the table, and waits impatiently, tapping his foot. Realizing that the only way to get rid of the intruding server was to pay him, the man pulls a credit card out of his wallet, which is quickly snatched away. Within seconds, the waiter returns, this time with reinforcements, and they begin clearing the table, carrying away a plate that clearly still has half of a piece of pie on it. The couple, perhaps too stunned to be angry, is quickly escorted to the door.

"Thank you, Larry," Fyre coos as we're led to the now-open table to a chorus of objections from others waiting in line. I decide to avoid looking in their direction for the remainder of the night.

I open my mouth to speak but Fyre beats me to it.

"I have to say, Mal, that this is a bit of a surprise. I normally don't give my number out to a man I've just met, but each time I have, I've received a call within a day or at most two. I'm quite hurt." Fyre pushes her bottom lip out in a pout that would make any toddler proud. I decide to play along.

"Well, you know, between dating supermodels and traveling to Sweden to accept the Nobel Prize, things have been a bit hectic. They're finally settling down a bit so I was able to work you into my schedule."

To my relief, a look of mild delight spreads across Fyre's face. I appear to have passed a test.

"Touché, Malcom. I really am glad you called." She reaches out to place her hand over mine. "I wondered what happened to you. I like to think that our time together in Nashville was memorable enough that you might want an encore."

"Believe me, it was. I've had a lot of loose ends to tie up." As I talk, Larry brings over two glasses of red wine that I don't remember ordering. Fyre and I simultaneously raise them and tap them together in a silent toast. We stare dreamily into each other's eyes. Or at least one of us does.

"Ahem." Larry breaks our trance, probably out of jealousy. "Are you ready to order or do you need a few minutes?" He addresses Fyre, apparently forgetting that I exist.

Fyre looks at me and I nod, ready to impress. Being the gentleman, I let her go first.

"I'll have the Arctic char."

I choke on my wine. Now what? I can't order the same thing she just did without looking like a childish copycat. Flustered, I deal with my dilemma by saying nothing.

Fyre looks amused. "I'm sorry, I thought you were ready. Do you want me to order for you? Maybe some cereal?" I follow her gaze to the wall behind the counter, where twenty-five colorful boxes of cereal from my childhood sit ready to add tooth decay to my list of problems.

She doesn't wait for an answer. "He'll have the Scottish salmon."

Larry finally acknowledges my presence, if only to snort at my ineptitude, then hustles away.

I need to move the conversation along. "Actually, I haven't been in Chicago long. I accepted a job teaching creative writing at UIC and have been busy moving in and preparing for classes when they start in January."

"Really?" The fact that Fyre is surprised at my employment reveals what she may have thought of my intelligence up to this point, but I let it pass. "Is that what you are, a teacher? Where were you before this?"

I look across the table warily. She seems sincere in her interest in my past and is probably just making conversation, but we're moving into an area I'd just as soon avoid—my past.

"Not entirely. I've done a little of this and a little of that. I don't like to stay in one place or do the same thing for too long. My life has been pretty dull and I don't want to bore you with it. Let's talk about you." Smooth. "What do you do?"

The discomfort I felt suddenly seems to have shifted across the table. Fyre is clearly uncertain about how to respond to my simple question. After a few minutes of heavy silence, she speaks.

"I guess you could call me a consultant, although no title really fits what I do very well. I have clients from around the country who hire me to help them with situations, and I use my resources to get the results they desire." I wait for her to go on but realize quickly that's all I'm going to get. I'm not satisfied.

"That sounds fascinating. Can you give me an example of what you've done to help a client? Something you're especially proud of?"

Fyre looks panicked and begins to mutter something about client confidentiality when she's saved by the return of Larry.

"Arctic char?" he intones pleasantly as he delicately places the plate of fish in front of Fyre. "Salmon." He drops my order from inches above the table, splattering sauce onto my shirt.

"My, Mal, maybe cereal and a bib would have been the way to go after all." Fyre slyly dips her napkin in her water glass and dabs at my stains. Despite my humiliation, I begin to feel familiar stirrings that have nothing to do with the fish, which by the way is excellent.

We continue our mundane conversation, made difficult for each of us by our efforts to avoid talking about our pasts. Eventually, Fyre tells a long tale of a vacation she once took to Mexico with a former boyfriend who pretended for four days to speak Spanish. She reveals that she attended an unnamed all-girls high school in Ohio and double-majored in Finance and History at an unnamed college in the Southeast. She's been involved in three serious relationships, only two of them with men. She's lived in Chicago and used it as the home base for her business for somewhere between eight and eleven years.

I nod and occasionally interpose a comment in order to keep her talking as a way of avoiding having to test my creative fiction abilities. The longer we sit, the more we use our hands and feet to flirt both above and below the table. By the time we decline Larry's proffer of a dessert menu, much to his disappointment, we know where this date is headed. I'm forced to ask myself what the hell I'm doing and whether I should be doing it. It's true that Fyre has opened up about her past and provided details that I didn't possess in Nashville. My doubts about what dark secrets lurk behind her mane of red should be satisfied with her detailed narrative about her past.

There's only one problem. As someone who has had to coerce critical information out of uncooperative captives when the lives of myself and others were at stake, I've had extensive experience in sorting out the truths, half-truths, and lies people tell. And my bullshit detector is clear that not a single thing Fyre told me about herself is true.

Chapter 9

Despite my reservations, I've continued to see Fyre. We actually exchanged Christmas gifts, which may or may not be significant, and on our last date, I discovered that we're enough of a couple that I'm supposed to know to celebrate the six-month anniversary of our first encounter in Nashville. The fact that she didn't buy me anything to commemorate the occasion apparently wasn't enough to keep me out of the doghouse. The evening ended early and with some unkind words. She did call this morning asking me out, though. I'm deciding if I need to bring a weapon.

Nearly two months into my foray into teaching, no one yet has stood up in class, pointed at me, and yelled "FAKE!" My strategy of letting the students learn by doing, rather than by having me tell them how to write, devised as a way of covering up my total ignorance on anything and everything literary, has actually been well-received by my students. Stuart's enthusiasm toward me cooled quickly, leading me to wonder if he did some research into me and became suspicious. He's never said anything, though, and I don't think he would report me to his superiors. It wouldn't reflect well on himself to have vigorously pursued the hiring of a fraud. Besides, my class has quickly become one of the most popular on campus.

It's bewildering to ponder the life I'm leading. I have a great apartment, a respectable job, at least for now, and if Fyre doesn't kill me tonight, a sexy and intriguing girlfriend. Life overall is good, bordering on great. I'm starting to relax. For the first time in a long time, I can get a good night's sleep. Unless you count this morning.

When I was a kid, maybe six or seven years old, I slept over at my friend Timmy's house. In the morning, still deep in slumber and dreaming of stepping up to the plate before hitting the game-winning grand slam in Game 7 of the

World Series, rain began to fall. Before the umpires could suspend play, my eyes opened upon the rear end of the household dog trotting away after marking his territory in my hair. Since then, in the course of various assignments for dear old Uncle Sam, I've been woken with a bucket of ice water in my face, falling out of a tree hammock, being stabbed, getting hit by a train (don't ask), a room-shattering explosion, and by the bite of a Chilean Recluse Spider which apparently took umbrage at sharing my blanket.

As unpleasant and nearly lethal as these awakenings were, none of them compares to taking a deep, open-mouthed breath and inhaling Leo's latest Cuban culinary creation. For at least the last ten or twelve years, he's owned a restaurant called the 'Kuban Kabana' on the near South Side where he does all of the cooking himself. I had the misfortune to eat there once, not long after I bought the building, at Leo's bidding. He pulled out all of the stops to impress his new landlord, insisting on preparing me a special, off-menu dish of which he was particularly proud. When it arrived, it looked like a cross between dog food and what I pull out of my kitchen sink's u-trap when it clogs. It tasted worse.

"Leo, what do you call this dish?" He beamed with pride as he peered at me out of the kitchen window, clearly unaware that I was asking as a protective measure so that I wouldn't ever order it by accident.

"Muh awn receipt. Two parts *ropa vieja,* un part *picadillo*, tre' parts my un creashun, an' muh saycrit sauce."

Okay, I'm breaking my promise but it's hard to truly describe Leo without also trying to duplicate his speech. Up front, I recognize that my efforts to capture his accent phonetically are futile, and I apologize to all Cubans for any perceived insult. In truth, I don't think his accent is Cuban at all. I'm about ninety percent sure that Leo himself isn't Cuban. One night after sharing too much of a bottle of rum in his apartment—the headache I had the next day in part due to my insistent declining his offers of food—he confessed that his job as a chef was a reluctant career choice forced upon him when the CIA gave him a new identity and relocated him for his own protection due to his role in a failed attempt to assassinate Fidel Castro. That would explain his lack of culinary prowess (and I'm certain it would take a government conspiracy to explain his 4-star Yelp reviews), but it also raised more questions than it answered. I'm pretty sure he's never been to Cuba nor been within 100 miles of Castro, but I would never doubt that he probably assassinated somebody somewhere. He has an iron grip and the kind of weathered skin common among para-military associates I once knew, but it's mainly his eyes. Most of the time, they appear dead as if they retired after seeing too much pain and violence over a lifetime, but twice now I've seen flashes of life in them that in an instant revealed a much deeper and more unsettling part of this erstwhile chef. Both times, I was so disturbed that I placed one of my sharper daggers under my pillow that night.

At first, I was determined to delve into Leo's past, a task made difficult by his reticence at discussing himself and by the fact that his physical age seemed to vary daily, ranging anywhere from 50 to 102. Ultimately, I came to accept his desire for privacy because he stopped asking questions about my past. We each have our secrets and know that the other knows we have secrets, but we've come to accept that there are good reasons they're kept private. If Leo wants me to believe that he's a Cuban rebel in hiding, so be it. He certainly doesn't believe that I started life in my 30s. We're linked by our unrevealed pasts, men whose personal histories go back to a certain point and then stop, as if we were born without a childhood.

My decision to respect Leo's privacy doesn't mean I have to similarly respect his cooking, however, or feel guilty about the resentment that consumes me when my morning begins with a big whiff of the world's worst food aromas. I sometimes dream about living over a donut shop. Those are nice dreams. To make matters worse, Leo sometimes pays his rent in food when business at the restaurant is slow. I used to donate it to the local homeless shelter until they asked me to stop. After that, I quietly set it out in the alley for the local feral cats. The cats have left the neighborhood, never to return.

As much as I'm tempted to pull the covers over my head and mask the aroma floating up from below with the stench of my morning breath, I have a job to get to. Early springtime in Chicago only means that we delude ourselves into thinking that the floor will welcome our feet with warmth when we roll out of bed, when in reality, every morning, we're shocked into wakefulness by the icy floorboards of the winter past. On the positive side, the shock to the soles usually swiftly propels me into the bathroom and tells my brain to join the rest of my body in waking up.

If I could skip the whole getting-shaved-and-showered-and-dressed-appropriately process in the morning and go straight to the kitchen, I might not have so much trouble getting out of bed. The best part of my day is when I get a few quiet minutes to sit in my large, retro kitchen sipping a cup of one of the world's best teas. No coffee maker for me, no mug of java to get me going. You can keep your soy hazelnut vanilla cinnamon white mocha with a dash of caramel made with beans that came out of the ass of an Asian feline, and don't expect me to take sides in a debate over whether or not Ethiopian beans are overrated. Muddy water, all of it. Let me luxuriate over a Gyokuro or in a pinch some Jasmine Pearls, and I can face the world. Today, it's a rare vintage of pu'er, worth the two weeks in a Chinese prison and the scar on my hip. Woody, earthy overtones with notes of dark fruit. Suck on this, coffee lovers.

My kitchen was the first area of my apartment I renovated, doing all of the work myself so that no one out there would know of a few irregularities built in for my protection. Windows of metallic glass, virtually impenetrable and impossible to break. A hidden compartment nestled underneath my silverware drawer is voice-activated to my voice only when I yell "Tequila," dropping down with a selection of knives, knuckles, canisters of mace, and one wicked, spiked cross between a hammer and a club. A reserve of cash, including dollars, yen, Yuan, and Euros, as well as multiple alternate IDs, are in a safe inside an orange juice container in the fridge, although the combination is entered from my bedroom closet, should the need arise to disappear. All of this is nice, but not what makes the room so special. I like it for the same reasons anyone else would. Lots of sunlight, enough cabinet space for my collection of pans, odd foods, and exotic spices, and counters that go on for miles. Sitting in the sunlight at the island, eyes closed, a steaming cup of tea under my nose, I'm at peace for a precious few moments.

Today, the peace is broken early by the vocal stylings of the second-floor tenant, Ted. He's some sort of a trader or corporate shill and must deal with a lot of 'fuckin' idiots' if his side of his early-morning phone conversations are to be believed. Apparently, these idiots are also hard of hearing. Ted was the first person to respond to my advertisement for a tenant, and every day, I have some regrets for taking him on. He's loud, arrogant, and unpleasant as hell, but on the other hand, he does pay his rent on time. With cash, not *Yuca con Mojo.*

And then there's Rebecca to consider, Ted's better half. No, not his wife. When he's not yelling at his clients or screaming at Leo or myself for some perceived aggrievement, or trampling over the flowerbeds, Ted transitions to Rebecca. He puts on a dress (and presumably the appropriate underthings, although I've never been tempted to ask), paints his face and his nails, puts on a mocha-colored wig with curls that frame his forehead, and he transforms. Somewhere in the process of removing his man-suit, the anger and aggressiveness of Ted disappears and a softer, gentler, more tolerable woman takes his place. Ted hid his crossdressing from us for a while but his cover was blown when he returned home in a formal gown the same night Leo and I, under the influence of too much rum, decided to try to fix the squeaky gate at 2:00 a.m. Rebecca has even joined Leo and me in our late-night talks in Leo's kitchen two or three times. Ted remains a world-class jerk, but Rebecca I kind of like. Even Leo agrees.

For now, though, I need to deal with Ted. On my way down the stairs as I leave for work, I bang hard on his door. "Ted, remember your promise. No high-volume coronaries before 10:00 a.m."

"WHAT? IS SOMEONE THERE? STOP THE GODDAM POUNDING!" Footsteps soon follow and the door opens a crack, just enough for Ted's narrow head to stick out. Ted's obsessively protective of his apartment. Even I've never seen it since he moved in. Maybe it's furnished in early Barbie doll, or he has a still in the bathroom. Everyone has secrets.

"Ted, keep it down. You'll cause Leo's cake to fall."

Ted scowls, says something that sounds like "Puck mew hitch," and slams the door. He does get quieter, though the profanities continue to hurl at the poor soul on the other side of his conversation. It's times like these I wonder if I can evict Ted but keep Rebecca.

I continue down the steps, shaking my head as I note that Ted once again propped the outside door open with a scrap of wood so that the UPS driver could leave his latest issue of *Modern Phone Etiquette* or perhaps a package of unmentionables for Rebecca safely inside. One more issue to bring up with him at some point. I hold my breath as I come within olfactory range of Leo's apartment then push my shoulder against the ancient iron gate to the outside, checking the multiple locks before I continue on. The sun is shining, a cold wind whips into my face, and the indecipherable cooking odor is behind me. Time to go to school.

Chapter 10

My first class today is a freshman-only Introduction to Creative Writing class. Their assignment from last week was to write a spellbinding first paragraph of a novel that makes the other students want to read the rest of the chapter. It could be any genre, any style, but each one had to include the words 'monkey,' 'thunder,' and 'breasts.' None of my students' efforts are putting this reader on pins and needles (although a couple make me blush), but a few have some potential, there's a lot of laughter, and the students seem engaged. More importantly, the exercise is getting the point across that each student could be given an identical assignment and their imaginations would go off in wildly different directions. I'm trying to build the idea that they shouldn't compare themselves to each other and to find their own voice. From that perspective, mission accomplished.

My next period is free. I have no papers to grade and my office walls give me claustrophobia, so I head down to the café to grab some tea. The place likes to brag up their tea but their matcha—their best option—is barely more than tolerable. In addition, any place that offers flavors (iced apple peach jasmine? seriously?) is missing the point of fine tea. Believe it or not, the manager here has accused me of being a snob.

I'm pleased to see a familiar figure sitting at a far table set against the window, her back to the door. I keep mostly to myself when at the school, partly to avoid wider exposure but mostly out of fear of discovery that I'm a phony. Vinn is the only faculty member with whom I've established any sort of friendship. Short in stature but tall in her field of molecular science, Vinn is simply brilliant. Talk to her for five minutes and you're either blown away by her intelligence or totally lost as to what she's talking about to the point that you assume that she must be a lot smarter than you. Or both, which is me most of the time.

Vinn isn't her real name. She goes by the initials of her first and middle name—V. N.—which when said fast enough sound like 'Vinn.' As far as I can tell, she's never told anyone what those names are because I broke into the personnel office once to pull her file (old habits die hard), and sure enough only 'V. N.' is listed on her employment records. Since then, we have a kind of tradition where whenever we're together, I get three guesses as to her real name. She's promised to tell me if I guess correctly, but I need both of them right or it's no go. I'm not sure she's thrilled with the game, but it provides amusement for me.

"Obnubilate," she says as soon as I sat down.

"Excuse me? Most people just say hello."

"Obnubilate," she repeats. "To cloud over, darken, or obscure."

Now it makes sense. To inject a little bit of excitement into academic life, we choose an obscure word, commit it to memory, and then the first one to insert it into a conversation in the proper context when talking with someone other than each other wins. The winner gets to pick the next word and occasionally buys dinner. Vinn's won twice to my once, which needs to change.

As I stir a few drops of stevia into my tea, I study her across the table. Vinn's jet-black hair and different colored eyes, one green and one brown, give her a mysterious, almost exotic look until you take in her whole face, which has all the innocence of the Minnesota farm girl she had been growing up. Unlike Fyre, the real thing. A few faded freckles have fueled my fantasies, but I've never pursued her in that way. There's no doubt that we have a chemistry here, and some repressed interest both ways, but Vinn has a sense of sadness that hangs around her along with a subtle scent of regret that has my brain screaming at me to give her some space. She clearly sees something in me that tells her the same thing, although I have no idea what that might be.

"Are you around after your last class?" she asks pleadingly. "How would you like to join me later for a lecture on mutant gene sequences in lower primates?" There was no hint of teasing or facetiousness in her request. She's serious. That's Vinn, and that's as close to a date as we ever get.

"Can't. I have a date tonight."

"Ah. Freida again?" she asks with one brow raised and a mischievous grin playing at the corners of her mouth.

"Fyre, as you well know. And speaking of names, 'Victoria Nancy.'"

Vinn's expression doesn't change as she gets up from the table, so I guess I haven't hit pay dirt.

I raise my voice slightly as Vinn picks up her tray and starts to walk off. "Vanessa Noodles?" Her pace appears to pick up.

"Vulgar Nursemaid?" I shout at her back. I'm not sure what words accompany the middle finger she raises as she walks away, but I've never seen anyone blush as deeply red as the mathematics teaching assistant passing her as he heads in my direction.

Chapter 11

You don't need a car to get around in Chicago. This normally suits me fine and I haven't bothered to buy one. It can create an uncomfortable moment or two in the early stages of a relationship, however, before you know if your date's social habits require far-flung travel, or, for that matter, to get to where she lives. Fortunately, Fyre lives in Streeterville in a condo overlooking Lake Michigan within easy reach by public transportation. Even better, she's like most locals in that she's more than happy to grab a bus or train to travel to where we're going. She also has her own car which she isn't hesitant to use if the situation calls for it.

Mostly, though, we walk. There are innumerable restaurants and bars within a few blocks of her building, and when the weather cooperates (a rare occurrence so far), we enjoy strolling further afield down Michigan Avenue to the Symphony or Millennium Park. She talks about having a picnic under the Bean when the weather gets warmer, which people swear it does. With a vengeance apparently. I'll believe it the first time I become concerned about sweating in her presence.

Tonight, though, we summon an Uber to drive us to the Rogers Park neighborhood to dine at a Senegalese restaurant which Fyre picked. In the few months that we've been getting together—six months, as I've been forcefully reminded—she's chosen most of our restaurants and activities. For the sake of my man card, I've convinced myself that it's because of her greater familiarity with the city, not because she's assumed the typically male role in the relationship. Then again, starting with our dalliance in Nashville, she has never been shy about taking the initiative.

We make small talk on the ride over but remnants of tension from our heated debate over the definition of 'anniversary' the last time we were together, prevent any meaningful conversation. I'd like to just pretend our argument never happened but sense that Fyre would like to bring it back out in the open to resolve it before putting it behind us. As a result, silence soon fills the air of the car.

The small storefront of the restaurant is indistinguishable from many of the dives I've eaten at over the years, mostly with extreme regret later that night. I eye the door with suspicion, although the smells drifting from within are enticing. We can't go the whole evening without saying a word, so I take the initiative with a scintillating first move.

"Have you been here before?" If she tells me she dined here once the night before she was rushed to the emergency room with mysterious gastric distress, I'm out of here.

"No, but I met the owner a few weeks ago. He promised that if I brought you by, he'd do something special for us. Well, for you anyway."

I'm not sure quite how to interpret that remark but resign myself to my fate, pull the door open, and follow her inside. Some places look small and unimpressive from the outside but boast a palatial interior fit for royalty. Not so here. The inside is a shoebox and the décor uninspiring despite the owner's obvious efforts to add as many festive touches as possible. The bright blue walls are covered with African artwork and masks. Unfamiliar music that I assume is native to Senegal floats across the room from speakers hidden within the walls.

A young man with some of the darkest skin I have ever seen, as well as one of the broadest smiles, literally bounds to the door when he sees us enter.

"Greetings, Miss! Please, welcome. I have your table ready."

Considering that there are only about eight tables in the joint, with seven of them unoccupied, we technically could choose to sit at any one of them. Each is covered with a blue tablecloth rivaling the walls for brightness, but only one along the far wall has been previously set with a trivet and pair of tall, matching glasses on either side of the table. The owner graciously pulls out our chairs, brimming with excitement to begin our adventure.

Fyre holds the two glasses on her side of the table out to the man. "Just for him," she tells the man as she nods in my direction. "I'll have a beer. You choose."

Momentary disappointment flickers across his eyes, but the smile instantly returns. He takes the proffered glasses with a slight bow and hustles away.

I eye Fyre with suspicion. "Just so you know, I don't have a fortune stashed away and what little money I do have is promised to my great-aunt in Topeka. She and her fifteen cats would be so disappointed."

Fyre lets out an amused snort. On anyone else, that would come across as crude, but from Fyre, it actually seems adorable. I begin to wonder if I'm smitten. "I'm not poisoning you, you idiot. This is my way of apologizing for the other night. I still feel I had every right to be a bit miffed at you, but I also overreacted. Besides, if I wanted you dead, there are a lot more fun ways to kill you than dropping powder into your drink."

I know she's joking, at least I think I do, but I'm so intent on looking for the slightest hint of a smile that I'm startled when a boy still years away from hitting the drinking age himself approaches the table. He carries a dark brown bottle with wisps of cloud escaping from its neck, which he sets down gingerly in front of Fyre. The owner follows close behind with a clay teapot adorned with graffiti-like drawings of various birds and animals.

"Tea is brewing. Do not touch. Do not pour. I come back."

Fyre smiles coyly as I lift the lid of the pot slightly to inhale what's inside, dropping it back quickly in reaction to the owner's apoplectic expression from behind the kitchen counter.

"Fascinating start to the meal. What is it?"

"I don't know exactly," she replies as she reaches for the laminated menu. "I understand that the Senegalese have an elaborate tea ceremony and I thought you might enjoy it."

"I do, thank you." I smile to prove that I really am appreciative and that as far as I'm concerned, our little tiff is forgotten. "While we're waiting, let's order. I'm starving."

As if on cue, or perhaps because he's listening in, the boy approaches our table.

Fyre turns to him. "Fataya to start. Then Diby Yap and Foufou."

The boy nods knowingly before backing away in the direction of the kitchen.

"I didn't order," I whine as I wave my menu over the table. My manhood is definitely being challenged.

"You didn't have to. I ordered for us."

"And he didn't write anything down. How will we know if he gets the order right?"

"I'll know. Haven't you ever been to Senegal?"

I lock eyes with Fyre, trying to decipher if this is an innocent question or if there's some more sinister intent behind it. We've been out together, not counting those times when there was only time for the main event and conversation was not a priority, maybe thirty times in all but never once have we delved into our lives prior to Nashville. I still know very little of her past and she knows nothing of mine. And while I've regaled her with tales of my exciting life as a teacher and anecdotes about my tenants, her revelations about what she does while she travels, and even what she does when she doesn't, have been virtually nonexistent and what she has said hasn't rung true. There's clearly an unspoken agreement that inquiries in those directions are off-limits and she may have crossed that line. I just decide to push back when we're interrupted.

"Ataya," the owner intones reverently as he picks up the warm pot. "Senegalese tea."

He signals me to move my hands away from the table then proceeds to pour the hot, greenish fluid into one of the glasses. Replacing the pot carefully, he picks up both glasses, pouring the contents of one into the other, then back again. For several minutes he repeats the process until a layer of foam begins to form on the top of the tea. Finally, with an almost religious fervor, he places one of the glasses in front of me. I'm not sure if I'm supposed to drink it or worship it.

"Drink," was all he said, as if he could read my thoughts.

Bringing the tea up to my lips, I can smell a hint of charcoal and can tell it's a green tea. Gunpowder, perhaps. While I would love to take my time to decipher more, the owner is standing in my personal space waiting impatiently for my reaction. In deference to my audience, I take a small, steamy sip.

It's bitter. Extremely bitter. Yet, there is also an overtone of fresh mint and a light sugaring that makes the bitterness barely tolerable and allows the flavor of the tea leaves to come through. It takes me a second to decide if I like it or hate it.

"It's wonderful," I tell the man, who grins happily as he exhales loudly. Has he been holding his breath waiting for me to speak?

Fyre looks at me suspiciously. "Do you really mean it?" she asks after our host has retreated to the kitchen. She looks worried as if she too is in need of affirmation that she's done well. It's one of the few times she's shown her vulnerable side.

"I do. It's different, not what I was expecting, and it takes a few sips to fully appreciate it. But it really is extraordinary. Thank you for arranging this."

I see Fyre relax as I say this, making me feel guilty as I follow through on my decision to push boundaries.

"To answer your question, no, I've never been to Senegal. Have you?"

Fyre looks at me with the same uneasy expression I had likely sent her way a few minutes before. "No," she finally responds. "But I've been to Mali, in college. Or maybe it was Bali," she says with a smile.

"Yes, those two are easily confused." I make it light. Mission 'Probe Background' temporarily derailed but not abandoned. I pause as a platter of crispy pastry is placed between us along with some fried plantains. "Fyre, we're always talking about my job, and I think I've run out of ways to pretend that it's interesting. We've never really discussed what you do. It's got to be better than teaching a bunch of wannabe writers."

Is that a moment of discomfort I notice? Maybe not, probably just my rusty observational skills overheating. "It's a little hard to describe," she finally says as she cuts into the Fataya, brown gravy spilling out onto the plate. "I'm kind of a freelance troubleshooter. People have a problem, they reach out to me and if I can help them, I do. I have a lot of contacts, so a lot of it is just putting the right people together. Sometimes, that requires that I make a personal introduction. That's why I travel a lot." Consistent with what she told me once before, but still conveniently vague.

My mouth is full of tender beef with tomato and onion sauce as she pauses. Goodness, this is tasty. Score one for Fyre. I swallow.

"Sounds more interesting than what I do. And more lucrative. Your apartment is marvelous."

If my mentioning income is crass, Fyre doesn't seem to mind. "Not as much as you might think. The condo I got after I inherited a little bit of cash a while back. It wasn't enough to retire on, but it got me the condo mortgage-free, so I've been very fortunate."

I regret having turned our chat to a discussion of money and the conversation stalls as the boy comes to collect our appetizer plates. The owner follows close behind with two entrees, one platter and one wide, deep bowl. It smells heavenly.

And it is. Seasoned, spicy grilled lamb on one plate and chicken and yam in a red sauce in the bowl. Our awkward silence vanishes as our conversation easily transitions over to the food. Any tension that may have existed floats away with the steam of our entrees.

Time passes quickly as we settle back into the comfort of our customary and mostly frivolous topics of discussion. Early-spring darkness begins to descend outside the windows. I've been so focused on Fyre and so hypnotized by her eyes that I'm shocked when I look up and see that the restaurant, which filled during our dinner, is now empty. I catch the owner's son impatiently looking at his watch. It's likely past closing time.

We try to pass on dessert, but our host has clearly decided that it's his duty to provide a complete meal for his favorite guests, despite the time. We both struggle through some sort of banana soup. As wonderful as it is, we can't finish it but vow to come back sometime just to order that.

No sooner do we leave the restaurant than I hear the click of the door locking behind us and the lights immediately dim. The air took on a decided chill while we ate and a light mist begins to fill the air as we shiver on the sidewalk. I use the weather as an excuse to put my arm around Fyre and pull her close as she punches her phone to call for an Uber back to her place.

Moments later, a black sedan with darkened windows approaches slowly down the street, stopping once, as if looking for an address, before continuing in our direction. Fyre looks puzzled as she pulls up the Uber app to check if it's our car. Warning bells ring inside my head, recalling other times and other situations with similar cars moving in similar ways.

It happens quickly. At the same time that the passenger side window begins to lower, from a million miles away I hear Fyre comment that she doesn't think that this is the right car. Instinct or my subconscious registering something my conscious mind doesn't see causes me to roughly pull her down with me as I fall to the ground behind a parked car, rolling over on top in a single motion as a loud crack echoes from the direction of the car. I worry that I reacted too slowly. The noise from the squealing tires as it speeds away is nearly drowned out by Fyre's angry protestations.

"What do you think you're doing? Do you think that was funny? Now my dress is filthy and my pantyhose is ruined!" She ignores the hand I extend as I stand, freeing her from beneath me. Clearly, I haven't been completely forgiven for the other night.

My adrenaline is still racing and I speak louder than I mean to. "Fyre, someone just took a shot at us. From that car. We could have been killed." I try, unsuccessfully, to sound calmer than I feel.

"Nonsense!" she scoffs, her voice filled with scorn and disgust and a few other bad adjectives that elude me. "Who would want to do that? Are you insane? Ah, here's our driver."

Wet and dirty, we pile into the back seat of a yellow Chevy Bolt. For a fleeting moment, I wonder how Fyre didn't recognize that the dark sedan wasn't our ride, and more baffling why she's pretending not to have heard the gunshot. The moment doesn't seem right to raise these questions so I wisely choose not to table them for now. The resulting silence on the drive back to the Gold Coast is intolerable, but every time I move to speak, Fyre puts her hand up, clearly still furious and not welcoming conversation. I reluctantly comply.

The ride seems interminable. We finally arrive outside of her building and exit the cramped back seat. I assume that this will not be a night of romance. Unfortunately, I'm right.

"Mal, I think we need to have an early end to the evening," Fyre tells me tersely as the Bolt drives off. She begins to walk across the plaza before turning back and drawing close to me, placing her hand gently on my chest. For the first time, I notice what I recognize as fear in her eyes. "Do me a favor. Don't take the el home tonight, Mal. Please."

With that said, Fyre runs as fast as she can toward her front door, not pausing to look back. For a moment, I stand in the rain, the adrenaline rush draining from my body, confusion setting in, a hundred questions screaming at my brain for answers.

I hail a cab.

Chapter 12

"So, there's no chance that it was a backfire?" Vinn asks sincerely as we sit in the café, where I had asked her to meet me before class. I'd had a restless night, replaying the car's approach in my mind countless times. Did I misinterpret what happened? Was there something else I should have done? Were there one or two shots? Was there a shot at all? If so, why was I the only person that seemed to hear it? It sounded loud enough to wake up the entire neighborhood. Every time I came close to sleep, I'd run the scene over again in my head to see if there's some detail that I missed. By morning, I was no closer to answering a single question than I had been when I went to bed.

"If you'd asked me last night, I'd have been one hundred percent positive it was a gunshot." I didn't volunteer that based on the acoustics; I was also sure it was a Glock. "But now, in the light of day, I'm starting to have my doubts. Why would anyone take a shot at us? Could it have been a case of mistaken identity? But then, why would Fyre have been so upset if she knew that I'd pulled her out of the way of gunfire? So much about her is a mystery, but I can't imagine that she'd try to deflect my attention away from attempted murder."

"It does seem strange," Vinn says sympathetically. "I could understand if you were caught in gang crossfire, or were the victims of a mugging. But being targeted from a car outside of a restaurant? You said that the street was deserted outside of the two of you. That would mean that the bullet was intended for either you or Fyre specifically. Is there something you're not telling me, Mal?" Vinn looks at me with a sly grin.

There's so much I'm not telling you that might explain this, I say to myself, but if anyone from my past was behind this, they wouldn't have missed and I wouldn't be sitting here now. That was another reason for my lack of sleep.

I'd wracked my brain going over every step I'd taken since I had come to Chicago to determine the likelihood that I'd been found. Not impossible, but the odds were long. Also, the shooting was definitely amateur hour. If it happened at all.

I try to keep it light. "Yeah, maybe one of the many broken hearts I've left behind. I'm probably mistaken and am overreacting. I guess I'll never know."

Vinn gives me an odd look as she rises from the table. "Well, if you need to talk further, you know where to find me. Right now, we're both late for class."

Despite my nonchalance at the end of my discussion with Vinn, I'm not any more at ease about the incident now than I was immediately after it happened. If it wasn't a gunshot, then I can relax and focus on patching things up with Fyre, not to mention get a good night's sleep. If it was a bullet aimed in our direction, though, there are so many questions that need to be answered and the most likely source of those answers hasn't been forthcoming about much of anything to date. I need to have a frank talk with Fyre. It will not be an easy discussion.

I manage to stay focused on fiction long enough to make it through my classes. A couple of students take advantage of my drop-in hours to initiate a discussion on whether writing genre fiction is a populist sell-out if limiting oneself to literary fiction means starving. I'm not sure the debate would interest me even on a good day, but today it's excruciating. Fortunately, the students are so intent on making their own arguments for both sides that they take little notice of my lack of input. A hallway bell eventually takes them away. As far as I can tell, the debate remains unsettled.

Time drags on, but school days ultimately do end. I beg off further discussion with Vinn, claiming that I'm convinced that I had imagined the gunshot, and that it's best simply to put the incident behind me. She gives me the same odd look as before but says nothing.

In truth, I'm more intent than ever in getting to the bottom of last night's events. Walking home from the el, I find myself continually glancing around and evaluating everyone else within sight. My heart involuntarily jumps with every passing car. I don't want to be constantly looking over my shoulder and sensing danger where it doesn't exist. That's the very life that I'm trying to leave behind.

Once back in the safety of my apartment, the first thing I do is to pull up Yelp on my laptop to verify the hours for the Senegalese restaurant and those of every other eatery and business on the same block. I need to know when the last one closes. I then begin to assemble my wardrobe for that evening's foray but discover that months of traveling with only a backpack, leaving most of my possessions behind me, has a price. I'm missing one essential item. I hate to do it but I don't have time to go shopping. I walk down a flight.

The lyrical humming emanating from inside the apartment indicates that it will be Rebecca answering the door, and after knocking a second time she does. Opening it up only as far as the chain allows, she gives me the once over before speaking. "Yes, Mal?"

"Rebecca, I'm hoping you can help me. Does Ted have a black sweatshirt that I could borrow?"

"Oooh, you need help with your wardrobe?" The door swings wide open. "Come right in and let's see what we have, shall we?"

There are times when I can too easily see Ted through Rebecca but tonight isn't one of them. Immaculately made-up, with eyelashes dark and thick with mascara, blushed cheeks, a pale peach lipstick, and a dark brown wig with hair curling at her shoulders, Rebecca may not look stunning but she definitely resembles a woman. My instinctual first question as to how she fills out the chest of her shift dress is immediately replaced with the thought that I don't ever want to get on intimate enough terms to find out. I try to clear my mind and focus on the business at hand.

I follow her into a bedroom, standing aside as she pulls back the louvered doors of one side of her closet, revealing a neatly hung row of men's pants and shirts. "Mmm, nothing here. Let me see…" Walking to the near wall, Rebecca opens up one dresser drawer after another before slamming each of them shut.

"I'm afraid we're out of luck, my dear," she says with sadness, clearly disappointed that she couldn't help me. As I turn to leave, though, her eyes suddenly light up. "Wait a minute! I might have just the thing."

With that, Rebecca moves quickly to the other side of her bedroom closet, enthusiastically pulling aside the door. Underneath a long, colorful line of dresses hanging from the rack sit stacks of plastic bins. Rebecca pulls the top off of one of the bins, rummaging through neatly folded layers of clothing, before emerging triumphant.

"Voila!" she exclaims happily. "I knew I had it." Like a cat proudly displaying the dead mouse it caught to its owner, Rebecca holds out a dreadful sweater clearly made of a fabric that wouldn't stand a chance in a duel with a match.

"Rebecca, it has sequins," I point out, earning a pout in response.

"I know what you're saying, that they are so last year. But really, don't you think that good fashion is timeless?"

I'm at least smart enough not to argue the point or to say what I'm thinking, that this particular garment would never fall in the category of good fashion. After all, it is black and I'm desperate. "You're absolutely right, thank you so much, Rebecca. If I can ever return the favor…"

The sneer I get in return doesn't need any editorial commentary along with it. I take the sweater, promising to treat it with care and retreat to my apartment.

The wind has picked up by the time I softly shut the door to my apartment and tread quietly down the stairs. Rebecca's sweater not only isn't fashionable, it isn't at all warm. I've been forced to bundle up underneath so much that I resemble a negative image of the Michelin man. It's a good thing my task for the evening requires stealth, not athleticism, so any restriction in my movements will be more than compensated by the warmth the many layers provide.

Not wishing to risk questions as to why I want to be dropped off outside a restaurant that had closed an hour earlier, I forsake the Uber and take the el up to Rogers Park, then walk from the station. I keep my head down and stride with a purpose to seem like I'm simply a commuter returning home after a late night of work. I probably don't need to be too concerned. The streets in that stretch appear deserted.

Still, as long as I'm dealing with improbabilities, if I really had been a target and it's true that criminals return to the scene of a crime, I don't want to give my assailant a second chance after his (or possibly her) practice round went high. Across from the Senegalese restaurant, which is now dark inside, lies a narrow passageway between buildings that provides a decent view of at least a block in either direction. It also acts as a much-needed windbreak. I slip into the mouth of the gangway to verify that the area is free of traffic and to make sure I won't be disturbed by a dog walker or nosy neighbor.

Instantly, I feel the presence of someone behind me. Weaponless and with limited options, I spin around quickly, ready to do whatever damage I can with my fists. My first glance straight ahead of me, though, only reveals the top of a head of hair as black as coal. I know immediately that a few inches farther down, if I'd been able to see them at all, were eyes of different colors.

"What in the hell took you so long?" Vinn mutters.

"What are you doing here?"

"Waiting for you. And freezing. Well, are we going to stand in this putrid spot all night or are we going to get to work?"

I have more questions but she's right. There's definitely a foul stench in the alleyway, the air is freezing, and I…we…have a job to do. Without another word, we move cautiously across the street, heads turning as we walk. When we arrive at the front of the restaurant, Vinn looks at me expectantly, and I know what question lurks in her eyes.

"No, a little more my way," I whisper. I put my hands on each of her arms and pull her gently toward me. "Now, about eight inches closer to the curb. And imagine that you're taller."

Vinn glares menacingly at me but does as I ask. I take my position at her side then move into the street and pace back about two car-lengths. When I'm almost alongside where Fyre had been standing, I use the parked car between us as a guide and hunch down roughly to the height I would be at, had I been driving and leaning over slightly to my right to aim a handgun out of the passenger window. While trying to keep my balance in this awkward position, I pull my tactical flashlight out of the pocket of my sweatpants. It's one of the few possessions I refused to part with when I left mostly everything else behind. It's saved my ass more than once and I owed it some loyalty. That and it cost me close to $400.00.

I direct the beam of light about six inches over Vinn's head, then reconsider. The shooter had probably been aiming for the body—mine or Fyre's was yet to be determined—so I bring my aim down slightly until it brushes the top of Vinn's hair. Repositioning myself to a more stable stance while carefully keeping the arm holding the flashlight steady, I adjust the beam until it's as narrow as a laser, then hold it there.

It shouldn't surprise me that Vinn knows just what to do. Turning, she quickly covers the three steps to the building, pulls an overturned trash can out from where it had been hidden in the shadows, and climbs on top of it before looking back at me expectantly. Too coincidental, I think. Vinn had been busy while she was waiting for me.

She reaches beneath her jacket and pulls out her own flashlight… not as nice as mine but adequate… and holds it up until the two beams intersect on a single brick a few inches below the roofline. Talking a piece of chalk from her pocket (if I'm ever shot at again, I'll have to remember to carry chalk), she marks an 'x' at the spot. I leave my post, position myself underneath where Vinn stands on her toes on the rusty can, and hold my light up to focus on the x. She shakes her head slightly. I begin to move the light very, very slowly in concentric circles outward.

It doesn't take long, maybe three minutes, but it seems much longer. Vinn raises her arm and lifts her finger, signaling me to keep still. Clutching her own light under her arm, she uses her other hand to bring out a switchblade and flicks it open. I watch, fascinated and more than a bit curious, as she digs something out of the front of the building before dropping it into a small plastic snack bag that she had also had the foresight to bring. I definitely have some questions for this woman when the time is right.

I hold out an arm to help Vinn down from the trash can, then right the can and roll it back to where it belongs. I join her in the doorway of the restaurant where both of us try to keep warm against the wind. She holds the bag out to me. I resist temptation and pocket it without fighting the dark to see what she had discovered.

"Congratulations," she comments dully. "You were shot at."

I nod as the realization of what she said washes over me and flushes the last drops of denial from my mind. I must have stood stupidly for several moments before Vinn hits my shoulder, hard.

"Come on, we'd better get going." She starts to move, then looks back at me quizzically. "What on earth are you wearing? And is that duct tape?"

With that, she grabs a loose end of the tape, and in one sweeping motion rips it off of the sweater, sending a cascade of sequins onto the ground. Damn it all. If this mysterious assassin doesn't kill me, Rebecca will.

Chapter 13

I don't even bother going to bed, knowing that sleep will never come as long as my mind continues to race. Who tracked me down and what did I ever do to him or her to make them want to kill me? The mental list I conjure up in response to my own question is a long one, but I methodically check each name off. Prison, several. Dead, even more. Brutal but too stupid to locate me, one. As dawn breaks, I've narrowed the possibilities down to six. At this point, though, I wonder what my night of evaluation has accomplished. In my list of six, if any one of them wants me dead, there may not be much I can do about it. Which raises yet another point. The shooting didn't have the feel of a professional job, more like the assailant used television crime shows as a primer. If I go with that assumption, I can eliminate the remaining six on my list.

But was I even the shooter's objective? Fyre has deftly avoided talking about her past, and much of her present for that matter. Is it possible that she's made enemies to such a degree that they would take potshots at her? Why would anyone want to hurt someone so personable and sexy? Even before that last thought finishes passing through my consciousness, I can see Vinn's blazing eyes ready to accuse me of sexism. Fine. Fyre's looks and personality don't disqualify her as a possible target. Maybe my personal involvement with her is shading my opinion, but I can't convince myself that she was the shooter's objective. Maybe a jealous ex-boyfriend, so that hitting either one of us would have satisfied him?

By the time I hear Ted cursing into the phone beneath me, signaling the start of the workday, the only conclusion that I've come to is that it would be unfair to keep Fyre ignorant about what Vinn and I discovered last night. If she was, in fact, the target, I owe it to her to put her on alert even if she's not ready to believe me. If it was me, she has the right to keep her distance for her own safety. Either way, if I keep quiet and something happens to her, I'll never forgive myself.

Sleep deprivation has made my mind fuzzy and it takes me twenty minutes to find my cell phone, which at some point during the night I thought was a good idea to store in the microwave. I begin scrolling through my contacts with the intent of not wasting any time before calling Fyre but stop suddenly as my mind starts to clear. What am I going to say? "Hello, my love, I found a bullet buried in the restaurant wall, so someone may be trying to kill you. Have a nice day." No matter how I work the words around, they either don't have sufficient gravity for her to take me seriously or are so extreme they would bring on full-blown panic. A creative writing teacher at a loss for words. Wonderful.

This clearly isn't a conversation to have long-distance and Fyre hasn't answered my last few calls or returned the pleading voice messages I left anyway. Texting seems to be an even less desirable option. I need to talk to her face-to-face. Problem is, I have my doubts about whether she'll agree to meet with me even if I can get through to her. I decide to breach social etiquette and stop by her place unannounced. For the immediate future, though, I need to get to work.

"You're procrastinating," Vinn tells me as she spreads cream cheese on her bagel, pointing out the obvious.

"Nonsense," I retort, denying the obvious. "This isn't a subject that should be discussed on the phone. Besides, she's not taking my calls."

Vinn raises an eyebrow. I wish she'd stop doing that. "Trouble in paradise? Can't imagine why. Most women adore men who push them down on the ground after a romantic meal of goat meat."

"I think my honorable intentions of giving her fair warning would be obnubilated by her memory of that night."

Vinn scowls. "Wrong context, I think. Also, there's no one else here. Doesn't count."

I ignore her and continue babbling. "I also have my adoring students to think about. I can't just take off in the middle of a class day to save a fair maiden's life." I sigh as my attempt at levity falls flat, even with me. "She's most likely working or surrounded by people. It's daylight. And she probably wasn't the target anyway. She'll be fine. Tomorrow's Saturday. I'll give her the bad news then."

"Okay, Mr. Rationalization, have it your way." Vinn pushes her chair back and rises from the table. I do the same. "Let's just hope that she's alive for you to tell her."

Vinn's last words haunt me as I make my way down the hallway to my afternoon class, which might explain why I almost walk right into Stuart just outside his office door.

"Mr. Winters," he sneers. Okay, maybe he didn't sneer. We creative types often have overactive imaginations, but it definitely fell on the uncongenial side of the facial spectrum. "Don't forget that mid-term grades are due by Wednesday."

"Of course, I haven't forgotten." How could I forget something I never knew in the first place? Maybe I need to start checking the faculty message boards once in a while. "I've already started on them."

Giving me a look that clearly shows he doesn't believe me, Stuart turns and ambles off in the other direction but not before calling over his shoulder, "Word among the students is that your class is one of their favorites. I'll have to sit in on one to find out why."

Great. Someone tries to shoot me and my boss wants to evaluate my teaching style. Life doesn't get any better than this. For a moment, I wish the assailant had taken better aim.

As it turns out, this afternoon's honors seminar would have been a good class for him to view. What starts out as a discussion of how genre can affect an author's characterization of his protagonist morphs into a spirited debate on point of view and whether certain types of novels by their very nature prohibit the use of the first person. I have some very intelligent students in this particular course and often find myself trying to keep up. I've found that as long as I nod and interject a cliché now and then, my students project their own levels of brilliance upon me.

For at least an hour of the ninety-minute class, my attention is diverted enough by the colloquy that I'm able to push my more pressing issues to the back of my mind. Even after class, when I usually discourage hangers-on, I stay back to listen to a few of my more enthusiastic students continue the debate. Once they leave, the emptiness of the classroom forces decisions I have to make to echo inside my head. I know I need to find a way in the near future to present the past in a way that is anything but tense. Just the thought alone gives me a headache.

I stop by Tryzub on the way home and request the daily dinner special to go without even asking what it is. Living life on the wild side, that's me. Approaching the front gate of the three-flat, I notice Leo peering out of his window. Before I can even make it to the stairs, he's out his front door peering up at me.

"You're tired. *Fatigado.* I see it. *Cena, amigo?*"

I begin to wonder what hours his restaurant keeps as he never seems to be there. I hold up my now-dripping bag in reply.

"Ah, Tryzub. Bonosh. *Esta bien.* Maybe drink later."

I nod, mostly just to get to the isolation my own apartment offers, and drag my fatigued body up the stairs. Only when I begin to unpack my dinner do I think to marvel at Leo's sense of smell because I need to open the bag before detecting the aroma of cornmeal and pork. After a terrible couple of days, some Ukrainian comfort food is just what I need.

The bonosh is more than *bien*, although I confess that I'm eating on auto-pilot. I'm not a stranger to being stalked but not knowing who my adversary is, if I even have one, added to my still-limited familiarity with the city, imparts an unfamiliar level of discomfort. The circumstances prevent me from going on the offensive, but how do I defend myself—and Fyre—against a mysterious stranger in a large city? Even in the direst of situations, I've always been able to visualize at least a couple of paths to saving my own skin. Here, nothing.

I find no answers in the food and my sleepless night continues to slow my thought processes. I consult with myself and come up with what I imagine every super-spy does in this situation. I lay down for a nap.

When I awake, it's dark. To my great disappointment, no answers miraculously appeared in my dreams. I find my phone under the covers, confirm that no one has texted me a solution, and sit up. It's just past midnight. With my mental fog beginning to lift, it occurs to me that Leo has never expressed concern about my level of energy before. He should be back from the restaurant by now if he was even there at all. Maybe what I need is a drink after all.

It doesn't surprise me that Leo is awake. I've seen his light on and movement behind his curtains well into the early morning hours several times. When the door is opened, though, I'm a bit unnerved to see that he has two shot glasses set out on the table with a bottle of the good stuff sitting between them. I was expected.

Leo's red eyes and whiskey-breath indicate that he may have gotten a bit of a head start on the drinking. He wordlessly ushers me in through the door and motions me toward the table. He's still wearing his food-stained shirt and equally filthy work pants. His hair is disheveled, his face drawn, and his nose is on its way to a shiny crimson hue. When he speaks, however, there's no wavering and his invitation to sit sounds very much like a command.

"So," he says simply, sitting back as if he had given me a clear indication of what I was supposed to do next. After a few moments of silence, he expounds. "Talk."

Not knowing why exactly, I fill him in on my last few days, finishing up by repeating to him all of the questions that have been occupying my mind. Pausing only long enough to throw back a healthy dose of amber courage, I look at him pleadingly as if he were the man on the mountain with all of the answers. "Leo, you know this city better than I do. What are the odds that this was a random act?"

He narrows his eyes at me, refilling my glass as well as his own. I haven't even noticed him drinking. "*Cero. Ninguna.*" He raises his glass toward me. I tip it with my own. We both swallow and he pours again. "You have *un problema major.*"

Even as my brain races rapidly toward intoxication, I still comprehend that he's not being a whole lot of help. I was hoping for better. "So what do I do? I can't call the cops."

"NO!" he explodes, spitting on the floor for emphasis and giving me a glare filled with disappointment. "Be *un hombre.* You must protect *su señora.* Go to her in morning. Stay with her. Wait."

"You want me to wait until the guy tries to kill us again?" My incredulity, mixed with the whiskey, might be making me sound hysterical. And maybe I am. It's crazy. Nuts. *Loco.* But there is also a certain amount of sense in Leo's walking orders. Maybe the only way to narrow the field from millions to one would be to flush him or her out again. Simple. On the other hand, doing so might result in one less *hombre* or *señora* in this world.

Leo watches the realization wash over me, then leans over and moves his hand to rest gently on my forearm. I can smell the whiskey on his breath even stronger than before. He speaks softly. "*Mi amigo*, you have experience in such things. I can tell. When time comes, you will know what to do." His tone is supportive, but the sadness in his eyes betrays him. He knows that he might be speaking with me for the last time, because I believe he, too, has had experience in such things.

"Tomorrow, you go to the woman. You will fix it. No worry."

He's right. Now that there's a plan in place…sort of… I feel a familiar confidence building inside of me. I can act now, to confront this man with a gun without fear. I'm not sure I can say the same thing about facing Fyre.

Chapter 14

Some plans don't last past the first few minutes and this is one of them. Fyre has apparently taken some precautions on her own initiative. Hal, the day shift manager at the front desk of her condo building, who knows me by sight from my many visits, tapped a few commands into his computer as I approach to verify that he could send me upstairs.

"I'm sorry, Mr. Winters, but you're not on the list." He seems genuinely puzzled, which is nothing compared to how I feel. The list? Since when does Fyre keep a list? And did she check it twice?

"But Hal, you know me. Can you just let her know I'm here?"

"I'm afraid not, Mr. Winters. She left specific instructions. You have to be on the list."

I throw a friendly nod his way to show that there are no hard feelings, stand looking stupid for a few moments, then reverse direction to the revolving door and step out into the early morning hours on the plaza abutting the building. Hal has at least confirmed that Fyre is home, otherwise, he would have simply told me that she isn't there. At least I think so. Lacking a better idea, I decide to settle in to wait for her to emerge.

The residents there clearly see tourists, vagrants, and jilted lovers as a major problem, as there is no place nearby for me to comfortably sit or even lean. Would a bench be too much trouble? Closer to the street sits a planter which had given up its holiday arrangement months ago and is still waiting for the City to plant its spring flowers. I perch on its side, feet dangling just above the ground. It isn't long before I pull the collar of my jacket up against the chill. I hadn't planned to be outside on a stakeout today and didn't dress for the cold.

The city awakens around me as I sit, minute after minute, hour after hour. Saturday shoppers, carrying their overpriced purchases in cheap paper bags, hurry past on their way to warmer environs. The sky brightens slightly as the sun rises higher in the sky. At least, I assume it's there behind the gray clouds. It's March in Chicago. From what I understand, it will be two more months before we actually see the sun again. I'm hoping that by then I can feel my toes.

I pass the time imagining Fyre standing at her window thirty-two floors up, watching me freeze while she sips her coffee. I debate whether such an action would justify allowing her to get shot. The jury's still out on that question as I push the thought away and begin scouting for a new location, preferably one with radiant heat, when a flash of familiar red catches the corner of my eye. Fyre is on the move.

I call out to her as she makes her way over the paneled concrete of the plaza in the direction of the sidewalk. She looks up, startled and clearly frightened, takes a quick glance around, then increases her pace, using her bright blue sneakers to their best advantage, as she runs toward a waiting sedan idling in the street. Before I can cover the gap to let her know that it's only me, the car pulls away from the curb into traffic.

I have two factors working in my favor at this point. First, traffic in this area of the city on a Saturday, or any other day for that matter, resembles a Wal-Mart parking lot on Christmas Eve. You're not going anywhere fast. I could probably just jog up to her car and pull open the door to join her as it waits for the light but quickly veto the idea. If she's keeping a list that excludes even me, she may also have taken other precautions such as carrying a handgun. Given that her nerves are probably even more frayed than my own, she might shoot first and look at a face second when a man tries to force his way into her car.

The second thing I have going for me is that ninety percent of the vehicles in the congested mass are taxicabs competing for the fares of ignorant tourists who don't know that the American Girl store is ten minutes away on foot, fifteen by cab. Any Chicagoan insane enough to own a car in this city would find an alternate route or take an Uber, which is exactly what I assume Fyre is doing. I flag down a Yellow, which easily blends into the dozens of other yellow taxis, just in case she's paranoid enough to think that she might be followed. A couple of minutes have passed, but Fyre is still only half a block ahead.

My Pakistani driver looks toward the back seat expectantly, probably hoping that I'll utter the magic words and ask him to take me to O'Hare. I hate to disappoint him.

"Do you see that dark gray Lexus in the left lane up there?" I point, as if that will help. "I need you to follow it."

The driver glares at me with darkened eyes. "You a stalker? Ex-husband? No thank you, sir. Get out of my cab."

He's serious. "Nothing like that," I reply quickly, hiding the panic in my voice as I watch the light up the street turn green. Just my luck to get the one socially responsible cabbie in the city. "She's my girlfriend. I was supposed to meet her here half an hour ago but I'm late. She left for our appointment without me and I don't know the address."

"You have a phone? Call her. Out of my cab."

With each passing second, Fyre's cab inches further away. I sigh in resignation and exit the driver's side into traffic, where another vacant Yellow Cab sits directly next to the one I just vacated. I open the door and jump in.

"Follow that Lexus!" I shout as my way of introduction. In response, the driver, who looks like Edwin G. Robinson on a bad day, turns around and grins. "I've always wanted someone to say that to me. First time in fourteen years. You going to offer me a sawbuck if I don't lose it?"

"You've seen too many movies, my good man. Let's see how it works out first." I grin to show that I'm in on the joke, trying my best to hide my rapidly rising alarm. The driver settles into his beaded seat cover and quickly pulls to our left, soliciting an angry blast of a horn from the cab in that lane.

"Hang on tight." More cabbie humor. We aren't moving.

Five slow motion but terrifying lane changes, two yellow lights, and one red one later, we're positioned only two cars back from the Lexus. The odds that Fyre can see me are slim, but I slide back into the shadows of the back seat. For whatever reason, she's made a point of keeping me at a distance and I don't know how she would react if she knows that I'm following her.

The Lexus driver seems uncertain about where to go, more than once signaling a left turn then continuing straight. My driver is nonplussed and seems to be enjoying the challenge of the chase, if it can be called that at speeds that top out at ten miles per hour. Eventually, we turn west onto Chicago Avenue where within a few blocks, we leave the tourist-saturated area behind. Traffic is still heavy but moving and it's easy to blend in while still maintaining a comfortable cushion.

The same can't be said when we turn south on LaSalle Street, passing over the river and into the business section of the Loop. Nowhere near as busy as it would be on a weekday; we've become much more visible. I ask the driver to hang back a little.

"Don't worry, buddy. They don't even know we're here. That moron's so lost, he ain't looked in his mirror once. Ride share. Phooey. He don't know the area. Probably from Schaumburg." He slows up and falls back a bit anyway, most likely in anticipation of getting that sawbuck. I find myself chewing my fingernails, which I never do.

We continue south, past the triangular prison, and for a moment, I think we're headed for the Eisenhower Expressway and a trip out to the west suburbs. Instead, our prey once more turns west, this time on Van Buren. Traffic is even more sparse here and for the first time, I feel totally exposed. My driver must sense my uneasiness. He drops back to keep a block between us.

Crossing the river once more, Fyre's car accelerates through a yellow light while we get caught by a red. I watch helplessly as the Lexus nearly disappears from sight. Showing he's either in the right spirit or is inspired by cop shows, my driver anticipates the green and peels after them, but then slams hard on his brakes and swings to the curb, throwing my body painfully against the side door.

Only then do I realize why he stopped so suddenly. Fyre is exiting the Lexus a block and a half ahead of us and would soon be impossible to find among the buildings crowding the area. I quickly throw money at my driver, who whistles between his teeth with satisfaction. I have a feeling when I check my wallet later, I'll regret not being more attentive.

I sprint to close the gap to about half a block. The temptation is to catch up to her, grab her by the shoulders, and tell her about finding the bullet and Leo's plan for drawing out the killer. Instead, I keep my distance. As my brain began to thaw in the cab and I could think rationally, I surmised that Fyre already knows that we were shot at, probably knows why, maybe knows who, but that she has no intention of confiding in me. If I'm to get to the bottom of what's going on here and get the information I need to help her, she's not going to be cooperative. My best bet is to let whatever she's up to play out while I assume the role of inobtrusive observer.

The entire area around us is devoid of both foot and vehicle traffic, which makes following Fyre easier but also increases the risk of being discovered. I edge behind a pillar of a dark glass monstrosity across the street that would have Daniel Burnham turning in his grave. Just in time. Fyre walks determinately, clearly knowing where she's headed, but at the same time nervously swings her head in all directions, as if looking for someone who may or may not be there.

She pauses, turns a full circle, then makes a quick dash into the shadow of the old post office. Do any travel around the city and it's hard not to have this massive, deserted building draw your attention. Early on in my tenure here, I was curious enough to look up its background. Built about one hundred years ago, this Art Deco behemoth stretches two long city blocks over the Eisenhower and rises maybe ten floors up. At one time, it was one of the busiest postal buildings anywhere in the world, but as with all good things, its life span was cut short. About twenty years ago, the feds determined that it had outlived its usefulness and moved on to a more functional and less visually appealing location. It's been vacant ever since.

I move down a couple of pillars to draw closer to Fyre as I watch to see what she'll do next. Trying her best to appear nonchalant, she sidles up to the wire fence that surrounds the building at the base of the stairs leading up to its former entrance, casually running her hand along it as she slowly walks westward. About three-quarters of the way down she freezes suddenly, again glances around nervously, more carefully this time, then stoops down to pull open a section of fence that appears to have been cut. Squeezing through with more than a few cuss words that carry across the street with the wind, she pauses only long enough to bend the section of the fence back, so that any passerby would have to be looking for the opening in order to find it.

Good thing this particular passerby now knows where to find it. I watch Fyre run up the steps before disappearing under the giant overhang and behind the broad stone pillars lining the building. I count slowly to ten before dashing across the street and over to the opening. Close up, it doesn't look nearly as accessible as it did from a distance. Worried about losing Fyre more than the risk of discovery, in a matter of seconds I scale the fence, drop to the ground, and run up the stairs in her direction. She's not here to mail a letter. Something is going down and I need to be there when it does. Whether as observer or protector remains to be seen.

Chapter 15

The side of the building facing Van Buren Street had obviously been the main entrance to the building. A long line of tall doors stretches across the entire north side of its façade. A few are boarded up and all of the others are presumably locked but Fyre is nowhere in sight. Unless she turned the corner of the building and jumped into the Chicago River, she found a way in. The first two doors I try don't budge, the boards on the third haven't been tampered with, and the fourth rattles as I try to first pull, then push, it open. I'm about to move on in frustration when I pause and look back at the door I had just abandoned. The other doors I tried didn't move as much as a millimeter. This one did. Leaning over to examine it more closely, I notice that the deadbolt is shinier than the rest of the mechanics of the lock, indicating a recent switch. I didn't anticipate having to break in when I left for Fyre's that morning so my lock picks are still hidden away in my kitchen. I'm never without my Swiss Army knife, though. I pull out the longest blade it has, stick it in past the end of the bolt, which is far shorter than the original one, and lever it back, pulling the door at the same time. It opens and I step inside.

Any doubts I have about the way Fyre gained entry are allayed by imprints of a pair of sneakers leading away from the door, clearly marked in two decades of dust that had accumulated on the floor. As I begin to follow them, I glance up and immediately wish that I were there for some other, less urgent purpose. Glints of light reflect off the marble walls rising from a stone base in which patterns of a compass had been carefully laid. Art deco light fixtures straight from the 1930s grace the lobby and a long line of teller booths sit empty after having sold their last sets of stamps when they were still thirty-two cents. Absolutely stunning. I wonder when the government stopped taking pride in its offices for a moment, before forcing myself back on task.

Hurrying onward, I'm startled to see a second set of footprints heading in the same direction. Assuming that Fyre didn't change out of her blue sneakers into a pair of extraordinarily large men's shoes, she and I aren't alone. Her prints are on top of the second set, indicating that the other intruder was here before her. I would have noticed if she had been following someone as I followed her, unless she's extraordinarily good at tailing from a distance, so this has to be a prearranged meeting. But why the secrecy and the isolated location? My level of concern rockets off the charts. Is this a meeting or a showdown? One way to find out.

The layer of dust diminishes and the prints fade away, leaving me to guess where the pair has gone for their rendezvous. Not as stupid as I look, I quickly eliminate the elevators and run frantically in all directions until I find a stairwell. Quietly opening the door and easing it shut, there's movement above me. Not footsteps or a door opening necessarily, I just sense more than hear that someone is on the stairs anywhere from two to five flights up. At this point, speed is more important than stealth. I abandon any efforts to keep my presence a secret as I fly up the stairs.

The door to the second level opens to an expansive area that appears to have served as a sorting area. Chutes leading to conveyors mix with abandoned compartmentalized tables. A few packages that will never make it to their destination still litter the floor. No sooner do I eliminate it as a possibility—it was too large for Fyre to have crossed before I arrived—than I hear a faint crash from one of the floors above. I continue upward.

Whoever I'm pursuing, whether it's Frye or the owner of the oversized shoes, is no longer making any effort to be quiet, perhaps because they now clearly hear me coming behind them and feel the need to move quickly. I don't bother to check out the third or fourth floors, as scuffling from above keeps me climbing. As I reach the fifth floor, an eerie silence greets me. A river of adrenaline urges me onward, but I stay motionless, listening for the slightest of creaks. Nothing. I'm not sure where to go from here but standing in the stairwell, waiting for Fyre to discover me, isn't an option. I cautiously open the door and step in.

Another large room, bigger than a football field, but this one shows more signs of its former purpose. Long tables where generations of men and women sorted mail extend most of the length of the room. Heavy carts stacked together with surprising care stand idle. Windows as tall as the room let in limited light, just enough for me to notice the peeling paint and buckled floors. If Fyre chose this room as her destination, her speed would be limited by the tiles rising up from rotting floorboards, which would work to my advantage. I step in and move to the end of a blue-tinted table, stare at the vast emptiness of the room, then bend down to see if she's hiding from view under the table.

Just as I lower myself to floor level, a loud crack shatters the air from somewhere near the windows farther into the room. I feel the air displace inches above my head and the wall behind where I had just stood explodes, scattering plaster all around me. Instinctually, I flatten myself into the dust on the floor and roll under the table. No second shot follows and the earlier silence returns, this time with a frightening portent of how it might be broken again. I keep still and concentrate on regulating my breathing.

Is Fyre the shooter? If so, there's a good chance she doesn't know that it's me she's using for target practice. I may not be on her list, but I don't think she wants to kill me. Assuming it's Fyre, all I need to do is to shout out to identify myself and I'm sure—well, eighty percent certain—that she won't shoot me. If it isn't her, though, any sort of sound will only give away my location and increase the odds that the rest of my life will now be measured in minutes. The gunman outside the restaurant didn't impress me with his or her accuracy, but that doesn't mean I want to help them out.

Past experience tells me that staying in one place until I'm found is never the best strategy, a thought confirmed when I hear light, cautious footfalls edging closer to my location. I take a deep breath then burst out from under the table, heading back in the direction of the door, keeping as low to the ground as I can. My efforts at escape are rewarded with a second shot which grazes my left sleeve and shatters the glass in the door as I push it open and tumble into the stairwell.

The smart move is to retrace my steps, scamper down the stairs as quickly as humanly possible, and leave the building. That's also what my pursuer will expect, which means it's not what I'll do. Besides, if the man with the large feet is the one with the gun, he couldn't have known that I would be in the building with him. Whether his intent is to shoot Fyre or he just thought it would be a good idea to bring a serious weapon to their rendezvous, the danger level is too high to risk leaving her on her own. I set out this morning with the goal of either warning or confronting Fyre and then using her to draw out the gunman, eliminate him, and bring some normalcy back into our lives. In some corner of my brain, I should have expected another bullet or two might be in the cards. Maybe not quite so soon or on the shooter's terms instead of my own, but this is, after all, what I had wanted. I just wish that the same corner of my brain had spoken up and suggested I bring a weapon of my own to the party. It's just this sort of sloppiness that weighed heavily in my decision to retire from this line of work. In any event, the opportunity may not come again.

So, upward I flee, for now in the role of the prey. I start to pass by the next floor, hoping that the gunman will assume that I'll seek a place to hide as quickly as possible, then realize that finding such a place makes a whole lot of sense. I use my shoulder to force the door open into the sixth floor. This room is crowded with gigantic pieces of mail-moving machinery, resembling slumbering monsters just waiting to be woken. Conveyor belts, chutes, and masses of metal extend the length of the room.

If they were subject to an awakening, the bullet that whizzes past my ear and buries itself into the machine just to my right would have done the trick. This guy may not be an Olympic-caliber marksman, but his tracking skills are enviable. He must have used the stairs on the opposite side of the room. I slide under a conveyor belt extending up to another belt nearly to the ceiling, then jump onto the next conveyor and dash up to the top. Here, narrow belts meant for packages run in all directions like the streets of a city, each lined with metal bands and posts evenly spaced along their entire length.

Even if the shooter knows where I am, it would take a phenomenally skillful aim to thread a bullet through all of the metal in order to reach warm flesh. On the other hand, a random shot could ricochet wildly and do some damage, so I keep moving, following the path of millions of packages before me. The crack of a distant shot gives me some comfort that my location is, for the moment, unknown.

As I crawl, I find myself battling an unfamiliar and unwelcome fatigue. At first, I presume that the adrenaline rush that accompanied the first shot ten minutes ago has ended and that my body is crashing, but a glance behind me at where I had just travelled reveals a trail of clearly defined droplets of blood marking the path, like so many of Hansel's bread crumbs. A hasty pat-down quickly finds its source, a small oozing wound in the fleshy part of my left bicep. It could be worse and isn't fatal, but any significant blood loss will send my body into shock. If the shooter doesn't find me to finish me off, a fainting spell followed by a fall to the ground from where I'm hiding would do his job for him. I need to stem the flow and let my body regain its equilibrium, and I can't do it where I am right now or while I'm under siege.

Putting pressure on my wound with my right hand, I take the chance that the gunman has deserted me to go back to his encounter with Fyre. Now that I'm on the sidelines until I can regain my energy, I try to take comfort from the fact that Fyre did come to this deserted spot for some reason, and a mutual agreement to meet with the mystery man is as plausible an explanation as any. The shots in my direction are because I'm an uninvited intruder. Under this scenario, it's likely that they'll both say what they came to say, then go their separate ways with no additional holes in them. In the meantime, I can recover and live to find our assailant, whether this man or someone else, another day.

I crawl for several minutes before descending along one of the conveyor belts near the end of the room. Another hundred feet past that stands a massive furnace that had been used to provide heat for the employees during the harsh Chicago winters of years past. Measuring maybe twenty feet on each side, its heavy, thick metal shows signs of rust at the base. A large door meant to give access seems promising but is stuck shut, barring my access. With each attempt to open it, I feel a cloud of dizziness descend upon me.

Abandoning the door, I look for other options. Around the corner, about six feet off of the ground are what I can only describe as the furnace's windows with shutters made of metal, eight inches thick. The lengthy hinge at the top of one of the panels covering the openings has nearly rusted away, leaving the panel hanging precariously even as it still protects the space within. Stepping onto the top of the door to a coal chute at ground level to bring myself closer, I use my last bit of strength to push the door aside before throwing my upper body into the opening. Turning on my back, I grab a sharp metal bar above me and pull my legs into the opening, just as the panel swings back into place. It doesn't completely block the opening, but I feel well-hidden in the darkness within.

My consciousness is fading and I know it's a race against time. Fighting the pain, I grab the right sleeve of my shirt with my teeth and maneuver my arm out, wrapping the loosened fabric tight around my bleeding bicep and tying it off by tucking the end into the makeshift bandage. Hopefully, it will provide enough compression to stem the flow.

I force myself to steady my breathing in order to be as quiet as possible while I turn my ears to the room outside. Within minutes, light footsteps approach, pause, then continue on, circling back twice. I find myself holding my breath and gently allow it to escape my lips. As blackness descends, I wonder if the immediate danger is past. That's the last thought I remember having before all goes dark.

Chapter 16

As I regain consciousness, all sense of time and place is uncomfortably fuzzy. My head rests against a honeycombed vent through which heated air once passed, while the remainder of my body sprawls across the debris-filled base of the furnace. One leg dangles down an opening that drops to the floor below. I'm uncontrollably shivering. The irony of being cold while inside a furnace isn't lost on me.

Shifting to try to pull myself into position to exit the boiler brings forth a sharp reminder of my injured arm. Long tendrils of intense pain shoot through the left side of my body and up into my head. Fighting to prevent myself from passing out again, I pause before attempting once more to leave my hiding place. The lure of remaining where I am and going back to sleep is overwhelming, but my need to find Fyre and to make sure she's okay is greater and forces me into action.

My own safety is also a priority. Pushing the heavy cover out slightly, slowly, I stick my head out just far enough to give myself a view of the room. Light still filters through the tall, dirty windows, so I haven't been out of it the entire day, but whether it's been minutes or hours, I can't say. My cell phone is in my left pocket and the price of reaching for it just to check the time is too high. Moving in frustratingly slow motion in order to minimize the pain, I slip off one of my shoes then inch my sock off before replacing the shoe. Wadding it into a ball, I stuff it into my mouth to give me something to bite on, and to muffle my screams as I prepare to drop out of my hiding spot onto the floor.

I slide my legs down as far as I can without falling, in order to reduce the distance to the floor to not more than three feet, but it might as well have been thirty. Riveting streams of heat radiate throughout my body as I land, enveloping my entire body in a blanket of agony. I can feel blood seep from

95

the hole in my arm, further soaking my already stained shirt. Waiting to find enough energy and the will to start moving, I glance back up to where I had been, making a mental note to thank the Kewannee company for the use of their Bulldog Firebox Boiler. If I live to see the day.

No shower of bullets greets my emergence, so I relax a bit as I shuffle to the windows to look outside at the position of the sun. It's well past its high point in the sky, meaning it's now sometime in the afternoon. I've been out of commission for at least a couple of hours. While that probably means that any threat is long past, it's with a grim foreboding that I realize that whatever was going to go down here today has already happened. I've been a complete failure in my chosen role as Fyre's protector. My job now is to search for the aftermath and hope for the best.

I toss my sock aside rather than face the agony of trying to get it back on. As I push through my body's resistance to movement, my mind also begins to short-circuit with periodic blackouts, forcing me to reboot and remind myself where I am and what I need to do. I find that I'm unconsciously wandering over the same areas two or three times, wasting what little energy I have. This isn't good. I need to be more methodical. I need a plan.

I drag myself to the closest set of doors. Exiting the sixth-floor, I cast my eyes upward, immediately feeling unfit for the task ahead. The only way this will work will be to start at the top so that as my legs began to fail, I won't face any more climbing. I rack my memory from this morning trying to recall how tall the building is. I figure at most there are three floors above me.

I'm wrong. Gritting my teeth, taking each step first with one leg and then using my good arm to literally pull my other leg onto the same step, it takes me thirty agonizing minutes to travel up three flights, only to collapse on the landing in clear sight of an equal number of flights still to conquer. I fight the blackness that begins to cloud my thoughts, using the pain to keep me awake as I crawl up the twenty-two steps to the tenth floor. Anger at myself helps propel me on. I've been shot before, more than once, each time in a part of my body that should have disabled me much more than this flesh wound, yet I managed to function at a high enough level to finish the job and survive. Going soft now, when the woman I may love needs me, is as infuriating as it is incomprehensible. Yet another reminder that my seeming invincibility, as well as my focus, had dissipated to such an extent that my days were numbered if I hadn't moved on.

As I reach the landing, the pain is so overwhelming that I make an executive decision. Death is preferable to going on. I willingly succumb to my brain's desire to float into a semi-conscious dreamland and invite the gunman, if he's still here, to find me and put me out of my misery. Or maybe Fyre will come, turn the tables, and rescue me. I lie there as the minutes pass until the remorse at my failure to be at Fyre's side if some shit went down propels me to stand and resume my search. I know I can't make it up any more stairs. If I don't get any answers from the tenth floor downward, I'll have to return to the top two floors another day. Better yet, maybe when I check my phone, there'll be a voice mail from Fyre asking if I want to meet her for dinner.

The tenth floor is mostly offices, whose partitions make my search more time-consuming than it would be on the other wide-open floors I had passed through, while dodging my would-be killer. It's oddly creepy to see hand-written wall charts listing vacation schedules for employees who probably died years ago. I push such thoughts from my mind although clearly death is preoccupying a good portion of it. Walking hesitantly down the faded and worn carpeted hallway, it's obvious within minutes that no other soul has passed this way for years. The echoes of ghosts from the past still haunt the hallways, but the living are nowhere to be found.

As I walk, adrenaline and a sense of purpose push my pain into the background. I descend to the ninth floor, a rising panic and impatience to reconstruct what happened while I lay inside the boiler beginning to occupy my every thought. It's critical that I gather specific information as my calling card to Fyre, to show her that all my actions have her best interests in mind. I need to convince her that I care enough for both of our futures to have scoured the deserted building to discover whatever information I could to make it easier for us, together, to plan how to ward off any danger in the future. The thought that her presence here may have been totally unrelated to the shooting outside of the restaurant, and that it has a perfectly innocent and non-dangerous explanation, flits at the edges of my mind but I stubbornly push them away.

The ninth floor begins the transition back to the blue-collar sections, with large machines occupying most of the space but with a few offices, including the Dead Letter Office, crammed into one end. I take more time here, finding what I think are a few areas of disturbance, but ultimately there's nothing that sheds the slightest bit of light on the events of that morning. The eighth floor is set up with long tables topped with motorized machines that appear to have been used to cancel stamps by hand or to mark each letter that passed through with a postmark. Another day under different circumstances and I would have found the antiquated process fascinating, but today my focus is elsewhere. I pay special attention to every corner and every hidden shadow of every machine, looking under every table. The afternoon light is beginning to dim. By the time I'm ready to leave the eighth floor, I have my flashlight out to aid my failing eyesight.

I find her on the seventh floor. Large machines similar to those I'd seen previously stand like guardians of the past, with rows of conveyors stretching between the belts near the ceiling and their cousins at waist level, ready to move precious packages to their post-sorting destinations. The machines cast eerie shadows across the room, each one seeming to dance as the angle of the sun changes.

Fyre's lifeless form lies beneath one of the conveyors near the center of the room, all but her shoeless feet hidden in the darkness. Her neck is twisted at a grotesque angle as her wide-open eyes stare into nothingness. A large crimson patch befouls the left side of her blouse and a small pond of congealing blood pools beneath her on the floor. It doesn't take an expert to reconstruct the events leading to her death. Shot in the shoulder and weakened, perhaps in shock from the loss of large amounts of blood, she could only watch helplessly as her assailant came close to finish the job with a ruthless grabbing and twisting of her neck until it snapped. Red finger marks stand out against her pale skin, causing me to shudder as unwanted images flood my senses.

An overwhelming feeling of fatigue and failure suddenly causes my legs to founder and my body to sag. I slide down onto the floor inches away from the body that I used to hold close. I stare at her for several long, tortuous minutes in sadness, at the same time committing to memory the brutal sight in front of me so that I will never waiver in my newly formed quest to discover who did this to her and to enact justice in my own way. This son-of-a-bitch will never see the inside of a courtroom. I was worse than worthless at protection, but I will not fail in retribution.

To bring the wrath of Mal to bear, though, I have to harness energy from somewhere to drag myself out of here or I'll soon be joining Fyre in endless slumber. I feel a dark cloud gathering at the edges of my consciousness and know I have to move soon, and quickly. Pulling myself to my feet inch by painful inch, I glance back once more at the body of the woman for whom I cared so deeply. It's only then that I notice markings near her right hand that resemble too much of a pattern to be simple smudges. Getting a closer look means moving back down to floor level again. I groan even before starting the painful journey to a position on all fours next to Frye's body.

Once I get closer, it's clear that the markings are crimson-colored. Several paths partially hidden by her torso give clear indication that Frye used the blood from what became the disabling bullet wound to her chest to try to write one final message. Her note begins with a clear '1' followed closely by the number 9. After that, as life drained from her body, the rest of the writing gets progressively shakier but still readable. Another 1 follows the 9, this time not as straight nor as solid as the blood on her finger began to dry, and then what appears to be the number 5, although I wouldn't bet on it. A gap precedes the next entry, a half-circle resembling either the letter 'c,' or the beginnings of an 's.' A full circle follows, then a straight-ish line that ends where Fyre's finger lay still, either after her energy failed or her attacker finished his job. '1915'? 'co' or 'so' or something else? Did it mean something significant or was Fyre reflecting on past events as her life played before her eyes?

Pondering those questions will have to wait as my own ability to function begins to fade. Using my good arm, I reach across to the left pocket of my jeans, inching my phone out and praying that it was undamaged and held a charge. The anticipated pain that kept me from grabbing my phone while in the furnace jolts me but only motivates me to get this done. Using just my right hand, I jab the camera icon, turn on the flash, and bring it as near to the message as I can manage, hoping that drawing attention to myself with the flash won't be my own last movement. I quickly take several close-up shots and a few from farther away before slipping the phone back where it will be safe.

Holding my phone gives me an idea. I roll Fyre's body into various positions as best I can in order to check her pockets. Finally, in the left pocket of her jeans, I find what I'm looking for. I place her phone in the same pocket as my own. Time to go. Standing up a second time is no less painful that the first. I take one final look at the lifeless form lying at my feet. What were you doing here, Fyre, and did you know the danger you would face? If this was meant to be a simple meeting, why here? Were you planning to do to him what he did to you? What was so important that you had to hide it from me and refuse my help? As I turn away, I wonder if I'll ever get answers.

I have to hope that the attacker—now murderer—has left the building. If I slow my escape with constant reconnaissance, I'll never make it to the door. It seems to take me hours to descend the stairs, which might actually be accurate because the skies outside are turning the deep purple-black that immediately precedes absolute darkness. With the help of my flashlight, I find the door to the lobby and gratefully pass through it, an open target if someone is waiting for my appearance. No shots. The lobby is deserted.

Anger fuels me now. I retrace the steps I took in a more innocent time of mere hours ago, reaching the fence and squirming through it. Two lifetimes have passed since I exited that cab to follow Fyre. Now I need to find another taxi to take me back home, where I can try to piece together the events of this day and figure out what they're telling me.

I see the lights of a Checker cab down the street and wait impatiently as it approaches. Raising my good arm and waving it over, I take a few tentative steps into the street as it slows. That's when everything once again goes blank.

Chapter 17

"He say he find your address in your wallet…" Leo says by way of explanation as I sit at his kitchen table, my head throbbing and bicep screaming in pain. "I pay for you."

He's pulled in close to my left side as he uses a stained rag to dab a foul-smelling yellow ointment out of an old tobacco tin and spreads it across the holes in my bicep. The wound is still trickling blood and the discomfort level hasn't diminished. The fact that there are two holes, front and back, is a good sign. At least the bullet passed through my arm and doesn't need to be removed. A trip to the hospital with a gunshot wound by law requires a doctor to notify the police, which is why I'm forced to trust Leo. The last thing I need right now is to have to explain my way out of a jail cell. What could I tell the cops anyway? I know almost nothing.

I bite down hard on my lip as the ointment begins to sting. A part of me wants to ask Leo what homemade concoction he's using so that I can tabulate the chances that the cure is worse than the injury itself, but something tells me that gratitude is the right attitude at this point. "Thanks," I squeak in a throaty whisper. "Let me know what I owe you for the taxi."

"Achhng," he says, and for the next ten minutes that's the extent of our conversation. He continues with the ointment for a few minutes more before taking out a primitive sewing kit. After threading a needle with a thick black thread, he hands me a freshly cut stick of wood, signaling me to put it into my mouth. When I hesitate, he pushes it into my mouth for me. Any hope that the ointment would act as a numbing agent quickly dissipates. I bite down on the stick. Hard.

The sewing lasts about three painful days, although the kitchen clock indicates that only a few minutes pass before Leo breaks off the thread. He stares at my arm, looking at it from all angles, before nodding to himself and putting the needle away. Before I can get up, he pulls another ointment from his seemingly endless collection of tobacco tins and begins spreading it all over the area he had just sewn. My squeal at the new excruciating sensation sounds a little girlish, so I pull the stick out of my mouth to show him that I can take it like a man. Leo raises an eyebrow at me. What is it about me that causes people to do that? The operation finally ends when Leo produces a large bandage and medical tape which he expertly wraps around my arm.

"*Hecho.* Done."

"Leo, thank you," I croak, still trying to find my voice. "Where did you learn to do this?" It isn't my first bullet wound, nor the first time I'd received treatment somewhere off the books. I know he had done a professional job.

He shrugs, then grunts, then moves away from the table. That's as much of an answer as I'll get, at least for today. Fair enough. Time to change the subject.

"Leo, I'd prefer if you don't tell anyone about this."

His eyes blaze as if I'd said something stupid, and maybe I had. After all, in the entire time I've been in his apartment, he's never once asked me to explain how I ended up with a gunshot wound. "No one. But she knows," he says as he nods his head upward.

"You told Rebecca?" I may have raised my voice a bit, but I'm incredulous. It turns out to be the second idiotic thing I've said in a row.

Leo again flashes me the evil eye, and I make a mental note that despite his age, I do not want to be on the wrong side of a knife fight with him. "Had to. Saw me carry you in."

I nod. That's something I'll deal with later. For right now, I need rest. I stand, shakily, and extend a hand to Leo, who takes it with questioning eyes. I know what he's asking. "No, I can make it on my own, thanks."

Memo to self: false bravado can be a painful thing. It takes me ten minutes and three rest stops to drag myself up two flights of stairs, but the thought of Rebecca—or worse yet, Ted—finding me on the steps and creating a further obligation keeps me moving upward. Stumbling forward through my apartment, my arm throbbing, the bedroom seems to be moving two steps away for everyone I take.

After forever, I land on my bed in one final lunge, legs hanging and my feet barely off the floor. I need to get out of my bloody, filthy clothes. I need to soak my sore muscles in a bath. I need to figure out what Fyre was trying to say. I need…

Later.

Chapter 18

Vinn can be a good listener when she wants to be. She sits across from me, expressionless and silent, while I recount the events as best I can, trying not to omit a single detail that might be relevant. I can be a good talker when I want to be. Even after I finish, she remains quiet, staring into my eyes as if she could look inside my mind to bring out details that I missed in the retelling. Part of me thinks she can. It's unnerving.

"You could have been killed," she finally says.

"I realize that now," I reply, a bit defensive. I take a sip of the Gyokuro I brought from home. "But how was I to know? For all I could tell, she was going off to meet a girlfriend for a beer. If I had any idea that gunshots and murder in an abandoned building were on the agenda, don't you think I would have taken precautions? I probably wouldn't have gone after her at all." My voice rises as I speak, maybe overplaying the incredulity I feel the need to convey to Vinn as a way of shielding the fact that yes, I used to do that all the time. I look around to make sure no one at one of the nearby tables is listening in. All good.

Vinn eyes me cautiously before leaning forward, taking my hands in hers, and speaking so softly that I have to lean in to hear her. "Yes, you would have. I know you, Mal. You care. Maybe too much sometimes, but it's a good bad habit to have. I respect you for it." She sighs, then leans back and lets out an exasperated breath. "The question is, what do we do now?"

"We?" I raise an eyebrow at her, my attempt to show her how annoying that is. No reaction. "I don't want you anywhere near this, Vinn. Some maniac is out there running around with a gun. He knows what I look like. He doesn't know you and I'd like to keep it that way. Besides, this doesn't concern you."

Again, the ten-second stare of death. "Fine. But it doesn't put either of us in harm's way to talk some of this through. Do you have any idea what she was trying to tell you?"

"Not a clue. And I'm not sure she knew that I'd be the one to see her message. Maybe it was meant for someone that would immediately understand what '1915' means and connect it to her killer."

Vinn nods thoughtfully. "Possible. You can start by asking her friends if it has any significance that they know about." She notices the blank expression on my face and frowns. "What? You do know who her best friends are, don't you? You were dating for what, six months? What were you doing that whole time if you never met her friends?"

I must be blushing, causing Vinn to snort and mutter "pig" under her breath as she shakes her head.

"Even if I did know where to start with her friends, co-workers, or family, which I don't, how would you suggest I approach them? 'Hello, you don't know me, but your best friend is dead and she wrote this note in her blood as she died. Can you tell me what it means?' Christ, Vinn, there are only three people in the world—you, me, and that bastard—that know that she's dead and if I want to stay off the cops' radar, I need to keep it that way."

Vinn compresses her lips, which I interpret as her way of reluctantly conceding my point. "Can you look back over the times you were together? Did she ever show an interest in history? Could it be the name of her favorite perfume? An address or part of a phone number? Anything come to mind, Mal? Anything at all?"

My turn to shake my head. "I don't think so. If so, I've forgotten. Then again, Fyre seems to have had her secrets." I can't keep the exasperation out of my voice. "So, where does this leave me? Someone killed her, Vinn, and tried to do the same to me. I can't just walk away."

"I know." She sounds sympathetic. "Look, you have a key to her apartment, don't you? And the doorman knows you?"

I couldn't keep the astonishment out of my voice, mostly because this idea is coming from Vinn. "First of all, I'm too much of a gentleman to ask for her key. And break into a dead woman's apartment? Are you serious?"

"What, are you afraid that her ghost will be in there making baloney sandwiches?" Vinn can be sarcastic sometimes. "Who's to know? If you need someplace to start cracking the case, Sherlock, her humble abode may have some answers."

"No, absolutely not. It just seems like a violation of her somehow, you know what I mean? No, no, no."

"Just trying to help, Mal. I've got to get to class. If you want to brainstorm some more, let me know."

I watch as Vinn exits the room. Her suggestion makes sense, and of course has already occurred to me, but how can I explain that it violates my principles to invade a private space of someone that was close to me, that everyone deserves to keep a part of themselves out of view of the world, especially their friends, even in death? I've known a lot of seemingly ordinary people who have anointed a special friend to be the first one into their home after they die to remove something they don't want anyone else to see. Ransacking Fyre's unit crosses a moral line for me, and I just won't do it.

"Hello, Hal, a little chilly out tonight, isn't it? Do you think Fyre will like these flowers?" I hold out the bouquet of yellow something-or-others in the deskman's general direction.

"Very nice, sir. Can you tell me, is Miss Stockton okay? I haven't seen her for a couple of days and I get concerned."

"Thanks for asking, Hal. She's actually been under the weather. I'm hoping these flowers will brighten her spirits as well as the room. She asked me to tell you not to bother calling up, as she's too ill to get to the phone and may be sleeping. I'll just let myself in."

Before the stalwart keeper of the doors can object and remind me that I'm not on Fyre's list, I double-time to the elevator and catch a break as the doors of one draw open just as I approach. I hastily punch the button and head up. It wasn't Vinn's look of contempt that changed my mind about searching Fyre's condo, although that did bother me for hours afterward. Finding justice for her by tracking down her killer trumps my moral objection to pawing through a dead woman's private affairs, and I have nowhere else to start.

I confess that I've broken into more than one place where I wasn't meant to be, some well-fortified with the express intent of keeping people like me out, but for all the practice I've had, I'm still terrible at picking locks. Even with a fancy set of picks in my arsenal to work on a relatively cheap lock, it takes a desperate final attempt with my Visa card before the bolt throws back and I step inside. On the negative side, my purchasing power just dipped as the chip on my card took one for the team.

I gently close the door behind me, turn around and almost have a heart attack. Vinn stands leaning against the wall of the entryway twirling a penlight in her hand, a bemused expression on her face.

"What in the hell took you so long? And who taught you to pick locks?"

"You could have at least let me in after the first few minutes," I retort, realizing as I say it that I need to work on my retorts. "And what are you doing here?"

"How was I to know that it was you? And I'm here because if you're as bad at looking for needles in haystacks as you are at breaking and entering, you need me. Now, are you going to stand there all night or can we get looking?"

I bite back a biting response—how's that for irony—and focus on the task ahead. Vinn is right, I can use all the help I can get, but one thought holds me back. "How do we know what to look for?"

She shrugs as she pulls on a pair of latex gloves. "Got me. We won't know until we see it. I guess if there's an envelope that's labeled 'Open if I'm mysteriously killed' or a box with '1915' written on the outside, we start with those. Otherwise, we take anything that may provide a clue and sort it out later. I'm going to start at her desk. I assume you want to begin in her panty drawer."

I take one step in the direction of the master bedroom before halting under an assault of giggles coming from Vinn's direction. Try to save face, Bozo. "As a matter of fact, multiple studies have shown that the average person keeps their most important and secretive documents hidden among their undies. It's the logical place to begin."

I don't look back as I take long strides to the bedroom to escape any taunts from my fellow felon, only pausing as I step inside its door and catch the faint scent of my sometime lover. Former lover, I think sadly. I look over at the rumpled sheets on the bed and NSFW thoughts flit through my consciousness. An overwhelming feeling of loss overcomes me. It takes all the effort I can muster to refocus on the reason I'm here.

In fact, Fyre did keep papers in her panty drawer, but they appear to be old love letters from someone that isn't me. The most recent postmarks are over three years old, which makes it unlikely that anything pertinent is inside, but I don't want to waste time reading them now to verify that assumption. I toss them on the bed.

Nothing else is hidden in any of the dresser drawers, or underneath them, or under or behind the dresser itself. The closet shelf yields one shoebox of shoes and a second box with piles of photographs, some yellowed with age but others look recent. I leave the shoes but add the box of pictures to the pile on the bed. I start to close the closet door, but hesitate as I view the long, neat row of clothing hanging from the wooden bar. With a sigh, I push them all to one side and begin patting down the clothes.

Thankfully, most skirts and blouses don't have pockets, so I'm able to push multiple hangers of garments to the end of the closet. For every other shirt, pair of pants, or jacket, I push my fingers down into the bottom of every opening. I have three pairs of pants and two jackets left when I feel a small piece of paper in the bottom of a pocket. Only as I pull it out do I recognize the jacket as the one Fyre wore the night I first met her in Nashville. The scrap of paper appears to have been torn from a notebook and had been folded in half. Opening it up, all I see is a name. "Clarise Knowlton." Probably meaningless or the name of her business contact there, but on the bed it goes.

I slide my fingers across the tops of the doorway, closet doors and windows. Shake the curtains to see if anything will fall out. Pick up her bedside lamp, crawl under the bed, massage every inch of the mattress looking for bumps that shouldn't be there. Finally, all that remains is the one spot that may be the most obvious: the drawer of the nightstand. Opening it with both hope and trepidation, only one item pops into sight. A diary. Fyre's diary. The overwhelming temptation is to sit down and read it right then and there in case certain pages need to be ripped out to keep them away from the prying eyes of a nosy molecular science professor, but instead I throw onto the growing stack. Priorities.

I vacate the bedroom and head to the kitchen in search of a trash bag. Vinn looks to be nearly done in the desk area and has her own pile atop the file cabinet. As I reverse course with bag in hand, she looks up and nods her approval. I sweep my treasures into the bag before joining Vinn, where she does the same with a messy mound of papers.

For the next two hours, we work side-by-side, leafing through cookbooks and looking for hiding places in cabinets, unstacking and restacking plates and bowls, moving furniture, and unzipping cushions. We rarely speak and neither one of us comments on the fact that each of us seems to have had experience in doing just what we're doing. That will have to be a conversation for another time. Maybe. If she goes first.

For all our efforts, nothing else turns up, but at least we have the satisfaction of knowing that we had done a thorough search in the time we had to do it. We sit to catch our breath, weary and dirty, before Vinn finally states the obvious.

"We'd better get out of here."

I nod my assent. Vinn picks up the trash bag, now sagging under the weight of the treasures deposited inside. She glances at the bag, then directly at me. "You'd better not be seen taking this out of the building. Go back out the front way and let me worry about the bag. I'll store it at my place and we'll sort through it later. Now go."

My first thought is to tell her not to look through the diary, but that would let her know that it's there. My second thought is a question. How did Vinn get in and out of the building without being seen? Another thing to table for now. I don't say a word and leave the unit for the elevator. Exhaustion, more emotional than physical, consumes me, and my arm is throbbing again. Looking through Fyre's life for clues will have to wait. I set course for home.

Chapter 19

"So where do we begin?" I've never been to Vinn's apartment before. Like myself, she lives on the top floor of a vintage three-flat, although hers is in the trendier DePaul area, nestled between two monstrous apartment buildings that flout all zoning laws. Know the right alderman and have enough cash and this is the result. Look out the kitchen window and all you see is cinder block. Gaze out the window of the master bedroom on the other side, more cinder block. It's claustrophobic.

Inside, however, Vinn shows impeccable taste. No IKEA here. I'm sitting on a floral-patterned couch which wouldn't have been out of place in a nineteenth-century parlor, although it's also surprisingly comfortable. Across from me, Vinn is perched on the edge of a museum-quality captain's chair with silk upholstery and engraved wood all around. The centerpiece of the room, though, is the multi-colored Persian rug, clearly hand-woven, in the center of which rests a thirty-cent Hefty bag bulging with the rubble we tossed into it earlier that week. I refuse to touch it and wait for Vinn to pour out its contents. I don't need the grief or the cleaning bill if something sullies the rug.

"I already started, kind of," she begins, putting her hand up to stifle the objection she sees forming in my mouth. "I know we agreed that I wouldn't look at any of this…" she pauses as she gestures toward the bag, "and I didn't. But I didn't see any harm in doing some online research. I Googled Fyre's name, and other than a few references that led nowhere, I came up empty. This girl led a very private life, which may be suggestive in itself. So I shifted gears and left her for now, looking into events that happened in 1915. Want me to run some of them by you?"

"Sure, why not?" I settle back onto the couch—did I mention how comfortable it is—and close my eyes to better concentrate. "Go ahead, shoot."

"Okay, tell me if any of these stand out from your time with Fyre. The sinking of the Lusitania?"

"Nope."

"Typhoid Mary?"

"No."

"Babe Ruth's first home run?"

I open my eyes and raise an eyebrow, which is becoming a habit. "Seriously? I tell you what, just keep going and I'll stop you if anything even remotely rings a bell."

"Fine. Houdini's famous straight jacket escape, the founding of the Kiwanis, premier of Birth of a Nation, the U.S. House rejects women's right to vote," Vinn stops briefly to frown, "publication of Kafka's *Metamorphosis*, first photo of Pluto, formation of the Coast Guard, Einstein's presentation of his theory of relativity."

Vinn pauses to catch her breath, which gives me the chance to jump in. "You can keep going if you want, but this doesn't seem to be helping."

"No stone unturned, right? Just a few more. Lynching of Leo Frank? Armenian genocide?" She looks at me and seems disappointed that I have no reaction. "Nation's first stop sign? World War I had just gotten going. A lot of ships being sunk, including an American submarine."

"Sorry, no. Earlier we speculated that it might not be a date at all. It could be an address or a coded message. Even if it is a date, how does what happened over a century ago tie into Fyre's death? And we're ignoring the other word that she tried to write, if that's what it was. I appreciate your research, but maybe we need to start going through all of this shit." I nod at the bag.

Vinn sighs. "Yeah, maybe. Hold on." She stands up, carries the coffee table to the edge of the room then leaves briefly, returning with a beige blanket which she spreads out over the rug. She tosses a pad of paper and pen at me, lowers herself to the floor, then points at my feet. "Sit."

I obey, sliding down with my back against the couch, and spread my legs in a wide 'v' to form an improvised border for the contents of our plastic bag of discoveries. Vinn reaches in and pulls out a handful of papers which she places in front of her on the blanket. I lean over to the bag and take out the shoebox of photographs. Still unsure of what to look for, I begin sifting through the pictures, placing those I've examined to one side. After a few minutes, I take the discard pile back in my hands and begin making smaller piles, doing my best to sort them either by approximate date or by the faces that are most prominent in the photo, in the hope that if they become relevant at some point, we can find whatever or whomever we'll be looking for quicker.

Each of us works silently, the only sound in the room that of papers being sifted through and an occasional sigh from one of us. I'm almost done with the pictures when Vinn reaches in for her second batch of documents. About ten minutes later, I pull the last few items from the bag, a checkbook and a few old copies of magazine articles which don't appear to be relevant to anything. Discouraged, I glance across at Vinn and am horrified to see her reading Fyre's diary, a cat-like grin spread wide across her face.

"Interesting," she says devilishly as she peers at me over the top of the diary. "I'd say your eyes are more green, but then she's seen them closer up than I have. Many times, in fact, and from very, very close according to what it says here. Either she's embellished your technique a bit for the sake of posterity or you're more of a stud than I would have guessed."

I lunge across in an attempt to grab the book from her hands, but Vinn is quicker than I am and leans away before leaping to her feet with a distinct giggle. I struggle to my feet, take two giant strides and grab her from behind as she scrambles to find sanctuary in the kitchen. She's still holding the diary tightly in both hands, but when I move my arms up in an effort to secure it, I only manage to get our upper bodies tangled in a pretzel-like configuration. Vinn goes limp thinking it would help her escape but is likewise unsuccessful, entwining our legs. As she flops, we each lose our balance and collapse in one unified crash to the floor.

In trying to break her fall, Vinn had twisted back toward me so that as we land, we end up eye to eye with arms wrapped around each other, our faces inches apart. I can smell a faint hint of perfume mingled with the scent of her shampoo as her hair falls from my forehead. For a few moments, neither one of us moves, our eyes locked and warm breath mixing together in the narrow space between our lips. My hands continue to grip the small of her back, while one of hers found its way into the back pocket of my jeans. For an all too brief moment, I lose all sense of the purpose of my being there.

It's Vinn who breaks the embrace, clearing her throat while pulling away from me and rising to her feet in one fluid motion. "I didn't see anything that would help us in here when I glanced through it, but I'll take a closer read later on." Running one hand through her hair in a vain attempt to straighten it, she walks quickly in the direction of her bedroom. I hear a drawer open and shut. As she reenters the room, I crawl back over to my spot against the couch, resisting the impulse to continue side by side.

"Did you find anything that gives us a place to start?" I ask, avoiding eye contact and trying to get us refocused. "I don't think these pictures help us, at least not yet, because I don't know who any of these people are. Some of the photos are really old and are probably from before Fyre was born. For now, anyway, I suggest that we set them aside."

"Agreed. There's a couple of interesting things in her paperwork although I'm not sure they'll lead us anywhere. They're not all here, but her bank statements show periodic deposits of some fairly large amounts, anywhere from about $20,000 up to almost double that."

"Wait, before you go on." I pull a small, green-covered ledger from my own smaller stack. "I have her checkbook here, which goes back just over two years." I skim through it. "I see the deposits you're talking about." As I flip the checkbook open to the last page containing any entries, Vinn ignores any impulses she may have and slides over beside me so that she can read it at the same time. Damn, her hair smells good.

"Okay, let's see. $22,850.00 in March. Before that, $39,000 in December, $34,500 in September…" Vinn reaches her hand over and turns the page back, "$29,000.00 in June and…wow…$52,300 in March of last year. See how the deposits are made every quarter?" She moves back across from me, picking up the bank statement she had dropped. "And they're automated deposits, so they're coming from somewhere else." She frowns. "Annuity? Investments?"

I shrug my shoulders. "Don't know. Finances aren't something we ever discussed, although she did mention that she paid cash for her condo. About the only other thing I have here is a list of names and phone numbers, all of them local numbers. I doubt these are her sugar daddies."

Vinn sticks her tongue out at me. "All right, so a dead end so far." She picks up a fistful of papers. "I found a few other oddities. There are several copies of articles here on cryonics and cryogenics. Hobby or something more?"

"You'll have to educate me, Mr. Peabody. They involve freezing things, right?"

113

Vinn rolls her eyes but stops short of calling me an idiot. Not everybody's a genius like she is. "Cryogenics is the study of extremely low temperatures and how matter behaves when subjected to them. It's legitimate. Cryonics is fake science at best. It's the idea that someone can be frozen after death and then brought back to life later following advancements in medicine. Absurd, but people like to believe that they can cheat the Reaper."

"So if I have a disease for which there's no cure, I seal myself inside an ice cube and then a century later when a cure is discovered, they thaw me out and bring me back to life?"

Vinn nods. "Essentially, yeah. If I recall, some guy wrote a book proposing it in the 1960s and when he died became the first person to be frozen. Cyronics has its devotees, but no basis in science."

"I guess I can read up on it, but I doubt it will lead anywhere. Oh, and as long as we're on the topic of things that don't lead anywhere…" I rise, retrieve Fyre's cell phone from my jacket pocket, and throw it on top of the pile. "Password protected. And before you ask, yes, I tried '1915' along with every possible combination of numbers I could think of. Her birthday, address numbers, the date we met, and so forth. No luck. Please tell me you have something else."

Vinn doesn't look happy at this news. "I'm not sure. The only other possibility is a name that your gal was fixated on. William Franklin Sales. She's got it written on some sheets of paper along with indecipherable notes. She ever mention him to you?"

"Nope, but look." I hold up a half-sheet of notebook paper. In the center of it, in red marker with asterisks and stars surrounding it, is the name William F. Sales. "I guess it's as good a place as any to start."

Without saying a word, Vinn pulls her laptop off of a chair and starts punching at keys. This time, it's me who moves over to her side to take a look, consequences be damned.

"Not much here, to be honest. Guy was some sort of an industrialist in the early and mid-1900s, made a pile of money and then died. Looks like he croaked long before Fyre was even born. I don't see a connection."

"Wait, is that him?" I point to an old photograph on the monitor of a figure in the forefront of a mob of pedestrians on a busy street, with what appears to be the Marshall Field's clock in the background. "Can you blow that up, or find a better picture?"

Vinn taps some keys, visiting several other websites before returning to the original one. "Apparently he was a bit of a recluse and a very unpleasant person. He valued his privacy and guarded it viciously, which is why there isn't much information out there about him. That and the fact that other than having a pile of cash, he wasn't very newsworthy. He was no Howard Hughes. No one in the press dug very hard even after he died and biographers weren't lining up to write his life's story. This is the best we can do." She zooms in on the photograph, trying to find a balance between getting a closer look and the fuzzier resolution that results when she enlarges it.

I shimmy back to the piles of photographs I had sorted and within seconds find what I'm looking for in the second stack. It was yellowed with age, tattered around the edges, and of a much younger man, but the resemblance its unmistakable. Even then, when Sales appeared to be voluntarily sitting for the photographer, his eyes flashed a defiant challenge. It's the only picture from the shoebox in which he appears. I'm convinced, but Vinn is not.

I hold it up next to the picture on Vinn's laptop. We both stare at it for several minutes, and at one point Vinn takes the photo from my hand and examines it from all angles just inches from her eyes.

"I dunno," she finally admits. "Could be. Probably is. But where does that get us?"

I drop my head, frustrated. "So that's it? We're stuck already?"

Vinn smiles. "Not quite. You're a Chicago newbie. I need to introduce you to the Newberry Library."

I look at her quizzically, but that's apparently all I'm going to get out of her today. I help myself to my coat but as I reach the door, I turn back to Vinn, who's still sprawled out on the floor.

"Phantasmagoria," I say as I begin to step outside.

"What? Wait...no, the last one didn't count, Winters. We're still—"

"A sequence of real or imagined events, like those seen in a dream." I close the door, muffling her protests.

Chapter 20

Our class schedules prevent us from taking our field trip to the Newberry until the weekend. I use the break from detecting to submit my mid-term grades on time but only because I gave my better students a B+ in the hope that angst over not getting an A will make them try harder, and my lesser students a B- as a bit of a gift so as not to discourage them from continuing the class. I haven't actually graded their midterm papers. I've put that task off given my time-consuming obsession outside of my teaching responsibilities, but I know that I can't avoid it much longer. Some devil in the back of my mind keeps reminding me that I may have promised the class that I would be returning their papers by the end of this week.

I cancel my office hours for the week, close my door with a battered 'Do Not Disturb' sign I'd purloined from the doorknob of a room other than my own in some sleazy hotel, and set to work. On the corner of my desk sits a generous supply of Da Hong Pao oolong tea, one of the rarest in my collection, to keep me going. Two hours later, I'm only on my fifth paper, but it's the second student who has no clue how to use the words 'their' and 'they're,' and on top of that has misused apostrophes throughout the work. Even as a fake creative writing professor, I'm questioning the intelligence of an entire generation as I fume, wondering if it's my responsibility to go back to the basics with my freshman class. Between slashing grammatical errors with my red pencil and pondering suggesting to the admissions office that they base their decisions solely on a question about the use of 'its' and 'it's' and denying admission to any applicant not using the Oxford comma, I look at the clock for about the ten thousandth time. It dawns on me that I'm not only taking my frustrations with the stalled investigation into Fyre out on my students, my mind has only been partly focused on grading papers, which then makes grading take twice as long and adds to my annoyance that I'd rather be pondering the significance of cryonics than reading essays. I push the stack of papers aside and open my laptop.

I relax once I begin browsing the web looking up whatever I can find on cryonics. Vinn's memory has proved sound. The idea that someone could be frozen at extremely low temperatures and brought back to life in a later generation was first proposed in the 1964 book *The Prospect of Immortality* by physics teacher Robert Ettinger. The idea gained a minor level of popularity, although why anyone would want to come back to this messed-up world escapes me. A 73-year-old psychologist, not Ettinger himself, is given the distinction of the first person to actually undergo the process, in 1967. No mention of William Sales so I go back to grading.

As before, only part of my mind is focused on the students' papers, which may have saved them from a bruising excoriation from which their egos would never recover. The rest of my brain keeps mentally examining the various bits of junk rescued from Fyre's condo. If there's any information there that can assist me in finding her killer, I can't fathom it. As far as I can guess, it all comes down to what Vinn and I can glean at the Newberry Library.

Vinn has a morning class on Saturdays so we agree to meet at the Newberry at noon. I enjoy the rare opportunity to laze a bit and am preparing a late breakfast when there's a gentle knock at my door. Not expecting anyone, my senses immediately go into overload and I grab the first heavy object that I can find, which turns out to be a rolling pin. I really need to make some of my more effective arsenal more readily accessible. I probably look ridiculous, but the main questions going through my mind are would a potential killer actually knock at my door, and since when do I own a rolling pin?

I return the kitchen accessory to the drawer, making a mental note of where it is in case I ever decide to make a pie crust, then quietly creep to the door. "Yes?"

A somewhat feminine voice with definite masculine overtones responds. Rebecca. "Open up, Peaches. I've got something for you."

I swing the door open only part way in the hope that whatever it is Rebecca has, she can just pass it through. She reaches out her left arm to finish pushing the door open wide then strides purposefully into the room and over to the kitchen island, a vision of green in her long, flowing dress. Black pumps adorn her feet. She looks ready to go clubbing, never mind that it's barely 10:30 in the morning. From one hand dangles her ever-present purse—Rebecca has a long way to go in learning the finer points of makeup, posture, and other feminine behaviors, but has the 'I need my purse even if I'm just going upstairs' bit down pat—while the other hand holds a paper bag from Whole Foods.

"I thought you might need some sustenance in order to get better, Sweetie. I made enough meals to get you through the week." As she speaks, she pulls several plastic containers covered with frost out of the bag, setting them on my kitchen table. As far as I know, Ted doesn't cook. Rebecca, however, likes to try to recreate dishes that Ted ate at one of his frequent dinners out with clients, normally three or four in the course of a single weekend afternoon. In nicer weather, when my windows are open, I choose those days to leave my apartment and run errands even if I don't have any to run. Let's just say that the odors that drift up from the apartment below are a testament to more failures than successes. All right, in truth, all failures. She could get a job as Leo's line cook.

All of which makes me a bit conflicted in my reaction to Rebecca's kindness. Her heart is certainly in the right place, and I'm touched at her response to my having been shot, although a part of me wonders if Ted in one of his nastier moods froze the worst-of-the-worst experiments and saved them for just the right occasion to pass them on to me.

"Uh, Rebecca, I don't know how to thank you." This much is true. "What are they?"

She looks down at the containers from under her heavily mascaraed lashes and appears momentarily flustered. "Oh dear, the Post-It Notes seem to have fallen off. Well, never you mind. They're all just absolutely scrumptious. You can't go wrong."

I smile at her as I begin to stack the meals in my heretofore-empty freezer, if you don't count two bottles of vodka. I'm about to make excuses for not inviting her to stay when Rebecca saves me the trouble with a quick 'ta ta' as she sashays out the door. Glancing up at the clock in my microwave, I notice that I'm now running late. Time to see if the Newberry is all that Vinn intimated it can be.

Chapter 21

Sitting not far from an el stop in the heart of the Gold Coast and across the street from Bughouse Square, for decades the nation's prime spot for free and often subversive speech, the Newberry Library is an imposing structure. Taking up most of a city block and rising several stories up, it's a severe structure of stone and masonry blocks with tall archways and windows to match. Standing outside the entrance, the building itself seems to scream at me that my mission here had better be serious. I briefly wonder if I should have put on a suit for the occasion.

"Are we going to go in or are you planning to stand there gawking all day?" Vinn seemingly appears out of nowhere, standing at the top of the steps impatiently tapping her foot. Her taunt breaks me out of my reverie and I ascend slowly to meet her.

More stairs inside the front doors bring us to the marble-tiled entryway, a large room that successfully mirrors the somber atmosphere of the exterior. To each side, though, are brightly lit rooms crowded with tall shelves crammed with the colorful litany of books so familiar to anyone with a library card. The familiar smell of paper and dust wafts out, bidding us to enter.

Vinn pauses at the front desk to ask the staunch woman sitting there if we might avail ourselves of the services of a reference librarian. With unexpected pleasantness, we're directed to the second floor and told to ask for Vivian. As we climb the broad staircase, a sudden inspiration strikes me.

"Vivian Newberry?" I whisper to Vinn, who glances back with a sour expression and shakes her head before doubling her pace up the stairs. It's almost as if she wants to avoid hearing my next two guesses. Some people just don't know how to have fun.

We find the reference desk and there sits Vivian, an attractive and impeccably dressed woman in her 40s. She greets us with a broad smile, shaking Vinn's hand while ignoring mine as she asks how she can be of assistance.

Vinn takes the lead. "We're doing research on a local businessman by the name of William Franklin Sales, who we believe was active in the first part of the last century. He seems to have been a recluse and there isn't a whole lot of material about him online. Do you have any resources that might help provide information that hasn't made it out into cyberspace?"

I can't keep my eyes off of Vinn. Something incredibly attractive about that woman when she's all business.

"Mmm," Vivian looks thoughtful, although I suspect that all librarians are taught that expression in library school. "The name sounds vaguely familiar but nothing pops into my memory. Fortunately, we have vast resources that should be able to help you. If you can't find what you need here, I'm afraid you may not find it anywhere."

What follows is a lengthy litany of recommendations involving electronic databases, bibliographical links, and directions to the most likely places to start as well as to obscure reference books that might contain information on the local citizenry. She ends by suggesting a look through the library's extensive genealogical collection.

Vinn puts up a good front by keeping her eyes focused and nodding her head at regular intervals. My eyes must have glazed over at some point and I apparently look as overwhelmed as I feel, because after a peek in my direction Vivian pauses, switches her gaze back to Vinn, and speaks softly in a tone normally reserved for mothers when talking about their clueless child. "Would you like me to help you get started?"

I blurt out, "Yes, please," earning an annoyed glance from Vinn, but she agrees that maybe we could use a little bit of help "for now."

Vivian directs us first to a computer where she explains how to access the areas that might be the most helpful, then describes where to find the books, periodicals, and other hard copies of reference materials revealed by the search. Barely stopping to catch her breath, she bids us follow as she glides up the stairs to the third floor. Vinn and I trudge behind her, struggling to absorb the quick lesson on the various sections ripe with biographical information not only on famous people, but ordinary citizens of whom the only memory lies within the pages of the materials on the shelves before us. I glance at the shelves with a tinge of sadness.

The next several hours are a blur. Vinn takes control of the computer to come up with possible places to look, after which she sends me off in a hundred different directions while she continues to mine whatever possible leads she can find electronically. Most of them are dead ends, but occasionally our efforts are rewarded with a sentence or two here and there, mostly found in contemporary writings from when Sales was building his business.

As the afternoon wears on, Vinn runs low on ideas of where else to look. Fatigue and frustration begin to set in. To relieve the monotony, we take a break to create a summary of what we've discovered about the life and times of William Franklin Sales. He was second-generation, his parents having come over from either Ireland or Wales in the late 1800s. Education is a bit of a mystery, but there didn't seem to be any indication that he attended college. No record of military service. In 1917, as a young man in his 20s, he started a company called 'Sales & Sons, Ltd.,' but information on exactly what it did is vague, and as far as we can tell at the time it was created there was no son. Whatever the firm did, it flourished and appeared to make William Sales a wealthy man. Estimates from blurbs in business journals ranged anywhere from three million during the Depression years to ten times that by the 1950s. Either he was successful in hiding his true wealth, or no one at the time cared enough to conduct a thorough investigation. What we don't find is any hint of a link to Fyre. I silently wonder if all of this effort is just a waste of time, but then we need to be as thorough as possible. Sales' name, as obscure as it is, remains our best and only lead into what happened to Fyre.

Despite being bone tired and more than a little disheartened, Vinn suggests that we at least see what we can find in the genealogical section. She correctly assumes that she's better with the computer searches than I am and sits right down and begins typing. William had three children: a son William Jr. (he exists after all, although what role he played in Sales & Sons as a toddler is up for debate), born in 1911, a daughter Sarah born a few years after that (exact date unknown), and a second girl, Margaret, in 1917. Links bring us to sites that post the birth certificates for William Jr. and Margaret, but Sarah's is missing. Not that it really matters. We're finding information we couldn't get online, sure, but where is it getting us? What was Fyre's interest in this mysterious man?

We're about to pack up and cut our losses when the ever-helpful Vivian approaches. "Are you still here?" she inquires. Reference librarians are apparently quite astute. "Have you had any success?"

Vinn shakes her head. "Not much, I'm afraid."

Vivian isn't about to let us give up that easily. "Have you checked the archives for the Chicago Tribune? We have a searchable index of articles from 1849 all the way through 1991. There might be something there. It doesn't hurt to check."

Without waiting for a response, Vivian turns and begins to walk swiftly off in the direction of the stairs, beckoning us to follow. We're led to yet another computer system and a room behind a locked door. "Much of it is stored electronically, but if you need something that isn't, you can ask a librarian to retrieve the original copy." She nods toward the locked room.

We thank her again and Vinn gets back to work. Remarkably, we actually find a few mentions. According to a brief blurb in a gossip column from 1954 noting that William Jr. was tossed out of a bar after having a few too many, Sales was one of the wealthiest men in the Chicago area. Vinn next pulls up his obituary from when he died in 1965 at the age of 74. I sit in the chair next to her and close my eyes, which are too strained at this point to read the fine print.

"Mal, listen to this. According to the Tribune, Sales was as secretive as we thought, but estimates of his wealth when he died put it at over $100 million." I give a low whistle as Vinn continues to read to herself, but bolt upright and open my eyes when she erupts with a burst of "oh my god!"

"There was no funeral service when he died. Listen to what the paper says: 'While the family was tight-lipped and did not respond to requests for comment, rumors indicate that Mr. Sales' body has been cryonically frozen.'"

We stare at each other, speechless. The cryonics articles now make sense, or at least Fyre's curiosity about the procedure does. But does anything we discovered today help us answer why she was killed or bring us any closer to the identity of the murderer? We get up to leave.

"Wait." I have a thought, which does happen now and then. "As long as we're here, is there a way to search the Tribune archive by date?"

Vinn nods, puzzled, then a sudden realization dawns that puts her on the same page, so to speak. She quickly sits back down and her fingers fly across the keyboard. The front page of the Chicago Tribune for January 1, 1915 quickly pops up on the screen.

We stick to the first few pages of each issue, figuring that if something was important enough to reference in your own blood as you lay dying, it should have been front-page news. As we scroll past each issue, our enthusiasm wanes just a little bit more. I take over the mouse when we reach the halfway point. Vinn takes her position at my shoulder.

It doesn't take long. The July 25 issue used large, bold type to report on a disaster in the Chicago River from the previous day. On July 24, 1915, a passenger ship named the *S. S. Eastland,* heavy with employees of Western Electric's Cicero plant, overturned just after loading, trapping everyone below deck. Despite being only feet from the dock and in a mere twenty feet of water, 844 people died, including twenty-two entire families. It was the greatest inland nautical tragedy in American history. Maybe the date refers to a sunken ship after all.

We continue on through the rest of the year, jot down notes on a few other noteworthy events, but no other story jumps out at us like the Eastland. Partly gut feeling, partly by default, we both think this is it. We return to the Tribune's coverage we skimmed earlier.

"My god," Vinn repeats as we stare at the photographs.

"Agreed," I reply. "Do you really think this is what '1915' refers to? If it is, what does it mean? How is it connected? And why would Fyre use her last moments to reference it?"

Good questions. We have no answers.

Chapter 22

Sleep is hard to come by that night as visions of drowning families swirl about in my brain along with too many unanswered, maybe unanswerable, questions. With the information we gathered, I feel as if we've put a couple of jigsaw pieces together but can't be sure that the pieces belong to the puzzle we're working on. Maybe the most important item of information from our trip to the Newberry is that Sales had money. A lot of it. That's usually a solid motive for murder, but the fact that he died over 40 years ago muddies the waters. I mean, don't murderers usually target the guy with the money before he dies? We also found a link to Fyre's interest in cryonics, but no clue as to how the fact that Sales' body might have been frozen means anything. We found the fuel to travel further down several roads, but at this point, all of them may just as well be leading to a plunge off a cliff to nowhere.

My thoughts return to the items we took from Fyre's condo. Is there anything that takes on new meaning given what we found yesterday? Again, nothing stands out. Maybe the only thing to do now is to stop trying to think logically and just gather facts and hope that at some point, they start to make sense or that one of us has a moment of clarity. I need to run something by Vinn and grab my phone from the bedside table.

She doesn't sound happy to hear from me. "Winters, are you mad? Do you know what time it is?"

"Actually, no. I've been up for a while."

Her tone softens. "Yeah, I haven't slept at all either. None of this make any sense."

"I know. Look, isn't there a list of phone numbers in our pile of documents? Maybe it's a sign of desperation, but I'm not sure where else to turn. Can you bring it with you on Monday? We can make some calls between classes." "Sure, why not. I guess it can't hurt." She pauses, but even through the phone I sense that there's something else she wants to say. I wait silently. When she comes back on again, there's a strong overtone of melancholy. "Mal? That *Eastland* thing. The pictures, those families…" her voice drifts off.

So she hasn't been able to get the images out of her head either, revealing a tender and vulnerable side to Vinn that I haven't seen before. "I know, Vinn. They're keeping me awake as well."

Vinn drops by my office at 11:00 Monday morning just as I'm making tea. Her droopy eyelids and pale complexion reveal that last night hadn't been any easier for her than the night before. She collapses heavily into a chair, waiting for me to finish brewing.

"Tea, Vinn? Looks like you could use it. It's a hard-to-find type of pu'er. Fermented tea. Not everybody likes it."

A flash of something brings a little color back into her cheeks. "You don't have any coffee in this place, like a normal human being?" She doesn't wait for my response, as she already knows the answer. "Fine, anything. Make it strong."

I pour two cups into mismatched mugs and slide one across the desk. Vinn takes a sip, raises her eyebrows, peers into the liquid in the cup, then sets it down.

"Let's get started. We'll take turns. I'll go first."

There are eight names on the list, all of them with a city or adjacent suburban area code. Vinn starts at the top. She uses my office phone so that we can put whoever answers on speaker.

"Good morning, Perl and Seitzman, may I help you?" I scribble the name down on a scratch pad on my desk.

"Oh, I'm sorry, hello. I'm not sure I have the right number. Can you tell me what kind of business this is?"

An exasperated sigh comes through the speaker. Rude. "This is a law firm. How may I direct your call?"

"My friend Felicity Stockton recommended that I use the same lawyer she did. Can you connect me please?"

The same sigh again. Must've been a long morning already. "Do you have a name?"

Vinn puts on her best damsel-in-distress voice. "She may have told me, but I don't remember, can you look it up for me?"

"Please hold."

After seven minutes, we realize no one is going to come back on the phone. Vinn presses disconnect.

My turn. "Law firm of Simpson and Mayer, may I help you?"

I try the same tactic Vinn had, with similar result. Either the names of clients are covered by attorney-client privilege, or Fyre had never retained their services.

We get variations of the same song and dance with the remaining six. All are lawyers or law firms. None would verify they knew Fyre.

"Well, that got us nowhere," I muse, disappointed but not surprised.

"Don't give up yet. She was calling lawyers for a reason. We have names connected to all of these phone numbers now. You take the first four, I'll take the rest."

It takes less than five minutes of online searches to determine what all of the firms have in common. Each of them either specializes in or does the bulk of their work in estate planning.

This time it's my turn to suggest the next step. Vinn looks at me curiously as I Google the Circuit Court of Cook County.

"It's worth a shot. Maybe a family member died recently." I navigate to the probate division's part of the website, which allows searching the court records by last name. I begin to type 'Stockton' into the search engine.

"No." Vinn stops me, reaching across and putting her hand on top of mine. A glimmer of excitement radiates from her eyes. "Type in William Sales."

I understand immediately and begin to catch her fever. We both subconsciously lean into the monitor as a list of possible matches appears on the screen. Only one is a perfect match, but there's a hitch that holds me back from clicking the link.

"Didn't he die in the 60s? This case number shows it was filed last year."

"We won't know until we look at it. Stop stalling and let's see what it says already."

Case information soon fills the screen. All it shows are the dates of document filing and court hearings along with short and cryptic descriptions of what was filed or what happened before the judge. Silence fills my office as Vinn and I peruse the list.

A lawsuit has been filed by 'certain heirs of William Franklin Sales,' although what's being adjudicated remains unclear. The attorneys acting on behalf of the estate are the first firm that Vinn called just twenty minutes ago. A few appearances have been filed as have some routine motions, but nothing of substance appears to have been done yet. The next court date is a simple status hearing in two months. The thrill I felt in finding the suit disappears. This is telling us nothing. Vinn is not as discouraged.

"Looks like another field trip, Winters. Tomorrow afternoon, 2:00, meet me outside the café. You and I are going to the Daley Center." Vinn takes a step to the door before turning around. "By the way, anytime you want to make more of that tea, I'll help you drink it."

As she leaves, I check. Her cup is empty.

Chapter 23

A tall, rust-colored building with a matching Picasso sculpture in its plaza, the Daley Center is the main courthouse for non-criminal cases in Cook County. As such, it's a bustling center of activity with streams of hopeful people going in and the same streams coming back out, many with expressions of despair lining their faces. Vinn and I enter a revolving door and join the line to pass through security, only one of us hopeful.

"What exactly are we looking for?" I ask as I strip off my belt and empty my pockets.

"We won't know until we see it," she replies vaguely. Déjà vu from Fyre's apartment. "We need to look at the court file to see why a millionaire's heirs opened up a probate case decades after his death."

Vinn has apparently done her homework as to where to go, because without any hesitation she leads me to a bank of elevators and pushes the button for the twelfth floor. We have a choice of two rooms on either side of the floor and only hesitate a moment before turning left.

Inside the room, we're faced with a long, L-shaped counter with several stations, some with lines and others without. Typically, it appears that the areas without lines are the only ones where an employee is stationed, each one looking like they'd rather be somewhere else. Men and women in expensive suits mix with others in sweats and jeans, and in one case orange short shorts, all queued before the empty counter spaces, looking restless and impatient.

We make our way down the counter slowly, eyeing each area as we search for the right place to go, a task made more difficult by a complete lack of signage. Finally, near the end of the counter, we notice a stack of forms requesting identification information and a file number. Using our finely honed talents at deduction, we assume that this is where we can request the court file.

Vinn fills out her name and phone number then pulls a slip of paper out of her pocket to copy down the docket number for the case. We try to look conspicuous as we stand with paper in hand, hoping that someone will at some point come to assist us.

Eventually, a middle-aged, hair-challenged man who had been scrolling on his phone at a nearby desk, and who had looked in our direction five minutes earlier, pushes back his chair with great effort and approaches slowly.

"Yes?" he says as if we've pulled him away from something far more important in his life than our need to see a file.

"Could you please retrieve this file for us?" Vinn coos in a coquettish voice laced with undertones of flirtation. She must have experience dealing with recalcitrant government employees and learned that the fastest way to get what she wants is an unstated promise of sex. I wonder if she would have given me the lead if a woman had approached the counter. I also wonder if she'll agree to talk to me in that voice sometime when we're alone.

"Hmmph," he replies, or something to that effect. He snatches the form, reluctantly glances at it, looks directly at Vinn for several seconds, sighs, then disappears into a jungle of shelving crammed with thick file folders behind him.

Just about the time I begin to wonder if he's gone on a coffee break, he returns with a thin Manilla folder and slaps it onto the counter. "I need your ID," he says gruffly at the same time he reaches out to take the driver's license Vinn has at the ready. "The file doesn't leave the room. You get this back when you return the file."

"You can really be a charmer when you try," I whisper to Vinn as we turn away from the counter. "And now he's got your address and phone number. Quite the catch."

Vinn mumbles something under her breath that doesn't sound like it should have been uttered in a public place. She drops the file onto another counter where several other people with similar files are already lost in piles of paper. "Let's see what we have here."

The first document she pulls from the file is titled 'Petition for Probate and for Declaration of Death of Decedent,' which is apparently the paperwork that was filed to begin the suit. Vinn and I look at each other, already puzzled. "Is this normal?" I ask rhetorically. "Wasn't it pretty clear over fifty years ago that Sales was dead?"

Vinn shrugs without comment. We both lean over to read the allegations listed in the petition. It's several pages long and we both read slowly to make sure we don't miss anything. The first twenty paragraphs or so are mostly legalese establishing jurisdiction and the authority of the woman who filed the action, a great-granddaughter of Sales, to do so. We read on, resisting the temptation to skip ahead.

"Holy crap," Vinn utters quietly about ten seconds later. I quickly catch up to her and let out a low whistle.

22. During the pendency of his life, at all times decedent William Franklin Sales was the founder, President, and sole shareholder of Sales & Sons, Ltd. Through prudent business acumen and conservative financial planning, the business grew from a single employee in 1917 to hundreds if not thousands of employees around the world in the 1950s.

23. In or about 1960, the decedent began to wind down his business and within the next few years sold off its assets and goodwill to various parties, choosing to devote himself to investing the profits of his life's work. At the time of his death in 1965, the decedent's assets in cash, property, and negotiable papers totaled approximately $350 Million.

Vinn stops turning pages, marking her spot with her finger, and looks directly at me. "We thought money might play a role in whatever is going on, but this takes it to another level. Would you kill someone for a share of that?"

"Not me," I lie, "but I know people who would. But isn't that enough to spread around in some pretty substantial amounts? You'd think the heirs would be satisfied. Who inherited it? And why is it an issue now? We need to keep reading."

It doesn't take long to get some of the answers, but they aren't anything we could have imagined. Vinn's mouth drops open in a very unladylike gape and mine may have done the same thing. For a long time, we don't say anything, staring at and re-reading the paragraphs before our eyes.

31. At the time of his death, the decedent was a devotee of the pseudo-science of cryonics, the belief that a human body can be frozen at extremely low temperatures in a sort of suspended state, to be brought back to life at a later time when a cure has been found for the illness that led to his death.

32. As a result of the aforesaid belief, the decedent left instructions for his body to be kept in a cryonic state in perpetuity until such time as medical science could bring him back to life and resolve the cancer that ravaged his body, and said instructions were carried out by those close to him at the time. His frozen body was stored at a facility in Palo Alto, California, and remains there to the present day.

"But I still don't…" I begin.
"Look here," Vinn replies. She's a faster reader than I am.

35. In the belief that he would one day be brought back to life, the terms of the decedent's will left the principal balance of his estate to himself, or more accurately his future self once he was brought back to a living state at an unknown time in the future.

Before we even have the time to react to that bombshell, Vinn pages quickly through the remainder of the document, speed reading as she goes. She's probably the type of person that reads the ending of a book when she's halfway through. It's annoying, but least she has the courtesy of summarizing it for me.

"So this wealthy-ass guy realizes his years are numbered and there's no way that he can spend all of his money, or maybe he worked himself to the bone to make his millions and now he thinks it's too late or his health is too poor to enjoy it. He latches on to this crazy idea that he can become a human Popsicle and come back to spend it later when he's brought back to life and his health woes are cured. Instead of doing what everyone else with common sense does, and leave his money to his family, he keeps it all to himself even in death.

"But he didn't leave his family completely out in the cold. He left instructions on how he wanted his principal amount to be invested. While the core amount can't be touched by anyone except himself when he returns from the dead, all of the interest and amounts gained through the investment are to be divided among each of his heirs and paid out quarterly."

She practically spits out her words. Vinn can be cute when she's morally offended and when basic science is being mocked. I decide that she wouldn't appreciate me pointing my infatuation out to her at this particular moment and stay on point. "That would explain the periodic deposits into Fyre's account. Is she one of the beneficiaries? This could be the link we've been searching for."

"Good question." Vinn dumps out the remaining few documents from the court file and flips through them, setting one aside. "Whenever an estate is opened, the petitioner needs to file an Affidavit of Heirship listing all of the heirs and their relationship to the deceased. I know that from when an uncle died. Take a look."

There aren't as many names as there could have been given how much time has passed since Sales died, but the list isn't short either. Vinn uses her finger to quickly scan the pages, finally landing on the name Felicity Stockton, born in 1986.

"She was his great-great-granddaughter."

Something about seeing it in black and white brings home the reality of my loss of Fyre and of the way her own life was violently cut short, emotions unexpectedly catching up to me at this odd moment. Moisture forms at the corners of my eyes as I struggle to keep my composure. Vinn pretends not to notice but puts her arm around me for a few moments. I find my voice to let her know I'm okay.

"Is there anything else in there?"

Vinn pages through a few legal documents that don't mean anything to us and places them back into the file. The last document we haven't looked at is Sales' will itself. There's something creepy about reading it, as if the old man is looking over our shoulders cackling a demand at us not to take any stock in that piece of nonsense, that he'd be back among us soon. I involuntarily shiver.

It begins with what I assume is standard language for the time, eventually getting to the disposition of his assets:

Notwithstanding the temporary cessation of my life as society currently construes it, I leave the principal balance of my estate as previously defined to myself, to be distributed at such time as I return from a suspended state of animation to a living being as is customarily defined by the narrow-minded members of this world.

No time limit is to be imposed upon my return. Only in the event of a catastrophic occurrence which leaves my body in a state which cryonic experts in the field affirm makes regeneration impossible shall the principal amounts be distributed to my heirs as designated and defined and in the percentages listed below. In such case, however, one-half of the principal shall be donated to scientific research into the area of cryonics before distribution to my heirs.

As to the proceeds generated from investment of the principal as outlined in Section 8.45 of this will, pursuant to the trust established in Section 5.85, above, such amounts shall be divided among my natural-born blood relatives as follows:

The will goes on to list a complex system for calculating the percentages to be distributed to his living heirs and how adjustments would be made as some heirs died and others were born. The afternoon is coming to an end and the Daley Center will close soon, so we don't take the time to calculate Fyre's percentage. According to the figures in her checkbook, though, even a great-great granddaughter was doing extremely well with her share of the interest.

Before we head to the copy machine, a thought crosses my mind. "Vinn, this is all really interesting, and maybe even helpful once we figure it out, but what's the purpose of the probate case?"

Vinn strikes her forehead with the palm of her hand. "Of course. Hold on." She pages through the petition once more, starting at the end this time and working backward.

"One of the heirs wants to have Sales declared legally dead on the basis that cryonics is quackery and that he'll never be coming back to life. She wants to have the entire principal of the estate distributed to the heirs and to cut off any future distributions."

This gives me pause, and a million thoughts of how that information is relevant floods my already-overworked mind. "What's the name of the heir that filed the petition?"

Vinn nods her approval. "Barbara Gooding. I think we need to talk with her."

Chapter 24

"The whole thing really is ridiculous, don't you think?" Barbara Gooding sits across from us at a small table in Caffe Streets, a coffee shop in the heart of the Wicker Park neighborhood. It has a hip but non-pretentious vibe to it, but its main attraction is that it's centrally located for the three of us to meet. Vinn seems pleased with her Peruvian blend. I give the café credit for offering a few selections of quality teas, although as with most coffee shops, they seem to be the poor cousins that are begrudgingly placed on the menu as an obligation, not a passion. They also have no clue as to how to brew it properly. Perhaps when I lose my job at UIC, I can offer my services as a tea consultant to coffee shops around the city.

After leaving the Daley Center a few days earlier, Vinn and I debated how to approach the woman. We quickly eliminated any mention of a connection to Fyre. There are few things like the death of a rich relative to bring out the fractures in an otherwise close family and we didn't want to risk that Barbara and Fyre are on opposite sides of a family feud. Besides, one day sooner or later, Fyre's body will be discovered and we don't want Barbara to suddenly recall a meeting she had with a couple of people who said they were friends of hers. We finally decide to use Vinn's status as a science professor to create a fictional class project studying mankind's desperate efforts to extend life throughout the ages, with a special emphasis on the misuse of science to flame false hopes. Not perfect, but it's the best we could devise. Due to the nature of the hook, Vinn takes the lead once again. I begin to feel like I'm in the back seat of my own investigation and wonder if I should throttle back Vinn's involvement.

As it turns out, our effort to create a plausible reason to ask about Sales' unusual bequest isn't necessary. Barbara appears to have been waiting for an opportunity to talk about the family scandal, and the issue now morphs into how to keep her focused. In the end, we find it easier to just let her go on. And on and on.

"I mean, who leaves their fortune to themselves? Have you ever heard of such a thing? And what kind of a lawyer would draft such a piece of tomfoolery? Isn't their job to talk sense into their client when he wants to do something crazy?" I nod my head as she says this. I've been wondering the same thing. She misinterprets my reaction as encouragement to belabor the point and looks directly at me as she continues. "The lawyer probably was willing to do anything to earn a fat fee. The ol' coot was his golden goose."

"Did you know your great-grandfather?" Vinn asks, clearly jealous of the attention Barbara is showering on me.

Barbara shakes her head. "He died the year I was born. I heard stories, though. From my parents.

"He was an only child of immigrants and grew up poor on the South Side of Chicago. I don't remember what his father did. I think he worked in the stockyards or maybe he cobbled shoes or something. Great-grandfather probably didn't have an easy childhood. Anyway, he didn't go to college. I'm not even sure he finished high school. When he was just a kid, he was forced to get a job to help out his family. At 14 or 15, he started working full-time for some manufacturing company in Cicero. I don't know the name.

"He started off as a stock boy, but my dad said he was forced to do whatever they needed him to do—sweep the floors, clean the equipment, or whatever. Family lore says that one time he was asked to deliver some parts across town and was given the keys to a brand-new company car. He was 14 and had never been in a car, much less driven one. He must have done okay, because he didn't lose his job."

Barbara pauses when she notices that I'm taking notes. "You're not going to quote me on some of this, are you? I'm not sure how much of it is true, really. The old man kept to himself a lot when he was older and didn't talk much about his early life. I'm just passing on stories that were passed down to me. Kind of like an oral family history, you see?"

I'm not sure if a response is required, so I just nod again and smile. That's all the encouragement Barbara needs to continue.

"My understanding," she emphasizes the latter word as she glances in my direction, "is that he was a smart kid and people took notice. He didn't stay a stock boy for long and got a few promotions, eventually ending up helping out in the R&D department." She looks directly at me. My assumption that she has me pegged as the intelligent one here is quickly dashed when she continues. "That's Research and Development." Vinn snickers at my new position as the village idiot.

"He stayed at the company for ten or fifteen years then left. Maybe he was asked to leave, because he wasn't the easiest person to get along with, or wasn't a team player. From what I've heard about him, either is possible. Or maybe he just thought he could do better on his own. So, somewhere along the line, around 1917 or 1918, he started his own company, Sales & Sons."

"Do you know what the company did?" Vinn asks, basking in her new role as the sharper mind on our side of the table.

Barbara shakes her head. "Not really. You have to understand that by the time I was born, the company had been out of business for a while. I think he focused on developing things, maybe engineering parts or stuff like that, and then manufacturing them. He did a lot of his business with other firms overseas. Whatever it was, the company was hugely successful."

"Do you know much about his family life?" My goal is to take Barbara back in time a little bit before we get into the present. Barbara responds, swiveling her head between the two of us as she speaks.

"He had three kids, two girls and a boy. We don't know much about his wife except what we found out through Ancestry.com." She turns to face Vinn directly and lowers her voice to almost a whisper, a conspiracy among the adults at the table. "A few years ago we had a family reunion, our first ever. Last ever, too, at least so far. We thought it would be fun to have everyone submit DNA samples and to trace the family history." Barbara shrugs her shoulders and resumes talking in her normal tone. "That's how we know that William married his wife in either 1910 or 1911. And her name was either Prudence or Pricilla. I guess it's not an exact science.

"The son, William Jr., joined his father in the family business but rumor has it he wasn't the brightest bulb in the universe. So when Sales Senior started getting up in age, he made the decision to wind down the company rather than turn it over to Junior. Turned out to be a good decision, at least financially.

137

Some wise investments multiplied his wealth more than keeping the company going ever would have."

Barbara sits back and sips her coffee, which by now must have been cold. She makes a face. Vinn uses the opportunity to try to bring the conversation back to more relevant matters, although she also has to keep up appearances that we're more interested in the cryonics than the will.

"So, what made him decide to freeze himself, if you know, and what made you decide to file a lawsuit after all of these years?"

Barbara finds her second wind and runs with it. "As I mentioned, William was never Mr. Personality, but things got worse. Margaret, his youngest daughter, died in childbirth. During the war, I think. The baby, her first, died too. After that, William cut off all ties with Margaret's husband. Gary was his name, I think. He may have blamed the husband for his daughter's death, which was irrational of course, but all he would say is that Gary wasn't related to him by blood, so he had no reason to continue relations or to offer support. He even forbade other relatives from having any contact with Gary under the threat of cutting them out of his will. His ultimatum created a lot of angst among the family, but in the end, money talks. Gary disappeared from view."

"Was Sales' true reason ever revealed, or was the whole matter obnubilated?" I ask innocently. Now Vinn has no excuse not to move on to my new word. Tie game.

"What?" If Barbara had ever given me the benefit of the doubt as to my intelligence, her look shows she's no longer on the fence. I'm officially a fool in her eyes. Vinn kicks me hard under the table. Sore loser.

Barbara ignores me and shifts slightly in her chair so that she now faces Vinn head on. "After that, his relations with the family deteriorated, although no one confronted him directly. I think that was a huge factor in his decision to shut the family out of his will. Leaving it to himself was genius, in its own way. What was idiotic was the way he did it.

"As his health began to fail in the early 60s, he became obsessed with finding ways he could be put into some sort of suspended state and return to the living at a later time. Or to be brought back from the dead. He looked into the occult, voodoo, Chinese medical sects, and areas even more bizarre that those. Then the year before he died, he discovered a book by Robert Ettinger called 'The Prospect of Immortality.' Cryonics. What a crock. Tomfoolery. You agree, don't you, Professor?"

"Absolutely," Vinn replies. "That's why we wanted to talk to you. To find out what motivates people to believe such wild ideas about being brought back from the dead."

Satisfied, Barbara continues. "He latched onto it as an answer to all of his dreams. Funded the construction of the world's first human freezer. Met several times with the author and some supposed scientists, probably fake. More opportunists looking to make a buck. All of this in a giant veil of secrecy. If you look it up, the first person to be cryonically frozen took the plunge in 1967. My great-grandfather beat him by two years."

Barbara sighs, a sudden pall of sadness darkening her features. She looks older than she did when we first sat down.

Vinn must sense that Barbara is nearing the end of her tale or losing her interest in sharing, but we still need to know what we came here for. "If you don't mind my asking, why did you file the lawsuit?"

Barbara looks up from the table. "Someone had to. Great-grandfather established a trust to disburse the funds that accrue from the investments, which has been a generous amount. But the shares are getting smaller as the family expands. It doesn't make sense to have all of that money, hundreds of millions, sitting untouched while William waits to defrost and make his grand return to the living. So I took the initiative to have him declared dead once and for all, to cancel his bequest to a cryonics company, and to get the principal divided among all of us right now." For the first time, a clear bitterness infects her voice. Maybe an undertone of greed.

"Does the rest of the family agree with what you're doing?"

Barbara practically spits. "No. Some think that, crazy as it is, we need to honor the wishes of the old man. There are even a few who drank the Kool Aid and believe in cryonics. Stupid.

"That was one of the reasons for the family reunion, if you can call it that because most of us had never seen each other before. To talk about this and to resolve any rifts. We were having such a great time at the beginning. Before we ate, everyone who wanted to participate lined up and got their DNA kits— there were a few holdouts—and we all laughed as we had a contest to see who could fill their tube with spit first. Then we barbecued, played some games, chatted and got to know people from sides of the family that we hadn't seen before.

"When we got down to business, though, things got ugly fast. Nasty comments, screaming at one another, insults. A couple of the women had to be separated from each other. Things broke up pretty quickly after that. Like I said, money brings out the worst in people. Why couldn't they just see that life would be better for everyone if we simply put an end to this nonsense?

"I waited a year, just to let things cool down, then consulted an attorney. Not a quack like great-grandfather's, but a real smart one. If I didn't do it, I'm not sure anyone would have." She sighs. "Not everyone is happy with me. But no regrets."

I start to ask for names of the heirs that expressed the most anger at her actions but stop myself. The question might make Barbara suspicious as to our true motives since it's irrelevant to the pretense we had created.

It may not have mattered, as Barbara rises and begins to put on her coat, a nice mohair that indicates she may be doing quite well from her shares of the trust. Our conversation is apparently over. We say our thank yous, shake hands, then sit back down as we watch her leave.

We don't say a word. Vinn finishes her coffee, but I simply stare off into the void, agitated inside. Something Barbara said was beyond disturbing and, if it means what I think it does, will lead us in a dark and potentially very dangerous direction. I wonder if Vinn had heard what I did.

After several more minutes of silence, Vinn looks up from her coffee. "Shit," she says.

So she had caught it too.

Chapter 25

We leave the coffee shop in a quiet daze, neither one of us speaking as we digest the significance of Barbara Gooding's disclosure about DNA sampling at the family picnic. Immediately behind us a man who had been sitting at a nearby table follows suit. Under normal circumstances, I might not have thought anything of it, but my nerves are on edge, the new information from Barbara has cast a more sinister shadow on our investigation, and even the smallest things ring alarm bells in my head. Looking back and replaying our time in the coffee shop, I realize that while we were talking with Barbara and I was working hard to concentrate on the conversation, my eyes were often focused in the general area of a nearby table occupied by a freakishly tall man. Red flags waved at the corner of my brain at the time, but I didn't want to divide my attention from what Barbara was saying to evaluate them. Only now do I recognize what was bothering me. During the entire time we sat there, an hour or more, the man never once took a sip from the cup sitting before him.

But there's something more nagging at me from those annoyingly elusive edges of my mind. I fall back from Vinn's frenetic pace, ostensibly to read a flyer taped to a lamppost, instead using the opportunity to steal a glimpse in the direction of the tall man. As I do so he quickly slips into an adjacent storefront, but the very fact that all I catch is a fleeting glance of his back as he hurries away is what I need to make the connection. Am I being paranoid? Did Barbara's unknowing revelation stimulate my already overactive imagination? Maybe. But if not, the man sitting in the coffee shop just feet away, within earshot, is the same man I had encountered in the Old Post Office. I only saw his back then, just like I did now. It's enough.

By this time, Vinn has retraced her steps and is looking at me oddly. "Is everything okay?"

"Yes. No. I'm not sure. Let's walk around the neighborhood a bit so that I can think."

I'm not looking for the exercise or for time to think. I want to see if we'll have company on our stroll. I give credit to Vinn that she doesn't ask questions, even when our walk suddenly turns in odd directions or backtracks, or any of the times I stop to tie my shoe or examine the leaves on a tree. Finally, though, after about half an hour, her patience has run thin.

"Winters, either fill me in on what's going on, or let's get somewhere where we can sort this out."

By this time, I'm convinced. I haven't seen the man, or observed a suspicious shadow, or even sensed an unseen presence. But I know. It's hard to explain. Whenever I've been tailed throughout the years, the surroundings become amplified and overly normal. The wind is too constant or the cars are parked too evenly apart, and the area around me resembles more of an artist's conception of the vicinity than the vicinity itself. I'm probably full of crap, but I've never been wrong.

"Okay, I'm ready. But we're not going back to your place. I'll explain when we get to mine." Up until now, despite the events at the old post office, I haven't thought there was any immediate danger in looking into the reasons behind Fyre's death. No one connected to it would know who I am and nothing we've been doing would draw us onto the family's radar, at least until our coffee klatch with Barbara. It hasn't been any different from researching a thesis paper. Libraries and online searches with a breaking and entering thrown in the mix. It's not like Vinn and I should be considered a threat, and we haven't done anything that would draw attention to ourselves, especially since no one that would care even knew that we're looking into this. That just changed. I assume Barbara had been followed to our meeting and now a dangerous man has our faces imprinted in his brain. Vinn didn't sign up for this and I can't let anything happen to her. I need to tell her that it's time for me to go it alone.

"You're trying to scare me, is that what this is?" We're back in my apartment, and the fire in Vinn's eyes is unmistakable. She's not happy and isn't afraid to show it.

"Frankly, yes. Vinn, I've appreciated your help, but up until now it's been a paper trail. This changes everything and it's not fair to ask you to risk your life over something that doesn't concern you. Fyre was my friend, girlfriend if you wish, and her death was my fault. What happens from now on is on me."

"It doesn't concern me?" If Vinn was upset before, she's absolutely livid now. "Winters, are you really as blind as you seem? Haven't you sensed that maybe my interest in this whole affair isn't just to solve a puzzle or to avenge Fyre's death? Do you think our meeting up in the café every day is because I couldn't find a better bagel somewhere else?" She stands up and leans into me until her face is inches from mine, her voice rising with every question, which I wisely assume are rhetorical, and flames appear to flare out from her nostrils as she continues. Okay, I'm probably imagining the flames, but you get my point.

"Maybe my concern is that I have some sort of feelings for you, God knows why, and that this is my way of helping someone to whom I'm attracted. If there's a killer out there who's on your trail and I'm sitting in my apartment drinking coffee while you're getting shot, which already happened once, what kind of fool am I? If caring for someone means putting myself in the danger zone in the pursuit of my man, then I'm your girl."

She sits back down in her chair, fury unabated, with a little stream of spittle hanging from the corner of her mouth. In some ways, she looks more adorable now than I've ever seen her but bringing up the 'you're beautiful when you're angry' line at this particular moment may be ill-advised. Besides that, I'm stunned at her confession. I've had dozens of crushes in my adult life but they've all been unspoken and unrequited, so the fact that my nascent feelings for Vinn are reciprocal has taken me completely by surprise. Granted, my focus lately has been first on Fyre and now on Fyre's killer, but have I really been that oblivious or has Vinn been that skilled at hiding her feelings? And why is my mind going back to how good her shampoo smells? Irrelevant in any case. I have unresolved issues from my past that makes getting too close to me, or even considering anything long-term, a grave mistake. I let my guard down with Fyre. While her death may not have anything to do with my past, it's a reminder of the dangers my baggage brings. Time for some transparency.

"Um, Vinn, I um…" I stammer, trying to figure out how to begin my sordid tale as I avoid looking her directly in her eyes. "We need to talk."

"Absolutely," she responds. We pull our chairs closer.

Chapter 26

"I guess the best way to start is to tell you that I'm not who I seem. Maybe that's not quite accurate…I am who I appear to be, now, but I'm not who I used to be. Does that make sense? No. I'm not putting this well. I can't explain this without going back in time, so please be patient with me. This is going to be difficult, so please let me get through it without interrupting.

"I wasn't one of the popular kids in high school and never tried to be. I preferred blending in, or more accurately being completely invisible. This will sound like bragging, but I felt I was more mature by years than any of my classmates and saw the whole high school experience as a nasty social experiment where dissimilar people form bonds as a means of survival. Kind of like prison. I don't think anyone was truly happy passing through school as a teenager, they only thought they were by fixating on momentary pleasure or by convincing themselves that they were better than some or all of the other students.

"So kids hid their insecurities behind a football uniform or the pom-poms of a cheerleader. My path to survival was to stay quiet, study hard, and not draw attention to myself. When that didn't work, I chose to pose as a rebel, the 'too cool for school' type. What I couldn't hide was the fact that I had a brain and knew how to use it. My grades were only okay—my teachers were constantly telling me that I would be a top student if only I'd apply myself—but my test scores were off the charts.

"Paradoxically, the quiet student who nobody at school knew existed attracted a lot of attention from colleges. Institutions most kids could only dream about were competing to convince me to enroll. I had my choice among any number of full-ride offers. True to form, as an erstwhile hermit and teenage moron, I chose a small college out in the middle of nowhere. It's not important which one. Just know that it was prestigious and not nearly as off the grid as I imagined. As I hoped.

"And that's where it all went south. I dropped my guard a bit, let my intelligence show through the sullen introverted act, and drew the attention of some unusual and powerful people who also make a point of being invisible. When I look back, I think they may have been tracking me even in my high school years. Anyway, by my sophomore year of college, I was getting visits from men and women who talked a lot about applying myself to projects that would be far more interesting than anything I'd find in the corporate world. I could look forward to extensive travel, be well-compensated, and most importantly work independently, only reporting to my superiors at designated intervals. What was frightening was that they knew things about me that even my parents didn't know, and also knew to appeal to my disdain for other people. I was resourceful enough to discover that the names on the business cards they left behind, which were blank except for the name and phone number, were fake. I know what you're thinking—certain covert departments in our government. Probably. Maybe. To this day, I'm not sure.

"I knew I shouldn't do it, but I kept the cards. With graduation on the horizon, I had been offered more jobs than I could count at salaries that would astound you. But with every visit to a prospective employer, I could feel the walls of the offices closing in around me. I'd have a near panic attack imagining the prospect of years working under a supervisor, whose sole objective was to fulfill goals handed down to him or her from above and who would expect me to be a means to that goal. Worse, just a few minutes of conversation with these grunts convinced me that I would wipe them off the map at Scrabble. Weeks passed and even the jobs that I hadn't turned down began to notify me that their opening was no longer available. Moving back in with my parents was beginning to transition from a remote possibility to a probability. Against my better judgment, I took the stack of cards from my mystery suitors, shuffled them, and drew one out. I made the call.

"I figured out later that it wouldn't have mattered which number I called, they all led to the same place. In any event, while I was dialing I decided to test a theory about the resourcefulness of these people. When someone picked up the phone, before they even spoke, all I said was "I'm ready," and I hung up. On my graduation day three weeks later, after the ceremony, a car with darkened windows pulled up as I was walking back to my apartment. The door opened, I entered, and life as I knew it ended forever.

"For the next six and a half years, all traces of my public life vanished behind false IDs, travel to countries no one has ever heard of and never will, constant uprooting and moving. You'll lose all respect for me if I tell you even a fraction of what I did. I know because over time I lost all respect for myself. My missions, for lack of a better word, got darker and dirtier. More dangerous. I was nearly killed three times. I changed the lives of scores of people around the globe, seldom for the better. Despite the clamoring of moral objections growing louder with each passing day, the flip side was the massive satisfaction that I felt each time I accomplished something few people in the world could have done. I felt made for the job and I was good at it. No, not just good. Exceptional.

"Then one day I was asked to take a life. It wasn't the first time they made this request, and I always rationalized that these other times were justified, but there was a difference. The target was not only a woman, she was one of us. I wasn't supposed to know that, but I vetted every job I was given, which was against the rules, but it was the only way I could live with what I was doing. I pressed further and violated all protocol by demanding justification. I got answers that were vague, so I pressed. I got answers that were evasive, so I pressed harder. I got answers that were lies, and I stopped. There were times during my 'career' that I felt invulnerable. It's part of what made me so good. Now, for the first time, I felt exposed. Not from the outside, that I could deal with, but from within. The reason they wanted her gone, as I pieced it together, was that she had outlived her usefulness. In another month, or year, or five years, that could be me.

"Don't ask if I did the job. Please don't ask or ever bring it up again. Try to erase it from your memory. Just know that it was the last thing they asked me to do. I had been smart. I kept a journal along with copies of the few documents I was ever given. Preserved a paper trail, both on real paper and electronically. When I told them I wanted out, I promised to forget everything about the past six and a half years. But I also told them about my notes. They weren't happy. I didn't care. They let me go and threw in a new identity as a going away gift. It was wrapped in colorful and explicit threats. No, it wasn't as a professor. I ditched the life they set up for me and tried to disappear.

"What I did has scarred me but you have to know that the things I did I did voluntarily. They would repulse you, as would the knowledge that I performed them with efficiency and lack of guilt, at least at the time. There is a dark part of me that may be buried beneath the surface, but it exists and is a part of who I am. I may be remorseful, yet it scares me that somewhere inside lurks the person who was capable of committing such acts. As I said at the beginning, I'm not who I appear to be. You're not showing signs of the disgust you must feel, and I appreciate that, but I can't believe that these revelations don't shock you. I pray that we can preserve our friendship—God knows I need it—and maybe it will even grow into something more. I hope so. No matter what our relationship, though, I didn't want it to go a single day further until you heard the truth about me. I'll understand if this is a deal-killer. If you walk away now, I'll understand."

A heavy silence permeates the room. Tears fill the corner of Vinn's eyes, and a tension so sharp that it's lethal divides the space between us. I move to the edge of my chair, take her hands in mine, then inhale deeply as she gazes uncertainly into my eyes.

"My turn," I say.

Chapter 27

Vinn's confession lessens some of my fears about revealing my own sordid history without being rejected and losing my only true friend, and she even seems to adopt an expression of knowing acceptance during some of the heavier stuff, perhaps recognizing herself in my tale. I do leave out a few things, and assume she did the same. Almost as important as laying all our dirty cards on the table is my newfound confidence in her ability to protect herself and continuing on as a team.

Fyre's killer still holds the advantage, however. He knows what we look like and most likely where I live, but all we know about him is that he's male and tall. And murderous. It takes some convincing, but Vinn finally agrees to stay the night if for no other reason than to shut me up. Okay, so I nagged her a bit. No sense in her being followed back to her place so that the tall man would know the locations of both of our homes. By mutual agreement, partly stated and partly not, we choose to postpone any pursuit of a possible romantic relationship indefinitely. I'm not sure I'm ready to change out my best and only friend for a lover and being in the crosshairs of a killer isn't the best scenario in which to make that decision. Vinn gets my bed, I get the couch.

We also put off discussing what to do with the new information we drew out of Barbara, but only until the morning when our heads are hopefully clearer and our emotions steadier. As I dish out my special apricot pancakes and pour Vinn her second cup of the coffee I had stocked just for her—I had to bite back a remark about how any woman who spends time with me had better learn to love tea—we discuss our next steps. During the night, we had both reached the same conclusion.

"We need to go back to her place and search again," Vinn sighs without enthusiasm. "The DNA results must be there somewhere. Hopefully she printed them out, rather than just leave them on her laptop. Most people do, I expect."

I mumble through my second bite. "At least this time we have something specific to look for." I'm no more eager than Vinn to go back to the condo and start over but it has to be done. We agree that exposing myself to the front desk would only serve to remind Hal as to Fyre's absence, which is too great a risk at this point. Vinn will take me in through the circuitous route that she used the first time.

Vinn borrows a toothbrush and runs a comb through her hair. As we walk to my door, Vinn in the lead, I can't help but think how good she looks first thing in the morning. Focus, Winters. We step outside and I reach to put my key into the deadbolt lock but stop short. "Vinn, come here a moment."

She retreats up the stairs to stand with me on the landing. Together, we peer at the lock, examining the light scratches near the key hole. As Vinn runs her hand down the wooden jam, I go back inside, returning with a professional-grade magnifying glass, one of the best made. It may be my imagination, but I think I see professional envy in her eyes as Vinn takes it in her hands.

We alternate turns with the glass, gradually widening our search area. After about five minutes, I return the glass to its place inside my apartment and rejoin Vinn outside.

"No question," she states matter-of-factly. "Scratches around and inside of the lock not made by a key. More of them farther down the jam. Oily smudges indicating someone leaned their weight and one hand against the door. Clearly, he tried to break in last night. Fortunately, you have some damn good locks on this door, with hidden back-ups, and he appears to be a bit of an amateur."

I nod. "Yep," I say, a master of understatement. There was nothing else to add. We descend silently down the stairs, each of us a bit more aware of our surroundings than the day before. It's not considered paranoia if you really are in the crosshairs of a killer. I note that Ted had propped open the downstairs door again and left it that way overnight. I'd procrastinated having that conversation with him for way too long and it could have cost us.

Fyre's apartment is exactly as we had left it although the air is a bit more stale I crack open a window. We agree that we'll flip our original searches, with Vinn starting in the bedroom and me in the living area. "I went over her room in great detail, so no need to check the usual spots," I tell Vinn's back as she heads in. She looks back at me in disgust; whether it was because I had stated the obvious, or because she doesn't have faith in my searching skills, I can't tell.

I do trust Vinn, more than ever after our talk last night, but end up duplicating what she had probably done anyway. I pull out drawers, turn them upside down, search for false bottoms, flip through papers, and unscrew light bulbs. An hour later, Vinn joins me in the kitchen, where we pour out stale milk looking for hidden secrets, examine every pot and pan, feel inside every glass and mug, pull out the stove, and dissemble the microwave. We draw a blank.

"Okay, Winters," she intones as we stand side-by-side surveying the apartment. "You knew her. You slept with her. According to her diary, you got inside her head." Vinn looks at me out of the corner of her eye, hoping for a reaction. I remain stone-faced, only blushing on the inside. "If Fyre wanted to hide something where no one would consider looking, where would she put it?"

I think out loud. "It has to be readily accessible in case she wants to get to it. But not where a visitor could accidentally discover it. She was a clever woman. She'd also hide it where it wouldn't be found on a reasonably thorough search, as we've discovered. Concealed where you could be holding its hiding spot in your hand and not even know it."

As I brainstorm, our eyes scan the room. We both know where it is at the same time. Not specifically, but where to look. Her bookshelf. I pulled books off the shelf on our first visit but wasn't looking for anything in particular, and, given the number of books, didn't have the time to do more. Now I am and I will. We both will.

There are probably two hundred volumes of various sizes, shapes and subjects on the shelf, which stretches from the floor to the ceiling. It's a centerpiece of the room, one I had commented on the first time I'd been to Fyre's place. So much a part of the room that it blends in, easy to overlook. At least that's my excuse.

"Let's try something first," Vinn says as I start to pull a history book out of the top left corner. "Might save us some time. Is there a volume here that doesn't belong? One that seems out of place?"

We take a quick census of the selections, Vinn dragging her finger along the spines. I pause suddenly on the shelf second from the top, look over at the kitchen, then pull out a paperback volume.

"This one," I suggest, holding *60 Dinners in Under 60 Minutes.* "She's got a row of cookbooks on the top of one of her kitchen cabinets and there's room for more. This is the only cookbook here, stuck in her contemporary novel section. And Fyre was a bit anal. She wouldn't keep a cookbook anywhere but the kitchen."

I hold the book in both hands, turn it upside down, and shake it. Nothing. Vinn grabs it from me and flips the pages with the identical result. Still, I'm sure that I'm right. As Vinn turns her attention back to books on the shelf, I sit on the couch and go through the cookbook, one page at a time.

Just as I get past the sixtieth meal—tofu Parmesan—and am ready to concede defeat, I find it. All of my focus has been on the inside of the book, looking for a piece of paper or bundle of documents. In fact, the palm of my hand has been resting against it the whole time. When I began to flip the book shut, I felt the slightest of bulges in the spine of the book. Now bringing it inches from my eyes, I can see a well-disguised, razor-thin cut.

"Vinn," I say, trying unsuccessfully to keep excitement out of my voice. "Do you have tweezers?"

"Yeah, sure, I love to pluck my eyebrows while breaking the law." Have I mentioned that Vinn can be sarcastic? She disappears into the bathroom, returning with tweezers in hand.

We sit together on the couch as I ply the cut open, using the tweezers to retrieve the thinnest flash drive I have ever seen. I swear Vinn gives out a little squeak. She'll deny it, but don't believe her.

"How stupid are we?" she asks rhetorically. "We've been looking for paper."

I retrieve a zippered plastic bag from the kitchen and drop the drive inside. We don't bother to look in the other books. Neither one of us thinks we'll ever have to come back.

Chapter 28

"Bingo!" Vinn exclaims with satisfaction. We're nestled in her apartment, having taken what could charitably be called an indirect route back to make sure we weren't being followed. Vinn sits at her kitchen counter in front of her laptop while I stand looking over her shoulder. There are only two files on the flash drive, one marked 'Ancestry' and the other 'Family,' with family in quotes. When Vinn opens the Ancestry file, we're greeted with several unnamed folders. In true scientific fashion, she opens the first one first. See? Genius.

In a rare bit of good luck, the exact information that we had returned to Fyre's apartment to find fills the screen—the results of the DNA test she submitted to at the family picnic. Not surprisingly, she was primarily of Irish origin although there were smatterings of Dutch and French as well. Vinn quickly scrolls through the details of the path to Ireland Fyre's ancestors took 10,000 years before and the chart of her distant relations' settlements in the U.S. It all might be interesting in another context, but isn't quite what we're hoping to find.

Vinn opens up the next folder. Blank. Same for the third folder. With some trepidation, she clicks on the final folder in the Ancestry file. Inside was a single document of one page, with one word written near the middle: PastaSalad321!!

"'PastaSalad321'? What in the hell does that mean?" I exclaim, a little too loudly.

"I was hoping you could tell me," Vinn sighs. "Doesn't it mean anything to you?"

I shake my head. "Nothing." My earlier optimism is fading fast.

Vinn stares at the document for a few moments. "Mal, I'm sure you've had to create passwords for websites hundreds of times. What do they require? Minimum eight digits long, at least one capital letter, and some numbers and a symbol. This is a password. Considering where it's hidden, and that it refers to a dish served at picnics and family get-togethers, I'll bet I know to what."

By that time, I'm actually way ahead of her but decide to let her bask in the glory of her deduction and the satisfaction of thinking she's the first to figure it out. Already acting like a couple. As I anticipate, Vinn opens up the Ancestry DNA site. She asks me for Fyre's email address then types in the password. We're in.

We ignore information similar to what we've already read on the flash drive and jump straight to the family tree. Fyre traced her roots back five generations on both her mother's and father's side. Vinn takes one parent's side, I take the other, then we switch off in order to make absolutely sure. Vinn takes the lead.

"So she traces back to Sarah, William's daughter, which should mean that she's related to William, Sarah's father. And that's what the chart based on public records shows, so no surprise there. But did you notice something curious?"

"Yep. Ancestry provides extensive contact information for other people who have taken the test who are in any way related to you. Look, there's mentions of other descendants of Sarah along with names of third and fourth-cousins, and even suggestions to link to people that would only be blood relatives through a handful of genes at best. One of my students was talking about this after class. The site tries to get you excited by connecting you to people both closely related as well as those barely related to you so that you can reach out to them. You could create a massively expansive family tree that way. When we check the relatives they list for Fyre, Sarah's descendants are all there. At least the ones who submitted a swab at the picnic. We should also expect to find links to the side of the family that descend from William, Jr. because they share his father's genes, but they don't show up anywhere. There's no mention of any of Junior's progeny, period."

"Let me try something." Vinn types Barbara Gooding's name into the search panel. "I'm coming at this in reverse." We look at the suggested relations for Barbara. This time, no one on Sarah's side of the family appears.

We sit, unspeaking, digesting this information for several minutes before Vinn breaks the silence. "This can only mean one thing. Either William Jr. or Sarah weren't sired by William Senior." She pauses. I can see her mind working and it's a sight to behold. She must be an absolute wonder in the lab. "Mal, don't you remember? We found a birth certificate for Junior, as well as one for Margaret, but not for Sarah." She opens up a new Ancestry page, types a few keys, and, after a few minutes of searching, points to the screen. "Here's Junior's birth certificate someone posted on the site. He was born in Cook County Hospital to William and Penelope Sales. The certificate was signed the day he was born, so unless Penelope was fooling around, which seems unlikely, Junior is Sales' biological son."

"Maybe, but we need something more. Let's work this out on Sarah. If Penelope didn't give birth to her, and they didn't adopt her, where did she come from?"

"Okay, think back. What was Sales doing around the time she was born—which was when?"

I have to take a moment. "Without the birth certificate we can't be exactly sure. The best estimate based on her placement as the middle child between Junior and Margaret would be 1913 or 1914. Possibly later but start with those."

Vinn's eyes grow wide. "Wait. When Fyre was dying, she wrote '1915' in her own blood, so that has to be important. We're working on the assumption it's related to the Eastland sinking—mainly because it got the biggest headlines that year and we don't really have anywhere else to begin—but we should also start down that road for another reason. I see a possible connection."

I catch her train of thought along with a heavy dose of her excitement. "Barbara said that Sales was working for some sort of manufacturing company in Cicero at that time, although she couldn't remember the name."

"Right. I don't remember—what sort of company was it that leased those ships for the annual picnic?" Vinn is racing ahead, typing furiously on her laptop and doesn't wait for an answer. "Here's the Eastland website. It was Western Electric, and its main plant was in…." She looks at me and grins.

"Cicero?"

"Cicero. What do you want to bet that Sales worked for Western Electric at the time of the Eastland disaster? But what's the connection with Sarah?"

I have an idea. As I said, I do get them occasionally. "Vinn, does that website have a phone number for the Eastland Historical Society?"

Vinn looks puzzled, but glances back to her screen and reads it to me. It's local. I dial and am momentarily taken aback when I don't get voice mail.

"Oh, hello, thanks for answering. My name is John Swanson and I'm a bit of a history buff. Who am I speaking to? Nice to meet you, Nancy. I'm hoping you can answer a question about the Eastland. I just read about it and it's fascinating. I don't know why I've never been aware of the disaster before. Anyway, was everyone that was on board accounted for after the sinking? Uh huh. Really? No, a rumor is okay. But never confirmed? Thank you, I really appreciate it. Yes, I'll consider a donation. Good bye."

I look at Vinn, sitting tense on the edge of her chair. I assume she knows where I'm going with this. "Records are fairly complete, although no one at the time kept track of who boarded which boat. Every employee and family member going on the picnic had to have a ticket and show it in order to board one of the boats. But there was an exception."

"Don't tell me," Vinn says quickly to show she's caught up. "No ticket was required for babies."

"Correct. Two years old and younger. And it gets better. There were rumors at the time, never substantiated, that a couple that were among the dead had brought their young daughter on board. The girl's body was never found."

Vinn lets out a low whistle, a habit we seem to share. "So Sales works for this company and is going on the picnic with Penelope and possibly Junior. They get on board the Eastland but aren't among the victims. Somehow, this girl, whose parents drowned, ends up in their possession. Penelope already has a son, is yearning to have a daughter, and a baby girl falls in her lap. No nine months of hell, and a decision is instantly made. No one sees them take her, no paperwork is filed, but all of a sudden they have another daughter. They're private people, antisocial, so no one would know that Penelope was never pregnant. Bingo, the family gets bigger and no one's the wiser."

"A lot of guesswork there, but let's assume that it's true," I grant her. "Sales raises Sarah as his own. What's the significance in whether she was or wasn't his biological daughter?"

We both cast our eyes at the stack of papers sitting on Vinn's coffee table. I walk over and pull out the copy of Sales' will that we made at the Daley Center, starting to page through it almost before I have it secured.

And there it is. I begin summarizing the highlights for Vinn. "In the event there's a catastrophe and he's unable to come back to life to retrieve his fortune, it's to be distributed, quote, 'to my heirs as defined and in the percentages listed below.' Then if I skip down...oh my." I stop, momentarily unable to proceed.

"What, you idiot? Tell me!"

"In the part he refers to in the section I just read, he specifically states that 'such amounts shall be divided among my natural-born, blood relatives.'"

Vinn will deny it, but her jaw definitely drops. I don't know if I can date a woman without manners. "So that confirms it. The DNA swabbing at the picnic was intended to be a fun activity. It was supposed to bring peace among family members warring over whether or not to contest Sales' will. Instead, to anyone who took the effort to figure it out, it revealed that the line of the family descended from Sarah aren't blood relatives at all because Sarah wasn't his biological daughter. But couldn't those heirs argue that he was just using boilerplate language in his will? That he couldn't possibly mean to cut off anyone who didn't have his genes running in their veins?"

"Maybe," I agree. "But remember what Barbara told us? That after his youngest daughter Margaret died, he cut off all ties to her husband by saying that he wasn't related by blood. Pretty strong argument that he knew exactly what he was doing."

Vinn sighs. "In the end, it really doesn't matter because someone, presumably one of Sarah's heirs, noticed exactly what we did on the Ancestry site and understood the potential for getting completely cut off. Barbara's lawsuit may have the consequence of bringing this all out into the open, and if she's successful, the entirety of Sales' estate will be distributed solely to Junior's heirs. No more quarterly payments, no share of the massive principal amount. From living easy to poverty all because of a DNA test."

Silence descends over the room as we consider this development and examine it from all angles. In a twisted sort of way, it makes sense. Still...

"Vinn, let's say that everything we just talked about is true. But it's one thing to face getting cut off from a substantial source of income and another to kill for it. You and I just discovered that each of us has a history that the other never suspected. Isn't it possible, likely even, that we've made enemies along the way that would be happy to see us dead? Maybe the same can be said for Fyre. Maybe the tall man isn't a relative at all and her murder involves something totally unrelated to Sales and his crazy will. I mean, why kill Fyre? She had no motivation to bring up the DNA results because she's one of the heirs that would get cut off."

"I can see your point," Vinn replies, "but something in my gut says we're on the right path. Unless we're out of our minds, Fyre may not have been the only victim. Why don't I call Barbara and ask about suspicious deaths in the family? I know…" she held up her hand as I began to protest, "She'll wonder why we're asking and what it has to do with our project on cryonics. At his point, what difference does it make if she sees through us?"

Vinn apparently reads my silence as my assent to make the call. She picks up her cell phone, checks her recent call directory, and pushes a button.

"Oh, I'm sorry. I thought this was Barbara's cell number. Is she there? She's been helping us out with a research project and I want to follow up on something with her. My name is… Oh, I see. Will she be back later?… I'm so sorry, I don't mean to upset you… Oh, I'm sorry… How? I see. Thank you, I'm sorry to have bothered you."

By the end of the conversation, Vinn's voice begins to tremble and with each word, she turns one more shade of pale. I sit impatiently and wait for her to compose herself. She finally looks at me, anguish in her eyes.

"Barbara Gooding died last night. She fell down a flight of stairs outside her apartment."

Chapter 29

"We're agreed, right?" I still haven't spoken and her tone is in-your-face challenging. "There is no way in hell that her death was an accident."

I find my voice. "Agreed. Although if I recall Barbara should have had nothing to worry about. Junior was her grandfather. My guess is that whoever is behind the killings wants this lawsuit to go away. To maintain the status quo and not draw attention to the language of the will or to lay the groundwork for an investigation as to which family members are true 'blood relatives.'"

True to form, Vinn's mind is already racing ahead of mine. "We need to go back on the Ancestry site and print out a chart of the family tree. Then do our own research to find out which heirs died ahead of their time, and whether they descended from Junior or Sarah. Maybe Fyre was an anomaly, because her death makes no sense."

Ten minutes later, we each have our own copy of the names of Sales' descendants arranged in the form of a family tree. Typical of any family history going back one hundred years, there are a lot of names. Twenty-two descendants of Sarah. Thirty on Junior's side. This will take some time. The good news is I know a scientist with an organized mind.

"You take Junior's heirs, I'll take Sarah's. I think we can safely ignore any children if Margaret's husband remarried and had kids." The anxiety that Vinn exhibited earlier after hearing of Barbara's death seems to have been temporarily suppressed beneath the urgency of the task ahead of us. "Start with the oldest and work your way down. Google them, then somewhere I've got the website for the Newberry which will give us remote access to the newspapers and other databases that may have useful information about the family members. Concentrate on how they died and how old they were. Write down as many facts about their deaths as possible. We'll go over them all together but make special note of any that seem even remotely suspicious."

Marching orders in hand, I set myself up at Vinn's desktop computer while she settles on the couch with her laptop. The work is laborious and slow and mostly frustrating. With enough persistence, though, and the sugar rush from a much-needed cookie break, we each make progress. Vinn finishes her list after close to five hours and offers to take a few names off of mine. It's late when we finish and darkness fell long ago, but neither one of us is ready for sleep. If anything, we're more wired now than when we started.

"I'll start," I volunteer after moving over to sit next to Vinn on the couch. "Getting much information on some of the older relatives on Junior's side wasn't easy and I wasn't always successful. I think we can assume, though, that anyone who died prior to the family picnic and the DNA test probably wasn't murdered. I also wasn't too concerned if I couldn't get a cause of death from someone who died prior to around 2000, which still gives us a huge cushion. Besides, all of the older ones seem to be either clearly accidental or natural from disease or old age. Three cancer deaths, one hit by car—that one was in 1980—one in France in WWII, dementia, remarkably two during routine surgery, and a few other causes."

Vinn raises her eyebrows—both this time—and starts to interrupt when I mention the deaths during surgery, but I shake my head. "We don't need to go there. They aren't close to within our time frame. There are some suspicious deaths, though. Barbara is a given, but I found four more, each within the last eighteen months. A nineteen-year-old girl disappeared on her way back from a sleepover and she was never found. Thirty-seven-year-old twin men were found slumped over at the kitchen table in the apartment they shared. The official cause of death was carbon monoxide poisoning. Defective detector. Finally, a sixty-year-old man with asthma suffocated in his sleep.

"Of course, they all could've been 'natural' deaths, not murders, and I couldn't find a single word to indicate that they were considered anything but routine. But I did a little more poking and eventually found a Facebook page for the family picnic. It's incredible what people post for anyone to see. Don't they know about privacy settings? Anyway, someone posted photographs of family members spitting into the Ancestry tubes and from comments on the page, I was able to compile a list of which members took the DNA test.

"And guess what? Each of the victims on my suspicious death list took the test. The odds of that are astronomical. Whoever's behind this killing spree, if that's what it is, clearly believes that the greatest risk will come from family members who submitted their DNA. They're the ones that will have access to the results, and if it didn't take us very long to discover something odd, others could find it too. Questions about who the true blood relatives are would arise. Silence the member, and no one else will bother taking a look at their dead relation's Ancestry results. Any questions die along with the family member."

Vinn looks pensive. "Impressive work, Winters. Five deaths within such a short period of time might raise some suspicions, don't you think?"

"Not necessarily. Remember, the deaths don't look suspicious to anyone without the knowledge that we have. Plus, the family isn't particularly close-knit. Fractures galore. A lot of them might not have even been notified of the death of a distant cousin or cared enough to pay much attention to it."

"I get that," Vinn admits. "But it's harder to ignore the number of deaths on Sarah's line. Within the last three years, I've got seven."

I confess I may have gasped. "That's got to be half of the descendants still alive! And what's to be gained from killing them? They have no motivation to spill the beans on the DNA."

"Not half, but close enough. These are people that don't keep close tabs on anyone outside of their immediate family. The animosity resulting from the picnic means that a lot of the family cut off all communication with other members even to the extent of notifications of a death. So it's possible that no one has put two and two together. We have the advantage of having had a lot of pieces of the puzzle placed before us within a short period of time. Easier to see a pattern when you know what you're looking for. As for your second question, maybe some of Sarah's heirs are actually honest enough to bring up the anomaly, or will accidentally say something to tip off the others, or maybe the killer just wants to reduce the number of beneficiaries so that if Barbara's lawsuit were successful, their share of the pie would be bigger.

"Can I move on to the possible victims? Names for now are immaterial so I'll just go by birth year, with the oldest first. Most but not all of these postdate the Sales family shindig. 1962, another plunge down the stairs, although these were icy and supposedly slippery. A month later, her 26-year-old son was killed in a drive-by shooting on the South Side. Cops theorize it was mistaken identity. No arrest. 1966, an only child with no kids, run over by a hit-and-run driver in Cincinnati, no one ever caught there either. Fyre we know about. She had a cousin, born two years before she was in 1984, skiing accident when his bindings broke. Both bindings, if you can believe that. No investigation. 1989: Clarise Knowlton, stabbed in her home in Nashville. Finally, 1993, a mere kid of twenty-four. Shot in the head in his apartment here in Chicago, case remains unsolved. Whoever this is may not be a professional killer, but he does try to vary his methods a bit. What's wrong?"

I'm shaking and my mouth is dry. I press the palms of my hands hard into my forehead, trying not to believe what I know has to be true. It takes time to compose myself, not wanting to confirm what an ignorant fool I've been. I can't put it off forever.

"Vinn, tell me about the Nashville woman. Did you make a note of the exact day that she died? And do you know about what time?"

Vinn consults her notes and tells me. Just to make sure, I check the calendar on my phone. Shit. I face Vinn and begin haltingly.

"We've been working under a false assumption, that one person—the tall man—is responsible for all of these deaths. Hard to believe, but I don't think we have a single murderer at work here. The night that woman was stabbed in Nashville, I sat at a table listening to music with her killer. Vinn, Fyre was in Nashville that night and left the venue before it closed for what she said was an appointment. Near midnight. When I saw her the next morning, she said she had gotten lucky and her work was done early, so she was leaving town."

As I speak, I look away from Vinn to sort through the pile of junk we pilfered from Fyre's condo. Finally finding what I'm searching for, I open it up and hold it out for Vinn to see. "When we searched her place, I pulled this from a pocket of the jacket that Fyre was wearing the night we met in the Nashville club. 'Clarise Knowlton.' Vinn, Fyre killed that woman. Then later the tall man killed her. They were both trying to protect their share of the spoils."

Chapter 30

"I don't know, Mal. There could be any number of explanations for Fyre having that name that don't involve murder. Before you jump to conclusions, we really need more." In part, Vinn is trying to console me by forcing me to consider alternatives, but she's also being who she is. A scientist who requires stronger proof than what I just provided.

But I'm not a scientist and I just know. The revelation that Fyre, a woman with whom I had shared a bed, was capable of stabbing a young woman to death for the sake of money leaves me dumbfounded and unable to continue our task. After several minutes of my staring unfocused onto the floor, Vinn moves to my side, puts her arm around my shoulder, and lets me process the news in silence. She drops her protests, knowing that nothing she can say will help, at least not yet. Hallmark doesn't make pithy cards for every occasion after all.

Finally, I raise my head, certain my red eyes betray my emotions. I don't care. An admittedly irrational guilt now fuels my insatiable determination to move forward quickly. I feel a newfound responsibility to be the one to put a halt to all of this, to stop the killings. I still want to find out who the tall man is and to personally confront him, no longer so much to avenge Fyre's death but to save faceless heirs to the Sales fortune from his killing spree.

"Vinn," my voice cracks a bit but I steady myself and continue. "I need to be absolutely certain that the guy who killed Fyre wasn't simply doing so to put a stop to her murderous rampage. Unlikely, I know, but someday—soon, I hope—I'm going to face him and I need to know exactly who he is and what he's done. His fate hinges on the answers to those questions."

Vinn stares deeply into my eyes before reluctantly sliding back over to her laptop where she consults her notes. She reaches over, takes mine, and does the same. "Assuming you're right, I think it's safe to say that both of them were at work, whether independently or as a team doesn't really matter. Two of these deaths, if at least one wasn't accidental, occurred 1,000 miles apart within six hours of each other. Two killers, not one. If not Fyre, someone else."

Strangely, I'm comforted by the news. Not that it absolves Fyre from being a heartless and horrible woman, but at least she wasn't responsible for every one of the deaths. The news also brings our mission into a sharper focus. We need to identify the tall man, confirm he's the other killer, and then do whatever needs to be done to take him out of the equation. At least on that point Vinn will agree. I think both of us know what that entails but we leave it unspoken.

It's now well into the early hours of the morning. Both the emotions of the evening and our long hours of work has left both of us totally drained. We'll have to finish another time.

I state the obvious. "Vinn, we need some rest. Let's reconvene between classes tomorrow."

Vinn looks at me sleepily. "You can stay here; save the time it takes to get back home." She senses my hesitation. "My couch is pretty comfortable."

"Thanks, but no. I need fresh clothes. Besides, your taste in tea is horrible." She snorts. "I'm going to get going." The idea of spending the night and starting the morning first thing with Vinn nearby is more than tempting, and I admit that forbidden thoughts of a nocturnal visit into her room enter my mind. It's this kind of thinking that convinces me I need to go home. That would be a distraction I can't afford right now.

Vinn gives me a brief hug and closes her door behind me. I wait to hear the locks turn before heading to the el. The trains run around the clock, although in the overnight hours, the time gap between them can stretch past what seems reasonable to someone who can only think of his head hitting a pillow. Despite my exhaustion, I take the precaution of walking south to a station other than the one nearest to Vinn's apartment just in case the tall man lies in wait for me at the closer stop.

Walking the deserted streets, I imagine trouble lurking in every shadow and the slightest rustle of a leaf blowing in the wind has me spinning around in a panic, looking for the glint of a gun or the blade of a knife. My paranoia makes the walk to the distant station take twice as long as it should have, but for all I know, it also might be keeping me alive.

As I approach the stairs to descend to the entrance, the unmistakable tread of steps echoes from the darkness below. Hugging the wall and slowing my pace, stepping carefully to mute my advance, I take each step with care, my senses rapidly shifting into overdrive. When I reach the bottom of the stairs with the turnstile in view I rapidly run to the opposite side, turn around in a crouch, and peer into the gloom. No one. Was I hearing things? Seeing things? All I know is that my exhaustion makes me too easy a target. I need to get home.

I dash to the turnstile, vaulting it to save time. The last thing I care about at this point is cheating the CTA out of a couple of bucks. I repeat my cautionary approach on the set of stairs down to the platform, easily taking fifteen or twenty seconds for each step. Two steps from the bottom I freeze, hanging back in the shadow, pressing myself against the wall.

I stay that way, motionless and barely breathing, for eleven, maybe twelve minutes. As far as I can see, the platform is deserted. No one passes me on the stairs. A train finally pulls into the station. Counting to five after the doors open, I sprint from my hiding spot into the nearest car just as the doors close again. Out of the corner of my eye I see a shadowy figure run to the door of the next car from somewhere out of the darkness, bang his hand on the closed panel, and then fade back into the gloom. He may have been tall. He may have worn a familiar coat. I can't be sure, but I think my caution was justified after all. I realize that I've been holding my breath and slowly release it. Happening a lot lately.

No one is waiting for me at my stop but I don't take any chances on my way home. I run an irregular route, halt, hide behind a tree or a bush until I can verify that I'm alone, then repeat. The open space between my front gate and the stairs isn't far but will expose me. I swear I can sense a presence, or maybe a slight body odor, somewhere nearby. I decide not to take a chance.

I edge sideways, hugging the fence, then take three giant and quick strides to Leo's steps, throwing myself down to the relative safety outside his front door. Just as I pull my wrist back to knock, crouching to provide a smaller target, the door swings open. Leo bends down, grabs me by the collar of my jacket, pulls me inside, then slams the door shut and bolts it. Either he has a sixth sense—which I've suspected since the day we met—or he knows something I don't know.

I stumble to my feet and over to my usual chair at the kitchen table, where a bottle of tequila and two glasses again sit waiting. I throw a questioning glance Leo's way as he joins me at the table. Rather than answer my unstated question, he simply shrugs his shoulders, glares at me for five seconds, and says "Talk."

So I do. I unload everything from my first encounter with Fyre—honoring our unspoken pact by keeping my life prior to that private—through the processes of investigation and discovery with Vinn, and finishing up with the conclusions we made earlier that night. It takes a long time, but Leo is patient. I find that simply reciting the history of the entire debacle helps organize it in my own mind. Hearing it out loud gives me a confidence that I didn't have an hour earlier that Vinn and I are dead on in our conclusions. As I finish, I cast my eyes down and am surprised to see my glass is empty. I don't remember taking a drink. Leo reaches over and pours a refill.

That task handled, he sits silently, his eyes boring into my skull. Unnerved and with nothing else to say, I shift positions so that I can focus on something else in the room. I don't need Leo's judgment right now. He finally breaks the tension and speaks.

"A man, stranger, been hanging around last few days." Leo raises his hand above his head to indicate the man's height. "I notice. He don't want to be seen but I see. Think he's a bad man. My gut. Was here tonight for long time. Don't know if he still here."

Such news would normally set my nerves on edge, but they've already fallen over that edge and I'm too fatigued and numb from the evening's earlier revelations for the full impact of what Leo is saying to hit me. It also isn't a surprise. I know I've been walking around with a bulls-eye on my back for days. I give a slight nod of my head to acknowledge that I've heard him.

Leo leans forward across the table. "I got help. Watch your back sometimes. Not always. You must be cautious."

Before I can ask what sort of help he's enlisted, he stands, grasps my forearm in his iron grip, and simply says "Go now."

I stagger to his door and feel him pushing a flashlight into my hands. As I climb his stairs I sweep the yard with its strong beam, see nothing out of the ordinary, then slide across the front of Leo's window facing outward, flashlight constantly scanning the yard. When I get to the top of the stairs, I hop out, flash the light upward, then run to the landing and shoulder open the door, thankful for the first time that Ted had left it propped open. I almost expect to encounter the tall man in wait, but there's no one there. Satisfied, I dash up the stairs to my unit, insert my key in the lock, and began to turn it.

Instinct is a funny thing. I like to think of it as part magical intuition but in reality, I believe it's my mind's subconscious drawing upon years of experience and in a microsecond piecing thousands of events and incidents together like a jigsaw, until a picture emerges from the individual scraps, then applying it to my current situation. Whatever it is, here it saves my life. I stop mid-turn, pull the key out, and step back from the door.

One of the first things I did when I moved into my apartment was to install professional safety measures that would prevent anyone but a handful of the world's best picklocks and other ne'er-do-wells from breaking in. Heavy door, some of the most sophisticated locks in the business, and a few unusual devices that no one would even suspect exist make my home nearly impenetrable. As an amateur bad guy, the tall man wouldn't be able to come close to getting inside and he didn't. He tried the night Vinn was over and failed. Unless he took an online course in breaking and entering in the meantime, he won't be waiting for me inside. But something doesn't feel right.

I use Leo's flashlight to scan the landing, first a quick look which reveals nothing, then a slow, methodical examination. I almost miss them this time around too, which would have been fatal. A pair of microscopic, barely visible wires the color of the door are nestled along its edge, running up and across the top of the jam where they wouldn't be as likely to be spotted than if they ran across the floor. I follow their path with the light, startling myself when they suddenly disappear into a small dark box pushed back into the shadows. In the daylight it would look like the world's clumsiest attempt at setting a trap. In the dark of the night, though, with a dog-tired and sloppy target, it almost worked.

I hustle back down to Leo's to request a wire cutter, which I don't doubt he'll have. This time, he accompanies me back up the stairs, partly to keep an eye on my back as I deactivate the device, partly to examine the creep's handiwork, but mostly to make sure I know what I'm doing. He lives in this building too, after all. Maybe he's worried that a loud explosion will deflate his soufflé.

Leo mutters accurate but unnecessary instructions as I cautiously begin a familiar process until he catches my glare and realizes that I do have some experience in this area. Again, no questions. As confident as I am, I still hold my breath and close my eyes as I position the tool to cut the final wire. I think Leo, whose rum-scented breath may be the last thing I ever smell, does too.

We don't blow up. I thank Leo for his 'assistance,' he nods his appreciation for staying alive, and I open the door. Leo peers over my shoulder past me, presumably to make sure a deadly viper isn't waiting for me, then turns without a word and lumbers down the stairs. I set the device aside for now, too tired to examine it for any clues as to its maker, and fall onto my bed. Minutes later my alarm sounds, interrupting a dream involving my defusing an explosive device the size of a large dog while a naked Fyre looks on. The blast of loud music from my phone brings on a slight panic attack given the dream but I recover enough to step into the shower, get dressed with nearly matching socks, and pack a large Thermos with hot oolong tea. It's time to get to class.

Chapter 31

Vinn's waiting for me in the café, her bloodshot eyes betraying her own restless night. I'm sure I look even worse. As soon as I sit down, I unload to her about the attempt on my life. On the trip in, I debated whether to burden her with this information and the worry that will accompany it but concluded that she needs to know for her own safety. Her reaction is exactly what I expected.

"My God, Mal! This has gone too far and neither one of us needs to be on pins and needles wondering if the next breath we take is our last. That's one of the reasons you and I each left our former lives. Maybe it's time to go to the police or the FBI or somebody."

I frown. "That's your frustration talking. You know we can't involve any of the authorities, Vinn. There's no way to tell them about the bomb without also revealing what I know about Fyre. Then I'd have to explain why I left a dead body in the old post office without notifying them about it, and chances are they'll take the easy route and decide I make a pretty good suspect for her killing." I take a breath. "Besides, if they start looking into my background, and they would, it would ring more than a few alarm bells. They might offer me protection from the killer but only because they'd put me in a cell."

"Yeah, that's what I figured, but I had to ask." Vinn sounds defeated. "So now what?"

"We can't warn the other relatives because they won't believe us unless we reveal what we know and how we know it. If we do that, they'll call the cops and we're right back to me in the slammer. Maybe you too. If we let them know anonymously, they won't have any reason to trust us, so that's no good. But we can't just sit back and watch them die from afar. We need to identify the killer and handle him ourselves."

There it is. What was an unspoken understanding last night is now out in the open. Vinn's only reaction to my pronouncement was a slight twitch at the corner of one eye. She understands what I mean by 'handle him.' It's probably part of what kept her awake. I know what thoughts are going through her mind because they're the same ones that have been haunting my own. Each of us has an unfortunate past that we thought we'd left behind and resent being pulled back into it. Despite that, she has to acknowledge that this is the right decision—the only option really. She also knows we each have the skill set to put things right. Vinn sits absolutely still as a debate rages within her while I sit impotently and watch.

My patience reaches its saturation point and I finally break into the silence to say what's on my mind. I lean in close and speak softly. "Vinn, you never signed up for this. If for no other reason than my own peace of mind, please back away now. I'm capable of doing this myself. Believe me, I won't think any less of you."

The flash in her eyes isn't the reaction I had hoped for but is exactly the one I expected. "What, and let you get all the glory? Or more likely, get killed? Not a chance, Winters. Let's do this." She's whispering, but her message comes through loud and clear.

I nod. "Yeah, that's what I figured, but I had to ask," which elicits a small smile from Vinn. For better or worse, till death do us part, we're in this together. I don't waste any time.

"Here's my thought. We need to go back to your place and look at the family tree again. We know that our target is male, and that he's no kid. We can probably narrow the list of possibilities to three or four, maybe even fewer. Then we make a list of the dates and locations of the suspicious deaths. Do you have a hacker?"

Vinn shakes her head. "Used to. Burned that bridge."

I look at her for a moment wondering if she would offer up an explanation. When none is forthcoming, I let it pass. "It's been a while, but assuming he's not behind bars, I think J.J. will help. It will cost me, but we don't have any other options. Anyway, we'll give him what we can dig up on the primary suspects and have him check their travel arrangements—airline tickets, hotel, whatever, then see who matches up."

Having a plan and something to do gives Vinn a little bit of life. Color returns to her cheeks. "Sounds good. How does tonight work for you?"

"Perfect. I'll be by at 7:00 with pizza."

"No pineapple or anchovies. See you then," she mumbles as she gets up to leave. She's walked about six steps away from the table when she pauses mid-stride and turns back with a slight smirk. "Oh, and Winters, try not to bring any uninvited company with you."

I smile at her back as she resumes her journey toward the exit.

"Velveeta Nachos?" I yell.

She has to do something about that middle finger.

Chapter 32

Vinn and I sit in her apartment at our now customary spots, impatiently waiting for a response from my hacker. You don't simply call J.J. up when you have a job, or even email him. There are certain message boards and chat rooms in which you leave a post with a reference to both a beef product and a city name beginning with the letter 'T,' then you wait for J.J. to get back to you if he so chooses. I got lucky, probably because J.J. owes me a favor. After sifting through several well-meaning responses for where to find the best cheeseburger in Tallahassee, I recognize a familiar bread crumb. Several trails to different boards and a couple of websites later, I piece together the email address he probably set up just for this one job.

We already did our homework and have our request prepared. We eliminated any relatives on Junior's side of the family tree, for now anyway, because they have little to gain from the killings. They have both the law and language of the will on their side. Anyone born before 1950 would be too old. Unless there's a third murderer out there, we know our target is male. That leaves only four possible names, with two of them being long-shots, one because a picture on Facebook shows he's wider than two average people and the other because his profile mentions how he's petrified of flying. Since I'm using up my favor with J.J. anyway, I add Fyre's information into the mix as well. Five names, including Fyre's, seven dates of death, not including Fyre's. I ask J.J. for travel records one week on either side of the death itself for all five of them.

It's now 1:14 a.m., an hour after we've polished off our second dinner of cold leftover pizza, when I get the email. Vinn asks me to forward it to her and immediately prints out two copies of the results. We eagerly dive right in.

"Who's Freddy?" Vinn asks in response to a side note from J.J. Two weeks after I got my new ID, Freddy was shot dead. Someone at his door used the phrase 'Key Largo' trying to gain entry and instantly lost his face. What Freddy hadn't counted on was the second man standing behind the first. He was right, you can't be too careful. I tell Vinn that it has nothing to do with what we're working on at the moment and that I'll fill her in later. We both read on.

There isn't much, partly because several of the victims lived in the Chicago area where no hotel or plane reservations would be necessary if the killer is local. There's enough, though, to give us confidence that we have our man. Richard Woodson, Fyre's cousin. He traveled to both Seattle and Austin before the death of two of the victims and returned a day later in each case. Vinn quickly Googles his name and comes up with a group picture from his accounting firm's staff retreat from ten years earlier. Woodson stands awkwardly in the back row, half a head taller than everyone else.

"Wait a minute," Vinn exclaims, her excitement pushing through her otherwise exhausted state. "Woodson. Not counting Fyre, the most recent victim was Paul Woodson. Less than six months ago." She clutches printouts from one of our earlier sessions in one hand and J.J.'s email in the other, checking the date and location of Paul's death against the hacker's email listing Fyre's itineraries. "Mal, look at this. Paul Woodson was Richard's younger brother. He died in San Diego last November. Guess who was in San Diego at the same time."

She knows I know the answer but I dutifully say it anyway. "Fyre."

"Yep. Mal, I'm sorry, I doubted you. She killed Clarise Knowlton and she killed Woodson's brother. He took revenge by moving her to the top of his list. A dangerous game she was playing. I wonder if she knew he was doing the same thing that she was, and if so, why would she agree to meet him? And in case you have any doubts, there's something else. Something we've overlooked." Vinn leans over to the plastic bag and pulls out the picture I took of the message Fyre scrawled as she was dying. "She didn't just write out a year, remember? She tried to give us a word too. It looks like a 'c' then a clear 'o' and that line could be the beginning of a 'u.' She died before she could finish 'Cou.' The first three letters of 'cousin.' That cinches it that our man is this Richard Woodson. No doubt about it. She kills his brother, he kills her."

It was hard enough to view Fyre as a one-time killer. The revised image of her as a mass murderer is giving me a headache. To cope, I deflect the conversation back to Vinn. "So any suggestions about how we proceed from here?"

She ponders it, her burst of energy starting to fade as she slumps into her chair. "We know what we have to do. Since we can't get the law involved, there's only one way to stop this. But despite what I just said about there being no doubts, we have to be absolutely positive that Woodson is our guy before taking the ultimate step. What would you say to some surveillance?"

I shake my head. "What, and wait until we can watch him kill another member of the family? I don't think so. Besides, we don't have the time or the manpower to do it properly. We only have to follow him to get his routine down, discover for certain when he'll be at work and safely out of his home. And if he's got a roommate or family, when they'll be out at the same time he is. We need to get into his place and see what we can find."

"Yeah, maybe we'll find a to-do list with 'kill Fyre' on it," Vinn replies with a mix of sarcasm and sleepiness. "But you're right. It's worth a try."

Vinn gathers the printouts, taps them on the desk into a neat stack, then sets them aside, closing her laptop. As she rises to head off to her bedroom, she again offers to let me stay the night. Considering my adventure the last time I left her apartment late at night, I only put up a feeble protest about not wanting to be any trouble before relenting.

I lay my head down on the couch while Vinn disappears to gather sheets and a pillow. She's right, her couch is as comfortable lying down as it is sitting. The next thing I know, I awake to the smell of breakfast cooking, a neat pile of bed sheets and a pillow stacked on the floor next to my head.

Chapter 33

It takes less than a minute for Vinn to track down Woodson's home address on the internet. Over the next several days, she and I juggle classes, department meetings, and personal obligations while taking turns watching his apartment in the morning and at night. We did the best we could, but each of us worried about what we were missing in the gaps when neither of us could be there. That, and the fact that on the third day I fell asleep leaning against a tree, called for drastic measures.

"Your tenants?" Vinn was the picture of incredulity. "Please tell me you're not serious or that sleep deprivation has caused you to lose brain cells."

"There's more to them than meets the eye. Leo is as tough as they come and I wouldn't be surprised if he's had experience in surveillance. The main problem will be keeping him from strangling Woodson himself. And Ted... no, Ted won't agree to help. But Rebecca would welcome the adventure. And she's...well, maybe asking her is a bit crazy. But four is better than two."

Vinn's not convinced so I drop it but make arrangements on my own. I'm careful not to disclose our end goal for Woodson. Leo only commits to a few shifts due to his responsibilities at the restaurant, although I have a feeling he's sometimes there in the shadows while I'm watching the building. He gives his reports verbally. They're terse but informative. Rebecca is thrilled to be asked but immediately begins obsessing about the proper fashion accessories for spies. In the end, plain skirts win out over jeans, and jewelry is kept to a minimum. She writes long, florid descriptions of her shifts in small, neat script with hearts dotting the i's. Neither discovers anything significant other than to confirm our own information, but I do get a little peace of mind that we aren't missing anything.

Both Vinn and I follow Woodson on separate mornings to his place of work, an accounting business in the Loop. By the end of the week, we're sufficiently confident that he's regularly at his job from 8:30 in the morning to at least 5:30 at night, sometimes later. As far as we can tell, he lives alone, which simplifies matters. Vinn's last class on Friday ends at noon. I post a note on the door of my 2:00 class canceling it so that I'll be free as well. Stuart won't be happy if he finds out, but on the flip side, it'll raise my score on my students' year-end class evaluations. I thank Leo and Rebecca for their help and tell them their services are no longer required. Only Rebecca seems disappointed.

"Are you sure you want to do this?" Vinn asks in a rare tone of uncertainty. Nothing like the specter of murder to cast a pall over breaking into a stranger's apartment.

"We have to be sure it's him for one thing, or more certain than we already are if that makes sense, and maybe we'll find something incriminating that we can report anonymously to the cops," I reply with a confidence that I don't feel. Vinn throws me a side glance. We've been through this; we both know the authorities aren't an option. "But you've already gone well beyond the call on this, so if you'd rather not go with me…"

"Drop dead, Winters," she cuts me off. "Let's get this over with."

Like Vinn, Woodson lives in the DePaul area, in a six-flat a short el ride north. I'd noticed during my surveillance time, pacing back and forth from the front to the rear of the building in an effort to stay warm, that workers are re-tiling the laundry room and keep the back door propped open with a brick. Ted would fit right in with that crew. It's with great relief that we find the same brick there when we arrive. Saves some time and lessens the risk of getting caught. A good start.

We brought paper shopping bags filled out with crumpled newspapers with us in anticipation of the presence of the workers. As we enter the door to pass by the opening to the laundry room, we hold them high both to hide our faces and to give us cover, loudly arguing as we walk as to whether it was necessary to have spent so much time and money in the stores. The bickering between us seems perfectly natural, which gives me pause. If Vinn and I decide to pursue a relationship once this is all over, I have to hope this isn't a portent of things to come.

We abruptly break off our discussion once past the danger point, take the stairs up one flight, and creep quietly to the front door of Woodson's unit. We stand quietly for several seconds to make sure the other unit owners aren't around before Vinn removes her set of lock picks from the bottom of one of the shopping bags. She'd insisted that she's better at this than I am and I knew better than to argue. Besides, she's right.

Just as she kneels down to one knee and selects what we hope is the right tool, the sound of footsteps from inside the door startles us. Vinn drops the pick back into the bag and scrambles to her feet as the doorknob begins to turn. We rush to the stairwell, entering it just as we hear the door squeak open. Peeking through a crack in the door, I watch as a vacuum cleaner emerges, followed by a foot pushing it, immediately followed after that by a woman carrying a basket of cleaning supplies. I breathe a sigh of relief and whisper the news to Vinn. She curses quietly and exhales loudly.

"So I peed my panties for a cleaning lady?" she whispers back unhappily.

I open the door wide once the woman disappears into the elevator. Vinn sheepishly returns to her position at the door, inserts the pick, and in seconds we're inside the unit, which does in fact smell quite clean.

There's no need to do the kind of thorough search we'd performed at Fyre's place because now we have a better idea of what we're looking for, or at least the form it will take, so this time we stick together. We conduct a quick tour of the layout before settling at the desk in Woodson's spare bedroom. Vinn pulls two pairs of nylon gloves out of a shopping bag and hands one to me.

The surface of the desk is completely clear of papers or any sign of a checklist entitled 'Relatives to Kill,' so we hurriedly move on to the drawers. The top drawer contains only stamps, envelopes, about a thousand pens and pencils, and nothing of interest. To be thorough, I feel the sides and bottom for false compartments, finding none. The next drawer down resists our efforts to pull it open. Locked.

"Lucky you have me here after all, Winters," Vinn teases as she pulls her picks out of the bag once more. One day I'll have to remind her that I do have some skills in that area, or challenge her to a contest, but this doesn't seem like the appropriate moment. Vinn has the drawer open in seconds. Okay, maybe not a contest.

The drawer contains a stack of mailing envelopes and a few folders. Anticipating my next move, Vinn pulls her hands away long enough for me to take a picture with my phone, then places them carefully on the top of the desk. I snap another photo to ensure that we replace every last document in the exact same order and position as we found them.

Vinn chooses the top envelope, leaving the second one for me. Each is closed with a binder clip and we carefully undo the cheap clips so as not to break them off. My envelope holds financial records, none of significance, along with a few tax forms. I look in Vinn's direction as she painstakingly places papers back into her envelope. She catches my eye and shakes her head. We carefully arrange her envelope on top of mine and place them on the far corner of the desk.

We repeat the process with the next two envelopes, placing both of them under the first two when we're done. Only a couple more to go. Vinn picks up the last envelope while I claim the file folder beneath it. I wait for Vinn to complete her unsuccessful examination before putting my hand on her arm.

"You need to see this," I whisper.

The folder contains a neatly stacked set of sheets torn from a legal pad which I spread out in fan-fashion on the desk. Hidden beneath them is the same type of family-tree printout we created ourselves, only this one has hand-written notations next to each name. Several of the names have red Xs through them. A couple of others have black ones. All of the Xs are so precise that Woodson must have used a ruler.

"My God," Vinn exclaims in a hushed tone in a combination of excitement and disgust, "it's like he's keeping score."

And he was. In no time, we discern that the three black Xs mark Woodson's brother, the woman in Nashville, and the young kid who was shot in the head in Chicago, so they're Fyre's kills. The red ones, we assume, are Woodson's. His small, neat printing next to the names contains details as to whether the individual had participated in the DNA test and their current location.

We continue on to the papers I'd fanned out, each of which lists detailed information for a particular family member, including their home address, occupation and work address, immediate family names and ages, habits for a couple of them, and a picture downloaded from the internet stapled to the upper left corner. Meticulous research prior to the kill. In the upper right corner of several pages are red checkmarks which correspond to the red Xs on the family tree.

"Dammit, look how precise he is. Just like an accountant," I mutter under my breath.

The sheet on top catches our eye, partly because it has small tears in spots and is wrinkled, indicating a lot of usage. It also contains much more information than the rest. Its condition, as well as its position on top of the pile, convince us that Woodson is giving this person special and active consideration. We do the same.

"Look at the name, Mal," Vinn says. "Franklin Stockton. Fyre's brother."

Before responding, I stack the rest of the paperwork in a neat pile then pick up the Stockton sheet, holding it out for both of us to examine together.

"From all of these notes, it looks like Woodson's spent a lot of time trying to track down Fyre's brother. Apparently more eye for an eye, even after he killed her. This is one sick individual. Let's see." I'm talking to myself as I quickly run my finger down the page, "here it is. Her brother lives in Chicago but seems to be homeless. That must be why Woodson can't find him. Vinn, do you have any doubt that he's Woodson's next target?"

"No," she replies. As she does, we hear footsteps in the hallway. We freeze, contemplating our next move. Seconds pass before the footsteps trail down the hallway. We listen as a door opens and then shuts. "Mal, take a picture of that and let's get out of here. We've stayed long enough."

I'm way ahead of her and am already pocketing my phone. We place Vinn's envelope and my file folder in the stack, check it against the photo I had taken earlier, and carefully place everything back in the drawer. Vinn relocks it, tugging it gently to make sure the lock caught. After that, we can't get out of the building fast enough.

Chapter 34

Saturday morning dawns wet and dreary, but for a late March day in Chicago what else is new? I seem to remember the sun shining for an hour or two on a Thursday morning sometime between Halloween and Thanksgiving, but I could be wrong. My perpetual lack of sleep, both from too many late nights working on the investigation with Vinn and tossing and turning in bed when my brain refuses to stop analyzing the macabre facts of the whole situation, makes my mood even more foul. I force down a piece of dry toast while I brew a large pot of Earl Gray. Not my favorite but it's a hardy tea with a lot of caffeine, which fits the occasion. I pour a cup of boiling water into my thermos and swirl it around to preheat the inside, then fastidiously dry it out before pouring in the tea.

I've just finished capping up the bottle when I receive a text from Vinn telling me that she's leaving her place. I hustle to put on two more layers over my warmest sweatshirt before zipping up my coat, checking to make sure I have my gloves, and head out the door. I have a bit of a walk to get to the closest el station, where we'd prearranged that I would meet her on the third car of whichever train she catches further up the line.

No assassin is waiting for me to exit my apartment, although I meet Rebecca on the stairs as she's shaking out a throw rug. She and I have had more 'accidental' encounters in the last week than in the many months before. I understand that my having been shot makes me a bit of a freakish curiosity to her, but I wish she would just bake me a cake or something and let me be. I feel Leo's steely stare bore into my back as I leave the yard, which is equally unsettling if not creepy. I'm glad to have an excuse to be away from the three-flat this morning.

The one person who seems to be leaving me alone today is Woodson, who must be sleeping in today. I still find myself looking over my shoulder every few seconds as I walk and assessing everyone whose path will intersect with my own. I remain cautious all the way to the train station and surprise myself when I expel a colossal lungful of air once I finally reach the platform at the top of the stairs. My vigilant pace almost causes me to miss Vinn's train, but once on board, there's no problem finding her. At that time of day on a weekend, the trains are rarely crowded. Our only travel companion this day is a homeless man sleeping while stretched out over four seats on the other side of the car. He is not Franklin Stockton.

We exit at Jackson Boulevard, simultaneously pull our hoods up both to guard against the chill and to hide our faces, then walk west. Finding a homeless person in Chicago won't be difficult. According to the official statistics I looked up last night, there are almost 6,000 homeless men, women, and children living in the city, which means there are probably a lot more than that. Around one-quarter of them live outside, shunning the shelters either for reasons of their own or because their temperament or mental illness has gotten them banned. It doesn't take a lot of skill to find cardboard boxes or blankets strung between posts serving as homes beneath underpasses or in isolated vacant lots.

Finding a particular homeless person, though, will be nearly impossible. The handwritten notations we found in Woodson's condo indicate that he has been at it for some time, presumably without success. He began his search long before he stalked Fyre and killed her. I wonder, not for the first time, how he lured Fyre to the old post office. Our guess is that he got impatient in trying to locate the brother to further his revenge scheme and went straight after Fyre herself by offering to join forces or some such pretense. Having accomplished that grisly task, he's refocused the target on her brother's back. Vinn and I agreed that before we go after Woodson, which may take time and meticulous planning, we owe it to Franklin Stockton to warn him of the danger he's in. To do that, we first have to find him.

In large part, the homeless in the city live in communities of various sizes in an effort to protect them from predators, which include other homeless, sick teenagers looking for someone no one will miss to harm, or even cops. Woodson's helped us out by already scouring some of the more accessible homesteads, dutifully noting their location. A woman he spoke to last week suggested he try Lower Wacker Drive, where many of the homeless abide during the colder months. If Stockton is there, we hope to get to him first. Today, if possible.

Lower Wacker Drive lies directly below Wacker Drive, a busy street that rings the West and North sides of the Loop along the Chicago River. Lower Wacker isn't nearly as popular a route with the locals as its above-ground namesake, with good reason. It's dark, dank, dirty, and can be dangerous. Two lanes in either direction, it's lined with an endless number of posts supporting the road above as well as concrete barriers on either side of its curvy, narrow lanes. No room for driver error down here. Distract yourself with a text or look away for a second and your car ends up totaled, maybe even in the river. On either side of the traffic lanes, behind the concrete dividers, are access roads for delivery trucks bringing supplies to the hotels and businesses above. Dead spots along these restricted routes where no loading docks exist, away from the glare of the superficial lighting, is where the homeless set up camp. Cops will roust them from time to time, but with nowhere else to go, they end up right back where they were.

There are no sidewalks along Lower Wacker but sticking to the inner service drive will allow us to avoid most of the traffic. Still, it's with no small share of foreboding that Vinn and I descend to the beginning of the road near Van Buren Street and the river. It's probably a few degrees warmer down here, and there's some shelter from the wind, but a damp and frigid chill immediately settles in my bones that sends shivers throughout my body. I retrieve my gloves from my jacket pockets.

As we start our trek, I take out my flashlight while Vinn has her pepper spray at the ready. The homeless are often mentally ill, or just plain mean, but even those with a heart of gold are justifiably suspicious of strangers and have homemade shanks and other weapons that they're not shy about using. The key to their survival conversely poses a threat to anyone approaching them and our good intentions will mean nothing. The area is also frequented by a violent element, intent on praying on those same homeless persons, a wayward tourist stopped too long at a red light, or anyone stupid enough to be wandering its streets. Like us.

For the first twenty minutes or so we don't encounter anyone, homeless or otherwise. Each of us raises scarves up over our mouths in a fruitless defense against the onslaught of car exhaust and the reek of garbage and urine.

We almost miss the first community, two men and a woman of indeterminable age huddled together outside a complex comprised of several large, intertwined cardboard boxes with filthy towels used to fill in any gaps. A shopping cart missing one of its wheels lies on its side nearby. I approach cautiously, Vinn just behind and to my right. I shine my light on a printout of a picture of Stockton we found online, one of many we packed with us.

"His name is Frank, or Franklin. We need to find him. His family is looking for him. Can you help us?"

The woman scowls, one of the men spits in our general direction, and all three retreat into the safety of the boxes, pulling a dark blanket across the opening to shield them from any further intrusion. Not an auspicious start, but not unexpected either. We could push harder, but instinctively know that it won't help. We move on.

Our next encounter is with a single man bundled in seven or eight layers of shirts and sweaters and huddled up against an exhaust vent for the building above. The slightest wave of heat weakly escapes from the vent, but it's clearly not enough for a body ravaged by the harshness of a Chicago winter. He shivers constantly as we draw near.

I repeat the same speech, holding out the picture. He snatches it from me, gives it a two-second glance, then balls it up and throws it at our feet. As before, not a word from him. I pick up the picture and smooth it out, dropping a dollar bill in its place. We continue walking.

Over the next two hours, we come in contact with over a hundred homeless people. A few shake their heads after looking at the picture, one or two verbally gave us a negative answer, and one threatens us with a large heavy pipe before we even have a chance to speak, only backing away when Vinn raises the hand carrying her pepper spray. We occasionally leave a few dollars, but with each encounter the weight of our helplessness feels heavier.

Time drags on. We drink hot tea to try to shake off the chill, but once it infiltrated our defenses, nothing seems to help. The morning passes to afternoon. I begin to feel the pangs of an unsatisfied hunger, but to complain about it to Vinn given what we're seeing down here feels wrong. She keeps her silence as well, although I'm sure she's as famished as I am. The granola bars in my pocket are a temptation, but they're not for us.

By late afternoon, as the sun dips toward the western horizon, we've curved to the east and are nearing the end of the encampments. At one of the larger groups, maybe eleven or twelve individuals, a ragged woman smelling of rancid body odor and booze grabs the photo and signals me to shine my flashlight on it. She holds it near to her eyes, then at arms' length, then close again before calling to a slight, hunched man to take a look. They whisper to each other in a language I can't quite figure out, then the old man fades away into the blackness. The woman holds the picture, now grimy at the edges, out to me.

"Down," she says firmly, pointing her finger to the cement at her feet. "Down," she repeats. She then shuffles toward the wall, instantly blending into its dirty facade. Clearly, that's all the information she's going to give us.

I turn to Vinn, puzzled. "Down? What does she want us to do, start digging?"

Vinn looks uneasy. "You've obviously never had a car towed by the city. We've been searching Lower Wacker Drive. Believe it or not, there's another level. Lower Lower Wacker. At one end of it is the City's impound lot, which is spooky enough. But there's also some streets down there which essentially lead to nowhere. Kids used to drag race there late at night because no one in their right mind drives down there willingly, but the city put up speed bumps to curtail the racing so now it's virtually deserted. There's the impound, the homeless I guess, the nasties praying upon the homeless, and any thrill seekers who accept a dare to enter the gates of hell. Word is that some of them don't come back."

Great, now I share her concern. I put on a brave front. "But we need to find him, right? We still need to go down there?" A part of me—a large part—is hoping that she'll talk me out of it. I'm frozen, starving, depressed, and don't have the energy to fight off any unexpected encounters.

"Yeah, it could be now or never. Stockton may move if he hasn't already, or Woodson may get to him before we can. I don't like it, but we need to do this. Now."

184

Chapter 35

When we discussed this little field trip, we agreed not to arm ourselves in case a cop got curious about our intentions down here. We take stock of our vast cache of weapons, which consist entirely of Vinn's single cannister of pepper spray and my flashlight. She gives me a quizzical look, probably wondering why I didn't ignore our own advice and come better prepared, but says nothing. Someday, I'll explain my aversion to guns to her, but moments before descending into the dark chasm of an underworld brimming with unseen demons doesn't seem like the right time. Consequently, we're walking into a possible battlefield with a tube of vegetable essence and a torch between us.

Rather than throw ourselves into a disorienting darkness by beginning our Lower Lower search smack in the middle of its length, we walk the couple of blocks to the end of the level we're on, near Columbus Drive, and after some difficulty locate the roadway down to the municipal tow lot. There appears to be no pedestrian walk down into the depths, begging the question of how the city expects people to get there after their cars are impounded, so we stick to the very edge of the street as we descend. There was no need for the precaution. We don't get passed by a single vehicle.

As we get closer to the bottom, the stink from decades of car fumes mixed with the fetid stench of rotting garbage assails our senses. We rush past the entrance to the auto pound, figuring the homeless would avoid an area with a continuous flow of people coming and going twenty-four hours a day. We'll also feel better if we don't draw the attention of the tow drivers or their victims on the off chance that we find a body rather than a living being.

Leaving the lot behind, a shadowy black mist immediately envelops us. I shine my flashlight ahead into the gloom but its beam is swallowed by the darkness and deflected away from the dingy corners of the Drive. The skies have been darkening for some time and will soon be devoid of any helpful light, but I have the sinking feeling that in this subterranean space the sun is a non-factor even on the brightest of days. We keep away from the walls, which are covered with a nasty, odorous slime. Walking in a straight line soon becomes impossible. The city apparently uses the streets down here to dump anything for which it can't find a use, including mounds of garbage. Rats and unidentifiable vermin scurry near our feet, adding yet another charming feature to this lost world.

We proceed slowly and cautiously as I move my light back and forth in an arc, partly to look for a homeless shelter and partly to warn us against anyone lying in wait. I know that the light, what there is of it, makes us an easy target, but without it we're even more vulnerable. Vinn quietly swears as she stumbles over a piece of twisted metal. Putting her hand down to prevent her fall, she's rewarded with a fistful of green, viscous muck.

As she throws me a nasty glance, probably memorizing a series of curses she can loudly hurl at me once it's safe to do so, a small huddle of cardboard and Styrofoam huts appear along the periphery of my beam on the other side of the street ahead of us. Vinn quickly uses her clean hand to lower my arm so that the light shines down at our feet.

"They'll think we're cops coming to roust them or someone else with no good in mind. They'll be ready for us with whatever clubs or shanks they keep for protection. We need to be careful."

We take our time approaching the makeshift village, advancing one or two steps at a time before stopping. I hold the beam of the flashlight focused on the ground a few feet ahead of us. We halt completely when we think we're ten feet or so from the nearest structure although with the lack of light, we could easily be twice that far or only inches away. Vinn uses two fingers to draw Frank's photo out of her jacket pocket.

"Hello," I call, repeating when there is no response. "We're not here to hurt you. We're looking—"

Before I can finish, a body flies at us from my right. I instinctively turn to face the attacker. As I do so, something sharp rips through the sleeve of my jacket, grazing my forearm. I kick my leg out and push hard against the back of the assailant in one swift move, causing him to stumble and fall at Vinn's feet. She quickly disarms him and twists his arm, putting her knee in the small of his back, eliciting a high-pitched squeak of pain.

Did I say 'him'? As I assist Vinn in turning our attacker over, all the time watching over our backs for others, I aim my light directly at the facial area, revealing the features of a woman who could have been anywhere from thirty to ninety. She screams as the light hits her eyes. It may be the first light she's seen in some time. I point the beam away to the side.

Vinn helps the woman to a sitting position, her arm around her shoulder, softly muttering calming words into her ear. I bring a granola bar out of my pocket, unwrap it, and tender it to her. After a moment of hesitation, she snatches it out of my hand, initially nibbles one corner as if it she suspects poison, then hurriedly stuffs the remainder into her mouth. I'm guessing that battles over food among her neighbors requires consuming any find quickly to avoid losing it.

Vinn continues to tell the woman that we have no intention of hurting her, and in a questionable move to gain her confidence returns her shiv. I retreat half a step as I squat down to pick Stockton's picture up off the ground. I use my glove to brush off the filth.

"We're looking for this man. His name is Frank. He's not in trouble, but we think a man is trying to find him to hurt him. We were told he's down here. Can you help us?"

The woman stares at me suspiciously, then back at Vinn, then me again. She appears to make a decision and turns back to face Vinn, nodding. "Frank," she says in a quiet, wavering voice, pointing toward the huts.

"Can you take us to him?" Vinn asks as I remove another granola bar from my pocket, standing as I do so.

The woman's eyes follow the snack. Vinn rises, helping our new friend to her feet at the same time. I hand her the bar, which she quickly hides inside the many layers of clothing that bundle her. She signals me to turn off the flashlight. Doing so, my limited vision is immediately reduced to almost nothing. Vinn follows her closely while I hold on to Vinn's elbow.

"Are you okay?" she whispers over her shoulder.

"Burns," is all I say. And it does. Badly. What worries me more, though, is the threat of infection. Who knows what filth that blade has been exposed to?

As we approach the boxes, the smell of urine, body odor, and desperation increases exponentially. I resist the temptation to cover my nose, worried that doing so would insult our hosts and hamper our mission. We're almost right on top of the first home before I can discern the scope of the community, about eight partitioned spaces in all. Although they abut a concrete barrier and have no direct exposure to the wind, there's little shelter from the cold and I find myself wondering how many of these residents won't make it through the winter.

We're led to the third structure, a refrigerator box connected to a few moving boxes with a filthy carpet remnant for a door. The woman leading us stoops down slightly, her movements slow and obviously painful. She mutters a few garbled words through the door then rises again and waits. After a moment, she bends back down and speaks again, just as softly but much more animated, waits a few seconds, then throws up her hands and retreats to her own set of boxes.

Vinn and I look at each other, unsure how to proceed or whether our status has reverted to that of uninvited intruders. Just as Vinn sighs and tentatively moves to approach the front of the structure, a figure emerges, crawling out before rising and unfolding his body limb by limb as if he's unused to standing. He stares at us warily, neither side sure as to who should go first.

The man standing before us bears a resemblance to our photograph, somewhat, but either the ravages of living on the street have aged Stockton by decades since it was taken or we're in the presence of a stranger who looks like our quarry in the way third cousins once removed resemble each other. Vinn holds out the picture at eye level. "Is this you?"

Stockton takes the photo in trembling hands, staring at it with vacant eyes before an overwhelming sadness suffuses his face. A tear forms at the corner of one eye. He nods slowly, almost imperceptibly, before handing the picture back to Vinn.

"That was me a long time ago," he responds in a raspy voice as if each word was filed with sandpaper. I wonder how long it's been since he felt the need to speak. "Frank Stockton was my name. No one uses it now." He pauses and grimaces, past memories intruding into his mind, before raising his suspicious eyes and meeting ours for the first time. "What do you want?"

I assume the lead this time. "Mr. Stockton, we were friends with your sister Felicity," I fib, feeling it necessary to bring Vinn in on equal footing. "After she died, we did some investigating. It would take a long time to explain, but we're certain that the man who killed her is looking to do the same to you."

Before I can continue, Stockton stares at me in shock. For the first time, I realize how badly sleep deprivation has affected my thought processes. Of the three people in the world who know that Fyre's dead, two of them are right here and neither is Franklin Stockton. I feel like a complete idiot but there's no way to take it back and start over. "Fyre, dead?" His voice wavers and his knees give way as he sinks to the ground, his hands covering his face. Vinn and I squat down next to him.

I put my hand on his shoulder but immediately pull it away when Stockton reacts as if he'd been burned, twisting his body away from my touch. We're losing him. "I'm sorry," I continue hurriedly, "to have brought you such sad news. I can explain more later. But for now, we need to get you away from here and somewhere safe."

Stockton remains crumpled in a heap on the ground, his body heaving in his grief. Vinn gives me a look and a shake of the head to tell me to back off for a moment. We sit silently for several minutes. I wonder if Stockton is thinking back to happier times when brother and sister were loving siblings, warm and safe inside of four clean walls. This should make me feel more charitable toward Fyre but doesn't. I can't share Frank's nostalgia.

Vinn eventually speaks up. "Sir, Mr. Stockton, I know this is a lot to take in, but you do have to believe us that your life is in danger. Would we have come all the way down here unless we were sure? Do you think you could gather up your belongings and come with us?"

After a few more quiet seconds, Stockton raises his head and glares at us with tear-streaked cheeks and a wild fury in his eyes, as if we were to blame for Fyre's death. He begins to scoot back to the safety of his home, never breaking eye contact, when I hear a distant pop. At the same moment, Stockton's body suddenly jumps several inches off the ground and falls back, a bloody hole in his chest.

Our first reaction is to fly to his side, but no amount of aid is going to help him now. Vinn and I move our eyes off Stockton's lifeless form to gaze back into the dark abyss. I see nothing. I flick the flashlight off and crouch low next to what used to be Frank. The odor of blood and freshly voided bowels permeates the air.

Neither of us says a word or moves a muscle, praying that the darkness that gives cover to the shooter hides us as well. This was no random act. Somewhere out in the gloom, Woodson is sitting with his rifle on his lap using a red marker to cross off one more victim. Outrage courses through my body. Nothing will ever relieve me of the guilt for our role in getting Stockton killed. We offered him protection but instead bought him a ticket to the grave. As the seconds tick by, I add to my angst by calculating the odds that in eliminating Stockton, Woodson won't feel the need to add to the body count and will leave Vinn and I alone.

Wishful thinking. As my knees begin to sound the alarm that they need to move and my calf muscles cramp, I contemplate standing and maybe even grabbing Vinn and hightailing it out of there. Before I make a decision, a tall, slow-moving figure appears out of the blackness, stopping mere feet in front of us. For a moment, no one speaks.

"I appreciate y'all finding him for me," Woodson says in a sort of lazy drawl that belies his Chicago upbringing. "Been at it myself for a while before I thought I'd let you do the work." As he speaks, Woodson keeps his shotgun level and his finger on the trigger, aiming it directly between Vinn and I.

"What threat was he to you?" Vinn asks angrily. "He probably would've died within a year or two anyway."

"But no one would know that, would they? Now an anonymous call will make sure his body gets discovered and identified. Won't raise an eyebrow under the circumstances. Perilous down here and no one wants to talk to the cops. Uh, I wouldn't do that."

I'd started to edge toward Vinn with the goal of pushing her down before charging at Woodson. She's smart. She would know to run. Maybe not the most sensible plan, but we don't have a lot of options. I'd brought Vinn into this mess so if one of us is to have a chance to survive it should be her. Woodson made short work of that option.

My mind reels with what to do now. Before I burned out, I survived some of the most evil and accomplished madmen in modern history. I may be rusty, but the prospect of dying at the hand of a rank amateur just doesn't seem fair or that it should be my fate, and my mind refuses to believe it. If there's any doubt that Woodson plans to silence us, however, and there really isn't, his next sentence removes it.

"Better if y'all aren't found here with him, though. Make ya a deal. If you don't mind walking a bit to my truck, I'll do it in one shot. If you'd rather make it hard, I'll do it slowly and you'll be in a world of hurt."

Vinn and I glance at one another, her eyes sad and resolved, yet determined. She's not ready to give up yet. As we turn back to face Woodson, confronting a smile I wanted to wipe off his face, his chest explodes and pieces of his lungs and heart smatter us in a gory shower. Woodson's eyes widen, his mouth opens slightly as if to speak, and he tumbles at our feet.

Vinn and I instinctively grab each other in a frightened embrace, a mixture of relief and uncertainty about what just happened washing over us. We don't move, unsure of what to do. Everything around me goes out of focus, the distant sounds of the city retreating and becoming even more muted, like in a dream. I feel myself floating away. A slap to my face instantly brings me out of my shock.

"Dammit, Malcom, pull yourself together," a vaguely familiar voice urges. "Unless you want to be found with two corpses and no good explanation for what you're doing in this godforsaken place, we have to get out of here. Now." Out of the dark emerges a large woman in a red party dress, her disheveled and sweat-soaked hair barely covering the diamond chandelier earrings which are a perfect match to her necklace. The look is hardly enhanced by her five o'clock shadow.

"Phantasmagoria," I mutter. I swear it's the first thing that enters my brain, which says something about my mindset at this moment. No reaction from Vinn and I don't plan to claim a point.

"Rebecca?" I squawk a second later. "What are you doing here?"

"Leo was concerned," she replies as if that explains everything. She seizes my arm with one hand and Vinn's with the other. Vinn has yet to say a word, staring at Rebecca uncomprehendingly. We're roughly dragged forward and stumble briskly away from the scene. I make out the profile of a thin rifle barrel extruding from near Rebecca's armpit. A scope sticks out from the other side of her arm.

"Winters," Vinn finally says. "Who is this uh…woman?"

"My tenant," I say simply. "The real question is, what kind of sniper wears heels on the job?"

Chapter 36

Driving a winding, random route out of San Diego through long stretches of desert, then to the north and west on the desolate highways leaving Las Vegas toward my destination in Utah, gives me plenty of time to contemplate the events of two months ago. My beat-up, old-model, rust-colored (and rusty) Altima, the best I could do paying cash with no identification, has a non-functioning radio, which is perfect to avoid distractions and to allow my mind to play back difficult memories, and to ponder what I might have done differently. Seven hours into the drive, the only conclusion I've reached is that it would have been better if I'd never met Fyre in the first place. If I'd kept it in my pants, I never would have been involved. Then again, if I hadn't been involved, who knows how many more victims Woodson would have claimed. The only answer I've come up with so far is that there is no answer. That's probably where I'll leave it.

Woodson's body was found by a sanitation crew four days after he died, lying in the shadows of where he fell. The story earned three short paragraphs on page five of the Tribune, two of them focused only on the well-documented violence of Lower Lower Wacker Drive, and no coverage at all in the Sun Times. No mention was made of a second body nor of the existence of a homeless community near where Woodson was located. The cops took the easy way out and labeled the death an unfortunate case of an innocent man getting caught in gang cross fire, which allowed them to avoid finding a reason that he'd be down there in the first place. Vinn and I figured that the rest of the homeless residents were gone within hours after Rebecca dragged us away, relocating in another dark spot just as desolate and odorous not far away. What they did with Frank is anyone's guess.

Yet another developer, one of a long line of companies with big dreams that will never be realized, went under contract to develop the old post office into shops, offices and condos about a month ago. I assume they walked through the whole building before committing their billions, but if they found Fyre, it doesn't appear to have made the papers. Dead bodies aren't good for business and would shift the focus away from their grandiose plans. Eventually I stopped looking, or caring for that matter. Any evidence that I'd been there would already be covered under a layer of dust, and Fyre forfeited the right to a decent burial. She'd be labeled as a transient woman trying to find a place to get warm so that her death, too, could be quickly swept under the rug.

For a while, it bothered me not knowing why Fyre would agree to meet Woodson, but figured that he tempted her with an offer that included leaving her brother alone, then each went to the post office with the intent of outmaneuvering and killing the other. Speculation, and ultimately I didn't really care about that either.

The night of the shooting, Vinn showed signs of disorientation, her skin got clammy, and her breathing was shallow and fast. She'd been away from this sort of violence longer than I had, so her reaction wasn't surprising. My memory of the immediate aftermath is sketchy, but I've been told that I wasn't much better. When I think about it, I was already starting to lose my ability to walk away unaffected by my actions before I left the government job. In any case, neither of us coped well with the evening's events in their immediate aftermath. Wisely, Rebecca avoided taking us to a hospital, instead driving to a quiet corner of the parking lot off Montrose Beach. She cranked up the heat to a setting on the far side of Hades, sitting quietly while we decompressed, digging into her voluminous purse to supply tissues when needed and a sewing kit for my wound. Not a treatment found in medical journals, but it was effective. We sat for hours without a word being exchanged. When the first rays of dawn peeked through the gray clouds settled over the lake, Rebecca put the car into gear and drove. Vinn chose to retreat to the familiarity of her home, declining my company in the few words she spoke all night. Rebecca brought me the rest of the way to Ukrainian Village in silence.

Leo was waiting in his kitchen upon our arrival with a bottle and three glasses. I don't remember much after that. I sipped something strong while they had a muted and short conversation. Rebecca cleaned the rifle while she drank before passing it over to Leo, who disassembled it. I've never seen it again. Unbelievably, other than a short discussion about my condition after the shooting, we've never spoken of that night. The only repercussion of the incident was that Rebecca joined us for our late-night booze-filled table sessions a few times over the next two weeks. Since then, it's just been Leo and I again. I'll admit I've gained a begrudging respect, along with a little fear, of Rebecca. Ted remains an asshole.

By mutual and unspoken understanding, Vinn and I have avoided rehashing the events, although they've occasionally intruded into our thoughts. For a month, Vinn worried about the police paying her a visit to ask why she checked out the Sales probate court file. The cops never materialized and Vinn no longer brings it up. Together, we burned all of the paperwork we'd stolen from Fyre's condo along with any of our own notes. We thoroughly wiped the search histories on any computer we'd used in connection with the matter and all traces of Fyre are gone from my phone. I was in favor of trashing every single device even after that, but didn't put up much resistance when Vinn suggested it would be overkill, so to speak. We did a meticulous search of her unit and then mine to make sure we hadn't missed anything. We'll probably both keep figuratively looking over our shoulders for the rest of our lives, waiting for someone with a badge to come calling, but with every day that passes, I'm starting to relax. At least as to the Fyre business. I continue to literally look over my shoulder for any number of other vestiges of my past to reappear. Those fears may never go away.

Our friendship has survived, but I won't say it's like it used to be. The proverbial elephant in the room is a large, intrusive, red-haired pachyderm and it's put a strain on our formerly easy familiarity. We continue to meet in the café and to play our silly word game (don't ask the score), and occasionally I'll risk a middle finger by tepidly venturing a guess as to her real name, but something from before is missing. My fantasies of going beyond friendship get emboldened by the weirdest little things such as the smell of that damn shampoo, but I don't want to push. Anyway, when the term ended, each of us seemed relieved.

I started job-hunting in April after not hearing from Stuart about how lovely it would be for me to transition from visiting professor to full-time teacher and to stick around for the next academic year. I assumed that my cover had been blown or that he simply didn't like me by the way he avoided my eyes whenever we passed in the hallway. Then, one day upon returning to my office after class, I found a copy of the fall class schedule sitting on my chair with half a dozen Post-It Notes complete with hand-drawn hearts stuck throughout its pages. Vinn.

The first marked page revealed that Malcom Winters would once again be teaching an Introduction to Writing Fiction course. The italicized class description even notes the course's popularity and that a lottery might be used to determine who gets into the class. Paging through to the other tabbed sections, I saw that I would also be teaching a class on crime fiction. The irony brought a smile to my lips for the first time in months. I sat in my chair, closed my eyes for five minutes, then opened my laptop and took my resume down from the job-search websites. Apparently my future, at least for now, is at UIC.

Starting two weeks before the end of the semester, the main topic of conversation among professors and teaching assistants alike involved everyone's summer plans. No one could wait to get away from the hallowed halls of academia. It bordered on an obsession. I soon learned that demurring that I hadn't decided on any specific plans yet only encouraged even more aggressive follow-ups. I couldn't reveal that what I really want is to be left alone. I need to evaluate my life, including where and what it's brought me, and to ask myself if I could ever escape the violence that seems to have followed me even through a change of identity. I especially want to reflect on whether I can, in good faith, establish close friendships if it means drawing people I care about into a danger zone that could cost them their lives. I've lived the life of a loner and don't care for it much, but if that's the role I need to inhabit, so be it.

To pacify the faculty members who continued to find their own form of happiness in making me miserable, I finally booked a flight to San Diego and a 14-day cruise to Hawaii. If I thought that would silence the crowd, I was sorely mistaken. Everyone at UIC turned their attention to giving me advice on which beaches were the most beautiful, what tourist traps to avoid, and which shops sold 'authentic' Hawaiian shirts. Sheila, a busty blond from the history department, passed on a critical tip about avoiding crab dip on cruise ship buffets. I got good at Hawaii-speak, although I won't actually set foot on a ship nor have a lei placed around my neck this summer. My destination is elsewhere.

I used one of my former aliases that hasn't been associated with too much baggage to book a remote cabin in the middle of a dense, nearly impenetrable forest in the middle of Utah, several hours' drive from the closest town and twenty miles or more from the nearest neighbor. All of my communications with the owner were by burner phone with the exception of a single confirmation email, which was sent to a Gmail address that I created solely for that purpose then deleted once his message was received. The phone has also been trashed. In the trunk of the car, I have one suitcase with clothes and a second with books and tea along with a shopping bag of food I picked up just outside Las Vegas. For the next six weeks, I'll have the isolation and privacy I need.

It's growing dark when I think I'm getting close to my turnoff onto an old logging road, making it difficult to see the hand-drawn map I made during my conversation with my host. There will be no posted sign to make my life easier. I pass by the entrance at first, forcing me to drive slowly in reverse so as not to miss the overgrown ruts of a long-forgotten logging road marked solely by a notch in a tree. Stopping the car as soon as I enter, I drag fallen branches over to hide the entrance from anyone and everyone. Not that anyone in their right mind would venture down this way. The road is a road in name only, jolting me and tipping the car from one side to the other even as I proceed at a slow, careful crawl.

Seventeen minutes later, coming around a bend, a small wooden cabin appears before me in a small clearing. Built in the 1920s out of huge logs from the local forest, it has an imposing yet welcoming vibe. Tall, majestic aspens encroach from three sides, leaning overhead as if to hide the cabin from the night sky. I pull around to the side next to the woodpile to hide the car from view. My muscles ache as I exit, the chill in the air leading me to give silent thanks to the owner for the white stream of smoke trailing from the stone chimney. Leaving my gear in the car for the moment and grabbing my flashlight, I find the key under the designated rock, twelve steps from the bottom step in the direction of the cottonwood tree, contemplating why it's even necessary to lock up. Clever bears, maybe.

I push open the heavy door, the welcome scent of burning wood greeting me. The interior of the cabin is as dark as the sky outside, the only light cast by the darting flames of the fire, but not dark enough for me to miss a slight movement from the rocking chair to the left of the fireplace. My eyes barely make out the outline of a figure as it straightens and begins to languidly move toward me. The instinctive danger signals flooding my mind dissipate, replaced by an entirely different reaction from an area far south of my brain as I realize that the trespasser is naked, her skin flushed from the fire and her breasts swaying gently as she approaches. She halts inches from me.

At first, neither one of us speaks. But I know she's going to say it. She knows I know she's going to say it. She says it anyway.

"What in the hell took you so long?"